PRAISE FOR R. MICHAEL BURNS

"Mr. Menace is a masterpiece of atmosphere and suspense that will leave readers second-guessing their own realities."

—Bret R. Wright, author of the Nate Jepson mystery series

"Burns will toss you into a smoke-filled pit of debauchery that will leave you breathless and hungry for more."

—Bret R. Wright, author of the Nate Jepson mystery series

"Detective Frank Orpheus should've left well enough alone … but you shouldn't. This is neo-noir at its finest."

—Bret R. Wright, author of the Nate Jepson mystery series

MR. MENACE

R. MICHAEL BURNS

WFP
WORDFIRE PRESS

EBook ISBN: 978-1-68057-147-9
Trade Paperback ISBN: 978-1-68057-146-2
Hardcover ISBN: 978-1-68057-148-6

Cover design by Janet McDonald
Cover artwork images by Adobe Stock
Kevin J. Anderson, Art Director
Published by
WordFire Press, LLC
PO Box 1840
Monument CO 80132
Kevin J. Anderson & Rebecca Moesta, Publishers
WordFire Press eBook Edition 2020
WordFire Press Trade Paperback Edition 2020
WordFire Press Hardcover Edition 2020
Printed in the USA
Join our WordFire Press Readers Group for
sneak previews, updates, new projects, and giveaways.
Sign up at wordfirepress.com

❀ Created with Vellum

CONTENTS

DEDICATION

For my bloodsister, Morgen

PART I: THE STRANGER IN GRAY

ONE

MISSING

I never truly understood the word "haunted" until I looked into the bottomless black eyes gazing at me from that ghost-white face.

I should have turned her away. I should have trusted my intuition, made some polite excuse, and ushered her out the door. I could read the calamity written in her expression the way a fortune teller reads tea leaves—promises of mean times ahead, and hard endings. But I'm a sap for lost souls, especially soft-featured ones with nice curves and hair the color of bedded embers, so I ignored my professional instinct and let the stranger in gray slip into my life, sly as a phantom.

I had no idea then how much a mistake like that could cost a man.

It seemed like such a small thing when the intercom buzzed and the voice of Cass O'Clare, my secretary and all-around go-to girl, crackled through. "Mister Orpheus, there's a lady here to see you. She doesn't have an appointment."

I glanced at the clock ticking away on the wall. Quitting time was coming fast and I didn't like to keep Cass late if I didn't have to. But my curiosity was up, so I tapped the reply button and said, "I can spare a few minutes. Send her in."

"Yes, Mister Orpheus," Cass's voice rattled. The formality gave me a chuckle—she only ever called me that when we had clients in the office.

A moment later the frosted glass door to my office opened on the woman who started me along the road into darkness of a kind I'd never imagined existed.

She hesitated a moment, lingered at the threshold as if she didn't quite trust the office, or the tall, gaunt figure seated behind the heavy oak desk.

"C'mon in," I prompted. "Tell me what I can do for you."

She drifted closer, smooth and silent as a specter. Her shadowed gaze took in the chair across the desk from me, but dismissed it. The lady remained standing.

"I ... need you to find someone for me."

I settled back in my stiff wooden chair and nodded at her, letting one hand wander lazily over the intercom box next to the phone. I wanted to look casual, like this was just any other day for me, but something about the slouch of her shoulders and the quiet resignation in her voice, the way the shadows wouldn't leave her eyes even when the light hit them, cooled me some. She had the look of someone who'd seen all the worst of life and didn't expect the rough patch to end anytime soon. Maybe never.

When she didn't continue, I spoke.

"Fair enough," I said, my fingers meandering over the desktop, playing the left-hand part of a favorite concerto of mine. "I do that from time to time, find people. Anyone special you had in mind, or do I get my pick?"

The woman standing across the desk from me stayed silent for a moment. She drifted to the window, gazed out past the dust-gathering blinds and the night-shrouded city. The neon sign on the hotel across the street splashed crimson light over her pale features, but the illumination never seemed to reach those eyes. I started to wonder if she planned to say anything at all. Then at last she spoke, without turning to face me, her voice so soft I scarcely heard it over the grumble of the traffic in the streets below.

"Me," she said.

That neon glow made her hair positively blaze, but her features, in profile, didn't warm up a bit.

"Say again?"

Now she turned, but slowly.

"I need you to find *me*."

I folded my hands under my chin and studied her face. Tired, pale, grave as a cemetery. Looking into those eyes was like staring into the windows of a house so full of restless ghosts the neighborhood kids would be too scared to even tell stories about it. But for all that, I didn't see any hint of crazy in her—and it doesn't take too many years in the sleuthing business to get pretty good at spotting the likely straight-jacket candidates. If you don't, you're bound to find yourself in the hospital, or worse.

The fact that her fancy duds suggested a healthy bank account didn't especially hurt my interest either.

"Okay," I said. "You're here in my office. Cain Building, suite five-thirteen. You can pay my secretary Miss O'Clare on the way out."

"Please don't take this for a joke, Mister Orpheus," my would-be client said. "I'm quite serious."

"Mmm," I agreed, nodding. "I can see that. But I can't say I understand exactly what you want me to do. Why don't you have a seat and tell me all about it?" I gestured at the padded-leather chair cocked in front of the desk.

She turned back to the window, watched the Hotel Moira sign wink on and off at her over the brick chasm between buildings.

"I don't know who I am," she said to the gloom outside the window. "I don't remember my name, or where I live, or where I've been lately. This morning I found myself in a dingy little diner in midtown with … with no idea of my name, or how I'd come to be there."

I could imagine her, dressed to the nines, sitting at a chipped Formica countertop alongside disheveled Hooverville dwellers who had to beg change to buy bad coffee. The picture in my head struck me as equal parts funny and tragic.

"I wandered around all day looking for anything or anyone familiar," my would-be client went on, "trying to somehow find my way back to myself. To find my way home or … to my job, perhaps, if I have one … I seemed to know my way around well enough, but couldn't remember ever having been to any of the places I saw today." She paused a second, two, as if questioning whether or not everything she'd told me was right. Then, still undecided, she went on. "I happened past this building by chance—or without any real idea where I was going, in any case. I saw your agency listed on the directory, and … I came up. On a whim, I suppose. Or maybe it was fate."

"Maybe it was," I allowed. "But I have to ask—why not go to the police, let them handle this?"

Something flickered across her face then, and it wasn't the neon from the flophouse across the street. I could see she was hiding things from me—maybe hiding them from herself, too.

"I … don't trust the police," she whispered.

"You and me both," I said, then sat up a bit straighter, businesslike, and waited for her to say what needed saying.

She was sharp enough to take the cue. "I don't know where else to turn."

It crossed my mind, then, to tell her I couldn't help her, maybe make up an excuse or just leave it at that. I didn't have any good reason for that impulse, but there it was.

In any case, I bit the words back.

More the fool me.

Instead, I hedged.

"I feel for you, sincerely. That's about as tough a story as I've ever heard, and I've heard some dandies. But I don't do this for a hobby, you understand? I expect to be paid for my services in these matters. Times are tough, and I have rent to make."

My nameless guest dipped a dainty hand into her jacket and withdrew a wad of cash that would've choked a horse. Large bills, well-circulated. I think my eyes went a bit wide despite my best effort to play it cool.

"I'm quite sure I can cover the expense," she said.

I raised an eyebrow. "So it seems."

"Can you help me?"

The question might've sounded strange coming from pretty much anyone else—after all, why bother telling her story and flashing her cash if she didn't already think I was up to the job? But she didn't mean just me—she was asking if *anyone* could help her, could make sense of such a cockeyed tale. Her voice held so little hope, so much loss, I couldn't help hurting for her. That alone should've told me the whole case would be trouble— any detective worth his license will tell you he never gets person- ally involved in a job. Too many angry husbands and jealous girlfriends, too many double-dealers and hidden agendas. Too many ways to get suckered. And emotions muddy the water, keep a man from seeing clearly and doing the job right.

But dammit—that voice, those eyes … What the hell else could I do?

From that moment, I was hung. And some part of me knew it.

I looked her up and down, slowly. Smart suit, gray woolen skirt and matched jacket over a white silk blouse. Red silk hand- kerchief in her breast pocket, stylish slouch hat atop those elegant auburn waves. Polished leather pumps that must've cost what I make in a good week. The pearls around her neck were the real deal, as best I could tell in the light from the banker's lamp on my desk. I'd seen enough fakes in my work to have a pretty good idea. No wedding ring, and no hint she'd been wearing one.

"Well, you didn't spend the night on the street or in any

greasy spoon, not looking like that. Anyone who can afford that get-up and carries that kinda cash doesn't live in midtown, either. You're an uptown girl, sure as I'm sitting here. Well brought up, too, by the way you talk. All of which means likely as not you'll be missed, and in short order—if you haven't been already. Someone will find you and once they do you'll get your name back. Then the trick'll be figuring out where you've been lately and where exactly you left your memory—and why you left it there."

My anonymous client stood statue-still, saying nothing, so I went on.

"Whoever's hunting for you, we know it's not a husband because you've got no ring and don't look like you've been wearing one. A father, maybe, or a high-class beau. Maybe someone you work with—you're certainly dressed for business. Society friends, brother, sister, personal secretary ... someone'll come looking soon enough. I'd bet *your* money on it."

The line didn't draw so much as a slim smile.

"I wish I could share your confidence," she said, looking out the window again as if there might be answers chalked on the sidewalks below. "Everything's blank. Like a diary with nothing written in it. As if I were no one. No one at all."

"You have anything else in your pockets, apart from that stack of cabbage?"

Again, she hesitated, the way a bad poker player does when he's thinking of bluffing, and I could see a shadow of fear in her eyes—fear of me, and what she might find out by hiring me. I wouldn't be surprised if she gave a second's thought to walking out my door right then and disappearing into the anonymity of the night.

Instead, she sighed, and slipped something from the hip pocket of that smart linen jacket.

"Only this," she said, and showed it to me.

I frowned at the thing resting in the smooth white palm of her dainty hand. It had the shape of a simple wedding band, but cut from jet-black obsidian, with a bright red vein running around it, just beneath the polished surface. Something about the way that crimson line flowed through it made it look almost liquid. The effect was weirdly hypnotic, made me feel giddy in a way liquor hadn't in a long time. It was the damnedest thing I'd ever seen, and I've seen plenty. Then I noticed a little jag poking out from one side of the thing, a kind of glass thorn, nasty-sharp. If it was meant to be jewelry, it was of a particularly mean sort.

"Any idea what it is?" I asked.

My client shook her head slowly, but something in those pretty black eyes of hers suggested that way down in the darkest parts of herself, she knew.

She slipped the black-and-red band back into the pocket it'd come out of.

"Well," I said, after a moment's pause, "there certainly are a lot of questions here. But I'm pretty sure we can tie all this up in a few days. Meantime, maybe you oughtta think about getting yourself to a doctor, see if—"

"No," she said, cutting me off clean as a razor. "No doctors."

"Don't trust them either, huh?" I asked, raising an eyebrow at her.

"No, I don't."

"Seems you're not a very trusting lady. Well, I suppose I can't blame you. It does make me wonder why you trust *me*, though."

My would-be client looked at me for what seemed a long time. "I don't know," she said after a moment. "Woman's intuition."

"Fair enough," I said. "Still, you might be hurt—a blow to the head, something like that—"

"Do I look hurt?"

She looked damn fine is how she looked.

"No," I admitted, "but—"

"I don't feel hurt, either. In fact, I feel just fine." Her words had taken on a sharp edge that set my nerves tingling once more.

When she spoke again it was with a different voice, distant and toneless. "No doctor can help me."

I felt tempted to press the point but knew it wouldn't buy me anything—I'd only talk her and her cash right out the door.

"Then I guess it's up to me," I offered.

She turned that lovely, haunted gaze on me full force then, and the tiny flicker of hope I saw in those eyes made my heart ache. "Yes," she said, oh-so-soft, "it is."

I took a moment to digest that. My line of work is mostly husbands wanting proof their wives are cheating on them—or more often, hoping for proof that their wives *aren't* cheating. I get the occasional low-life politician with a problem he doesn't want to take to the cops, and once in a while an insurance group'll hire me to check up on someone they think is ripping them off. Mostly it's pretty tame stuff. A few broken hearts, sure, but none of those fellas is ever counting on me to put his whole world back together.

This case wasn't ten minutes old and already I knew I'd never had another one like it.

"Tell you what," I said, picking up the stub of a pencil and jotting notes in a leather-bound pad I kept handy, "I have business tonight, so I can't start the legwork on your case until tomorrow. If that's acceptable to you, you can arrange things with Miss O'Clare out there in the front office, and we can start filling in those blank pages in your diary. Meantime, I'll have Miss O'Clare set you up with a hotel for the night. It'll be on your dime, of course, but I'd say you can afford it. Unless you have somewhere else to go."

"I—" she began, then stopped. Something passed over her face then, and I saw the first hint of light in her eyes. But it was gone before it could catch fire there. "No," she said. "No place at all. None that I remember."

She started toward the door, then stopped, lingering a moment on the threshold, as she had when she'd first come in, and turned back to face me.

"What happens if ... if I have another blackout or ... or whatever, and can't remember you, or my coming here?"

I plucked a card from my breast pocket, rose to hand it to her.

Frank Orpheus, Licensed Private Investigator, it said, in raised black letters that had cost a pretty penny. My office address and phone number followed beneath.

"Keep this with you, maybe it'll trigger your memory if you *do* forget. In any case, I'll have Miss O'Clare give you a call first thing in the morning. We'll make sure you get back here. After all, I'm not likely to make any money on this case if you up and vanish on me."

She nodded, slowly, and slipped the card into her inner jacket pocket—close to her heart, I couldn't help thinking.

What a sap.

I gave her nod back to her and our eyes met for an instant, really met, and I felt something stir between us, like the air just before a major crack of lightning when the sky is dangerous with electricity. I turned away and dropped back into the chair behind my desk before the thunder had a chance to crash.

I tapped the intercom. "Cass, set Miss—"

I hesitated, groping for any convenient name to stick on the case file, something more imaginative than Jane Doe.

"—Set Miss Gray up with the standard contract."

I glanced at my client to see if the name I'd picked out for her met with her approval. She nodded slightly and I thought I saw the tiniest hint of a smile pluck at her full red lips.

"Yes, Mister Orpheus," I heard Cass reply. Maybe it was the intercom, but her voice right then seemed to be ... missing something.

"And get her a decent hotel for the night, will you?" I added. "And not that dump across the street. Someplace where the bell-boys outnumber the roaches."

"Right away, Mister Orpheus," Cass answered.

I clicked off. "You're all set," I told the erstwhile Miss Gray.

"Thank you, Mister Orpheus," she said, and slipped out of my office, drawing the door closed behind her.

As soon as she was gone, I tugged open my top desk drawer and pulled out the nice little government-issue spy camera I'd picked up from a G-man pal of mine a couple years back. Small enough to slip in a pack of cigarettes, and not the kind of toy John Q. Public was likely to see at his local department store anytime soon. I tucked the gadget away in my front pocket.

Then for a while I sat with my feet up on the desk blotter and stared vacantly at the door with the word PRIVATE painted in efficient gold letters across the frosted glass, as if some traces of her silhouette might linger there, while soft female voices exchanged words I couldn't quite make out.

Less than a minute after I heard my strange client leave the outer office, I got up and opened my door. Cass regarded me with her big hazel eyes. She was the sort of girl some guys might've called a Plain Jane, I suppose, with her dishwater blond hair up in a spinster's bun and her stodgy office clothes that looked like they could belong to a woman twice her age. But she was smart, and damn good at her job, and willing to do it for what a lug like me could pay. Plucking her straight out of secretarial school had been better luck than I had any right to hope for.

"Where'd you put her up, Cass?" I asked.

She didn't smile as she answered. "Uptown a few blocks, at the Chandler."

I nodded. I knew the place—one of the few decent hotels in midtown, but easy walking distance, which was good because it meant maybe my client wouldn't take a cab. She'd be a hell of a lot easier to follow on foot. If I had to deal with the midtown traffic, I'd be in poor shape in a taxi.

"You gave her good directions?" I asked Cass as I pulled my overcoat from the rack near the door to the hall and tugged it on.

"Sure, of course," Cass said, nodding, one hand subtly

adjusting the position of the framed picture of her smiling mother. She did that sometimes, when she had something on her mind but wasn't sure she wanted to share it.

I waited a second or two, but she stayed clammed up, so I plucked my gray felt fedora off the rack and settled it on my combed-back brown hair, tugging the brim down over my eyes. I'd lied about having business that night, of course. I wanted to follow my mystery lady around a bit without her knowing, see if I could catch her keeping more secrets from me—or from herself, for that matter. It was fifty-fifty she'd figure out my ruse, but worth the shot.

"I'm gonna play shadow for our new client," I told Cass, though I'm sure she'd already gathered as much. "I'll probably be out all night, so go ahead and lock up early if you want."

"Sure, Frank," Cass agreed, her voice distant. She shifted Mom's frame again.

"Something on your mind, Cass?"

Cass shrugged, making the gesture elegant in her simple way. "There's something about that woman," she said, staring off through the hallway door, the one with my name on the glass. The one our newest client had disappeared through about ninety seconds ago. Miss Gray would still be waiting for the elevator, I guessed. Thinking again of that smoldering hair and those tragic eyes, I almost lost track of what Cass was saying. "I don't trust her, Frank. She's bad news. I can tell these things—you know I got a little gift like that. Just like how I knew my father was gonna walk out on mom 'n me even before he knew. Just like when I warned you about that crazy girl with the nails … Maybe you ought to give this case back."

I touched the scar, the one the crazy girl with the nails had given me—no more than an inch from my left eye. It itched some.

"Miss Gray's money's as good as anyone's," I said.

"We've got money coming in," Cass said. "That check from

Hughes, McDonald, and Crumley finally got here, so we're set for a while."

"You got something against bringing in a little more?" I asked, raising an eyebrow at her. "Tough times like these, you don't say no to a case. Even an odd one."

Cass sighed. "We both know it wasn't her money you were looking at when you decided to take her case."

That stung a bit, not least because of the thorn of truth in it. Still, I liked to think I ran a bit deeper than that.

"Sure, she's a looker," I agreed. "But she's also got an interesting story. And cheating spouse cases get dull fast. I could do with some variety."

"She spooks me, Frank," Cass said, with a little shake of her head. "I really think—"

I cut her off, something I almost never do.

"We can talk about your woman's intuition later," I told her, hearing those words come from Miss Gray's lips even as I repeated them. "But I'm gonna lose her if I stand around here gabbing any longer. So—good night, Cass." With that, I headed out the door.

TWO

TAIL

A steady, sullen rain fell as I drifted the night streets, traffic snarling and honking along at my right, soot-black buildings looming on my left, uptown skyscrapers in the distance prodding the clouds with their gleaming art deco steel spires. Ahead, my mysterious client wove her way through the crowds, dodging clusters of raincoated businessmen and umbrella-wielding office-ladies, shying away from the working girls and occasional dubious men lingering at the corners under the rain-haloed streetlamps, slipping around the huddled figures outside a soup kitchen. I kept losing sight of her in the throng but didn't dare wander too close in case she stole a backward glance, the way a woman in her circumstances might be smart to do. Fortunately that red-as-embers hair of hers shone like a beacon in the crush of people and I had no trouble finding her again.

She walked tentatively at first, staring up at the street signs and the dark buildings like a lost tourist, and I had to slow my usual pace to keep from overtaking her. Then somewhere between Exeter Street and Dempster—halfway between my office and the hotel Cass'd set her up with—a change came over her. She came to a dead halt in the middle of the sidewalk under the dark of a coffee shop awning, and stood there a moment like an eerily realistic department store mannequin that had somehow escaped its window display. Then she started walking again, her pace quick, her posture straight. All that tentativeness had vanished from her demeanor. She moved with a sense of purpose, of *direction*.

It gave me pause. Had she caught me tailing her? Hell, was she *counting* on it, leading me into some kind of ambush? The idea didn't make much sense, but what did? I couldn't afford to take the possibility too lightly.

At the next intersection, instead of heading right, toward the Chandler, she went left, and damn near lost me. I put on a little extra steam and made it around the corner in time to see her sliding into a bright yellow taxi.

I muttered a curse under my breath and flagged down the next cab I could.

"There's a tenspot for ya if you can keep up with that cab," I told the driver.

"You got it, Mac," he answered, like he got that sort of request every other day, and got us moving.

It was no easy trick, following that other car through the tangle of traffic in the labyrinthine city streets, cutting corners and cheating our way through red lights, but the slouch-shouldered fella behind the wheel proved equal to the task and kept us always in sight of the glowing plastic FOR HIRE bubble on top of my client's taxi. It wound its way west, deeper and deeper into the ugly part of town, streets where all the shops had bars over their windows and half the storefronts stood empty and dark, where there were never too many people on the pavement and the ones that hung around looked like characters fresh out of the Holes over on Aeacus Island, thugs and pimps and chump-change grifters. I could hardly guess what business a classy lady like my Miss Gray had in this neighborhood.

The traffic thinned out a lot here and I told the cabbie to fall back a couple of blocks, lest the woman in the other car catch our scent—her, or anyone else. If she had any reason to be here, there was no telling who might be watching.

Between the buildings ahead I could see the gray towers of the West River Narrows Bridge. The coppery odor of dark, brackish water reached me even among the smells of rain and exhaust.

"Buddy, I think you're gonna hafta getcherself another ride," the cabbie said. "I don't go to th'other side of the river."

"I'll make it worth your while," I said, and flashed a sawbuck. I was blowing my retainer fast, but I was damned if I'd lose her just because my driver had a streak down his spine as yellow as his jalopy.

The cabbie frowned at me in the rearview, then shrugged. "Your dime, Mac. But don't expect me to wait around for ya. Soon as you step out, I'm making tracks."

"Of course," I agreed, watching the other cab disappear over the rise of the bridge, taillights shimmering like fresh-spilled blood on the rain-puddled blacktop. I scratched absently at the knotted scar over my left eye, the one I got from "the crazy girl with the nails"—a young wife who wasn't too happy to find me and my camera in her bedroom closet. Damn near lost my eye that time, and the pale white groove she left in my flesh has a tendency to gnaw at me now and again, especially when I'm looking into stuff I shouldn't. I dropped my hand and tried to ignore the prickling.

A moment later we descended the far side of the bridge, the maze of dark buildings and darker streets stretching away ahead of us—and the other cab nowhere to be seen.

The cabbie muttered some choice words and thumped the steering wheel with the heel of one thick hand, probably picturing his bonus circling the drain.

"Make a left, first intersection," I said. It was barely even a hunch, but it was all I had.

The cabbie shrugged and did what I said. Sure enough, my

client's cab—or its twin brother—was just pulling away from the curb two blocks away.

"Let me out here," I told the driver. He stopped without bothering to nose his car toward the sidewalk for me. I paid the fare plus the incentive and watched my paycheck vanish into his pocket, bidding farewell to the good bourbon I'd planned to buy with that chunk, and climbed out of the cab. I hardly had the door closed before the driver pulled away, sped down the street, and went tires-screeching around the corner, back toward the bridge. The rain had let up, at least, but it had left behind a chilly fog that clung like an unwanted embrace.

I looked around at the vacant, graffiti-scrawled brick buildings, the winos snoring in corners under blankets of yellow newspaper, the trash going to rot in the gutters. I was starting to wish I had something bigger than the snub-nosed Harpe .38 revolver I wore in the shoulder holster inside my coat. A gun like that worked well enough to intimidate your average two-timing pencil-pusher, but this wasn't exactly the part of town you read about in the society pages. The folks around here didn't scare so easily.

The block ahead pretended to be deserted but for one place with a red neon sign flickering over the recessed door. Club Erebus, the sign said, the first word winking on and off in buzzing electric spasms. My client, the erstwhile Miss Gray, could've ducked into one of the other entryways, I supposed—most were boarded but a few doors and windows dangled open here and there. I didn't doubt that a number of felonious transactions happened in those supposedly-abandoned pits, but I couldn't imagine my well-dressed client in any place like that—not while keeping her duds in that kind of shape.

Then again, I couldn't imagine her in this part of town at all, so what the hell did I know?

I paused a moment right outside the building with the sign and looked it over. Dingy stone, heavy door, no windows on the street level. The narrow ones on the floors above were all dark, maybe shut-up blind with black-painted plywood; in the sanguine radiance of neon and the feeble glow of the lamp at the corner half a block away, I couldn't be sure. From somewhere inside came the heavy notes of music, all thudding percussion and deep thumping bass, somehow dark and insidious. I felt it slinking over me like a living thing, making me squirm a little in my suit.

The dive's door was a faceless black; I didn't see a knob or handle.

I thumped the heavy wood with the heel of my fist, loud.

A narrow slot raked open, dark eyes glared at me. The slot rammed shut.

The door remained closed.

I sighed. This case was gonna blow a gaping hole in my wallet, the way things were shaping up. I fished a large bill out and held it at the level of the slot. I doubted this little blind pig was so exclusive the gorilla on the door wouldn't take bribes.

I pounded again, keeping the bill nice and high.

The slot dragged open, slowly this time. The eyes squinted at me, at the cash. Then a thick, calloused hand poked out, pinched the bill between two stubby fingers, and withdrew into darkness. The slot rattled closed and the door swung open.

I stepped inside, keeping my hat on and taking a good look at the goon on the door as I slipped by. I'm no stub, but this goon towered over me by a solid foot and his shoulders looked wide enough to park a truck on. He wore his black hair slicked straight back and had a jaw someone had chiseled out of granite. His pinstripe suit looked fresh-pressed but gave off an odor I didn't want to think too much about, like maybe he'd borrowed it from someone recently embalmed. His beady black eyes had a watchful glint to them that made me think of a mean-tempered dog. He gave me a look that said *one wrong move and I'll break you in half and toss the pieces to the rats in the back alley.* I couldn't imagine any good answer to that gaze, so I ignored it.

I wandered away from the door and the big Bruno guarding it, into the crowd and the gloom.

The interior of the place looked like it had never had as much as a passing conversation with the exterior. Everything about it—the art deco tile floor, the fancy wallpaper and the chrome trim on all the fixtures—suggested a club that belonged in a much nicer part of town, on the other side of the river. And if the style felt about ten years out of date, it had been kept up nicely enough that a high-class crowd wouldn't mind it a bit.

The joint wasn't exactly packed, but enough people milled and slunk and sauntered around that it seemed plenty busy. Off to my left, a sallow man dressed all in black poured drinks into cut crystal glasses behind a chrome and polished mahogany bar. Beyond, the other rooms meandered away into a smoky gloom; shadow-eyed people crouched in dimly lit booths mumbling at one another over black-lacquered tables. That thudding music droned on from somewhere deeper inside, resonating in my bones, making my teeth ache. The pressed-tin ceilings seemed a shade too low, the hardwood floors scuffed and lusterless, the glamour of the front room swiftly abandoned once you poked a little further in. A dull gray smell hung thick in the air, under the odor of smoke—the stink of things rotting in dark places, moldy carpet and stagnant water. The whole damn place rubbed me the wrong way, especially those damn tunes; I felt the scar over my eye itching. I resisted the urge to scratch.

The clientele in this dive wasn't what I expected. There were plenty of dubious looking characters keeping to the deeper shadows like spiders in their webs, sure, but also folks in pricey glad rags, old boys and businessman types puffing sweet-smelling imported cigars, ladies drinking dark wine from long-stemmed crystal glasses. The layers of society mixed so completely here it got so I could hardly tell the high-class dames from the hookers, the bankers from the crooks. If you care to say there's much difference.

My mystery woman was nowhere to be seen, but I would've bet another couple of sawbucks I'd come to the right place.

I wandered back and slouched against the bar, keeping my eyes on the room beyond. The smoke shifted and wavered like a living thing, almost pulsing with the thumps of the bass and drums. My head hurt.

"Hey, pal," I said, tugging the bartender my way with a waggle of my finger. "Gimme a double bourbon, neat."

The fella—bald as a cue-ball and about as white—gave me a nod and poured the drink. As he set it down, I dropped yet another large bill on the polished wood and pushed it his way, clamping it there with my fingers. The bartender raised a black eyebrow at me.

"You seen my friend here?" I asked. "Good lookin' lady, gray suit, red hair? The classy type."

"I couldn't say," the bartender said, voice thick as a slab of slate.

I tapped the bill, already feeling sure it wouldn't help. A fella who paid his bills pouring bootleg hooch knew how to keep his lips zipped.

"None of my business who drinks here," the barkeep said. His voice was flat as cheap gin and tap water, and I thought it had sort of an echo to it. The sound of it set the short hairs on the back of my neck bristling. I played it cool, as much as I could.

"C'mon, pal, help a fella out. She's an old friend, and I know she came in here …"

"That'll be four," he said, nodding at my glass. I managed not to wince at the fact that this one drink cost as much as the cheap bottles I managed to acquire. With a forced shrug, I slipped the bill back into my pocket and tucked it away, dropped a handful of change on the bar. The bartender swept the coins up and turned his back to drop them into the register.

He hadn't said anything useful but he'd told me what I needed to know and it'd only cost me the price of a fancy double bourbon. I'd watched his eyes when I'd described my client and for just a second he'd given her away, sneaking the slightest gaze off to the left, further into the meandering club. The kind of tell any half-decent poker player would've caught.

I swallowed my bourbon whole—and hell, it was worth every penny—then headed off the way the barman's eyes had pointed me.

It took some doing—the club twisted and turned around on itself like a maze—but at last I spotted her, sitting in a booth among a group of women, all gathered around two men. The women presented an interesting mix—my client and two others looked like society girls, ones that had more business sipping champagne in some ritzy uptown boutique than guzzling wine in this dump. Of the other three, two wore too-short, too-revealing dresses and I made them for working girls for sure. The last was hard to place, decked out like some nice suburbanite's daughter or college girl looking for a questionable night on the wrong side of town, the kind she'd regret when the sun came up.

The two Jakes they all fawned over made an interesting pair as well. The fella book-ending the bunch was tall and gaunt, sunken cheeks and deep-set eyes, skin chalky white. His charcoal suit was immaculate, creases all razor-sharp, his bowtie perfectly knotted. Something about the figure he cut got me thinking of an undertaker who never went off duty.

The other fella—the one the girls' eyes all kept going back to —was older, his hair silver at the temples and salt-and-pepper on top. Distinguished looking, you might even say. His dove-gray duds didn't call attention to themselves the way the undertaker's sackcloth suit did, but I guessed they cost five times as much. The fella reclined in the center of the little harem, now stroking one girl's hand, now lazily playing with another girl's long blond hair, now sliding an idle paw under the table and doing who-knew-what with it ... Even without the girls constantly batting their eyelashes at him for his approval, his sheer casualness would've made it instantly clear he was in charge here. The other fella, the undertaker, sat never smiling, mostly watching the action beyond the crowded booth but now and then glancing at the boss and nodding mildly; everything about the man said "lackey." He might as well have had the word pinned on his lapel.

I hung my coat on a brass hook between two booths and slipped in behind a table kitty-corner to theirs, fairly sure I could keep an eye on the weird little crew without getting spotted. I had no idea how my client would react if she saw me, and the idea of finding out definitely tempted me. For now, though, I decided to play it cool and see what developed.

I ordered another drink and cocked my head toward Miss Gray's table, trying to snatch bits and pieces of the conversation out of the smoke-dense air, but that lousy music droned on and on and muted everything else away to meaningless static. As I watched the girls chattering away—probably nothing but empty chitchat in any case—I started to think maybe their enthusiasm wasn't what they pretended. They nodded to the older man, laughed at one another's witty little quips, and smiled … But the more I spied on them, the more I sensed a strained quality to the whole show, as if it was all just a game they were playing, and not a very enjoyable one at that. They seemed too eager to chat, almost desperate to fill in all the empty spaces with noise, to keep their jaws working and their heads bobbing for fear of what'd happen if they stayed still for even a second. They smiled readily but their eyes never lit up and after a while I saw their grins almost as grimaces, veiled misery painted in shades of rouge and bright red lipstick. I wondered what kind of a man could sink such deep fear into those girls—the kind of fear that kept them close and kept them dancing. Then again, as far as I could tell my Miss Gray had come here on her own—gone out of her way to be here, in fact.

Sometimes fear had its attractions, too, I supposed.

My bourbon arrived and I sipped it slowly with one hand while the other crept into my pocket and tugged out that nifty little G-man camera. I set it flat on the table and, keeping it as hidden as I could under my long broad hand, took blind aim and clicked. The tiny camera only held enough film for half a dozen exposures, so I had to be choosy, but one good shot and the wad of cash I'd blown on this little excursion would all be worth it.

The girls chattered away with the older fella, whose cold-as-steel gaze never flickered, whose stoic face hardly changed, even when he responded. I clicked.

The girls all laughed at some clever remark he'd made but his façade didn't crack.

Click.

He turned his head and nuzzled my client's long lovely throat, lashing her peach-fuzz flesh with his tongue in a distinctly predatory way, all hunger and no affection, all power without passion or intimacy. It turned my stomach a little.

Click.

The woman I'd called Miss Gray returned the kiss with compound interest, even as another girl, eager not to be left out or ignored, mauled the man's throat from the other side. He seemed hardly to notice.

Click.

I polished off the bourbon and wanted another one—anydamnthing to blot out that lousy infernal music, the thumping in my head, the churning in my gut. That knot of scar over my eye tried its best to drive me around the bend, but I forced myself to ignore it.

The booze hadn't helped. The crowd, the smoke, the noise, the music—it was all getting to be more than I could take. I had to get out of this dive, fast.

But not before I got a good look at whatever happened next.

I'd finished my third bourbon and was about to start on the fourth when all at once the girls scooted out of the booth, trailing along after the undertaker—who stood fully a foot higher than I'd guessed he would, almost a match for the goon on the door—in a direction I calculated led deeper into the club. Mr. Dapper with the silver at his temples followed like a shepherd keeping his sheep in a flock. The girls kept looking back to him and chattering or batting their eyelashes and tossing their hair, as if making sure he was still behind them, pretending they wanted him to be.

I waited until they'd passed, then tossed a couple bucks change on the table and went after them.

Somehow, they got far enough ahead of me that I damn near lost them in the gloom, among all the milling strangers. They passed through the room where the little combo thumped the drums and made the bass and brass groan like tortured banshees, and I thought my head would split. The fella on the piano wasn't so much tickling the ivories as tormenting them, and I wanted to shove him off his stool and play an aria or two to save my own sanity. Instead I hung back, as inconspicuous as I could make myself, and watched as the goon—either the same fella who'd been up front, or his twin brother warts and all—opened a narrow door through which the gaunt man disappeared down what I took to be a dimly-lit flight of stairs. The harem followed close behind him, Mr. Dapper close at their heels like he meant to be sure they stayed in line.

I stood frozen, watching the crew stumble down and out of sight, each girl wearing a smile with all the warmth of a death rictus. At the last instant, my client, she of the ember-red hair and fresh-cream skin, turned back to steal a kiss from the older man—and for an instant our eyes met, and locked, and I saw a glimmer of fear in her face, a desperate plea, though I felt absolutely certain she didn't know my face at that moment any more than she'd known her own name when she walked into my office. Then she kissed Mr. Dapper's neck and he slipped a long arm around her and they slunk away through the door. I got the impression of dank cellars and steep stairs, but it was more an instinct than an observation.

The goon closed the door after them and I thought I caught

a glimpse of something painted there—a large circle, bright red against the black mahogany of the door. The goon dropped a red satin curtain over it, then stood in front of it with his arms crossed over his huge chest and his lantern-jaw jutting menacingly.

I touched the piece inside my coat, feeling its compact deadliness. No point even thinking about it. I couldn't get past that thug, not without making the kind of scene that wouldn't help my cause at all. And a round from a .38 would only make a fella his size mad, unless I managed to put it right between his peepers.

I studied the curtain and the goon in front of it for a minute, out of the corner of my eye, then ambled casually away, in a direction I hoped was out.

It seemed to take damn near forever to wend my way through the labyrinth of booths and rooms, the cigarette smoke growing dense as a fog, the music writhing over and through me. The faces of the people around me hung in the gloom like dozens of gray balloons, their eyes too big, with features drawn on by a mediocre artist. I felt like a man wandering through an ugly dream. Probably it was the booze warping my thoughts, though hooch usually didn't have that effect on me unless I'd consumed a lot more of it. All I wanted was to get out of this rotten gin joint.

Somehow, the fella who'd blocked the door where my client and her crew vanished had made it back to the front ahead of me, because he stood there watching as I slunk past. He gave me another black look, like maybe he knew or half-knew or almost knew what I'd been up to, and I thought of the camera in my pocket, and the gun in my holster.

Big Bruno met my eyes. I met his.

I looked away first. Let the man have this little contest. No point in giving him anything else to remember me by.

Then I pushed out into the street and hurried toward the bridge, hoping it wouldn't take too long to get myself a cab on the other side. I'd be plenty happy never to see this part of town again.

Even so, I paused halfway across the river, looking back into the depths of that shadowy brick canyonland. I didn't care for the feeling that I'd abandoned her, that I was giving up on the woman, my erstwhile Miss Gray. Sure she was just some gal who'd paid me a retainer to dig into her own life and I didn't know her from Adam or a street tramp. But those eyes, they left afterimages in my mind—so much fear, so much loss. I could hardly reconcile those eyes with the woman I'd seen in that creepy speakeasy. Whatever was behind those eyes, the ones she'd gazed at me with when I first saw her, that was the person I'd been hired to find, and I hated abandoning her with those shady men and their peculiar harem. All of a sudden the money didn't seem like such a big worry. I had to solve this case to banish the ghosts from those haunted eyes.

I thought for a second of turning my shoes around and walking right on back into that dingy neighborhood, right back into that so-called club, and nursing a bourbon or two until either my client or the morning sun put in an appearance. But I had a gut feeling I'd only be wasting my time and frittering away my cash.

A languid breeze came up off the river, carrying a rotten black odor with it.

"Hell with it," I muttered, out loud so maybe I'd believe I meant it. Then I went on down the bridge towards the lights and the traffic on the eastern side and grabbed the first cab I saw.

THREE

SNAPSHOT

I t was plenty late but I didn't go home right away. Instead, I stopped off at the Cain Building and used my passkey to let myself into the little darkroom adjoining my office. Maybe I felt guilty and needed to do some kind of penance by working myself all night, or maybe I just wanted to get this case over and done with as soon as possible. Either way I knew I wasn't about to get any sleep until I had the things hung and drying, ready to print and study in the light of day.

I poured the chemicals then killed the overhead light. I'd done this kind of work dozens of times, but tonight the perfect darkness of the room and the eerie quiet of my empty office got to me in a way it never had before. I kept imagining I could still hear that skin-crawling music from Club Erebus—but the place was dead silent except for my own breathing. Even the sounds of traffic five stories below didn't make it in here. No light, no noise, hardly even a sense of up and down. I felt like a man swimming in a sea of India ink.

Working blind, I popped the film out of the camera, prepped it, dropped it into the developing fluid and sealed the tank. Then I clicked the light back on, set my little egg timer, and paced until it rang.

Developing fluid out, stop bath in, shake like a watered-down martini—I knew the routine by heart. All the shots I'd snapped over the years of insurance cases whose injuries miraculously healed when they thought no one was looking, of cheating spouses and their paramours, of businessmen meeting with the wrong people in the wrong places—the vital tools of my trade, and not exactly the sort of stuff you trusted to the corner drugstore. Still, in all my years I'd never been quite so crazy to get my hands on the finished product, and even now I can't say exactly why.

I swapped stop bath for fixer, shook up the canister again and then dumped the last of the chemicals out and gave the negatives a good long shower under the tap. Then at last I hoisted the strip and pinned it to the line strung over the counter to dry. I thought about digging out the loupe I'd acquired from a grateful jeweler not long ago (it'd turned out his brother *wasn't* swapping phonies for the real things), but I knew that it wouldn't be enough to reveal much detail in the tiny frames of the government-issue film. I'd have to wait until the negatives could go into the enlarger—a few hours at least, if I didn't want to risk scratching the not-quite-dry emulsion.

The pricey timepiece on my left wrist informed me that midnight had already come and gone. A smart man would've headed home, caught a couple dozen winks, and come back rested and ready to solve the world's mysteries in the morning.

Instead, I shambled out into my office, dropped myself into my desk chair, put my feet up on the big paper blotter, and shut my eyes for a while.

Sleep kept drifting close, but my mind was too occupied by everything that had happened the night before for it to take hold. In the dark behind my eyelids I re-watched the events from the moment Miss Gray showed up to the minute I'd climbed into that cab headed away from the club where she and the rest of the strange party had disappeared through the door with the red circle on it. The more I pushed the pieces around in my brain, the less they added up to a picture I could make any sense of. She clearly knew those folks—Mr. Dapper and the undertaker and the harem—but didn't know herself? Hard to buy. But then why pay me to look into her doings? I couldn't figure. Some kind of game, or a plot to tangle me up in something ugly? Who'd bother? Sure, I had a few enemies—probably two dozen angry wives, husbands, and various lovers who'd been less than happy with the results of work I'd done at some time or other, and a fistful of conmen I'd caught in the act. But the trap scenario didn't play. Anyone who really wanted to give me the kiss-off would just show up at my office with a Roscoe in his hand and take his frustrations out with a few rounds of hot lead. As far as I could tell, that left me with two possibilities. Either the poor girl was plain crackers, or I'd gotten myself into something much weirder than anything I'd ever seen before. And thinking of her face, her voice, her eyes, I felt sure as ever she wasn't crazy.

Those eyes … Lord help me.

The first light of morning sneaking in through the Venetian blinds roused me from my nap. I sat up blinking, my stomach grumbling. The Half Moon Diner a block away would already be slinging hash and pouring strong hot joe, but hungry as I was, I didn't even think about leaving.

I dragged myself out of my chair and shuffled back into the darkroom. In the gore-red gloom of the safety light, I plucked the negatives from the line and gave them a quick look, but the tiny images, light swapped for dark, were no more than meaningless semi-transparent shapes, ghosts spied through a keyhole. I dropped some photo paper into the enlarger and fed in the negatives.

A dozen sheets of photo paper and a lot of chemicals and water later, I had my eight-by-tens.

The first shot was nothing but shadows, a bunch of black and gray with no meaningful shapes to be seen. Ditto the second. The third had some hints of light in it, but nothing I could make any sense of. The fourth was better. The fifth was pitch black.

I played with the timing, I underexposed the print sheets. I adjusted and readjusted. Images swam out of the dark, but mostly nothing more than vague blurs, shapes that were probably faces hovering over a candlelit table, but not so's anyone could recognize them. But there was that one. The one good print of the bunch.

That one bugged me.

In it I could pretty much make out the girls, all gazing raptly at the spruced-up sultan in the middle of their queer little harem, those same vapid smiles etched on their waxen features. But the fella himself, good ol' Mr. Dapper, was a blur, his features smeared as if he'd shaken his head wildly the second I'd snapped the picture. That didn't track with anything I'd seen of the fella—seemed to me he'd hardly batted an eyelash the whole night, except when he'd bent to one of the ladies to indulge in a long hungry kiss. I frowned at the picture, at the various others dangling from the drying line. So many meaningless smudges of light in pools of dark, all of it painted blood-red by the dark-room light. For no good reason I thought again of that endlessly thumping music, and the stale stink in the air of that grim gin joint, and my stomach flopped. All at once I wanted to get out of the darkroom almost as much as I'd wanted to get out of that club, pretend I'd never seen those crazy photos, maybe come back in the bright light of day and take them all out and dump them down the incinerator chute. Or better, have Cass do it for me, and never have to look at them—never have to *think* of them—again.

I closed my eyes and tried to rub the exhaustion out of them while I breathed slow and deep. The fumes from the chemicals got inside my head, made my thoughts swim. I wanted a breath of fresh air more than anything in the world, but I knew damn well if I walked out of that darkroom I wouldn't walk back in unless it was with a book of matches. So instead I opened my eyes and shoved a negative into the enlarger and set the focus and exposed it.

It was the same one I'd just done, I thought, but as I watched the image come together out of the chemical bath, it looked like the damn thing had changed. Now the girls' faces blurred into uselessness, seemed almost to melt toward Mr. Dapper in the center of the shot. This time, it was him I could almost make out, face turned about one-quarter profile toward one of the indistinguishable girls. And something else that got those short hairs on the back of my neck prickling all over again, something I thought I saw but couldn't trust my tired eyes to tell me truthfully. There was a kind of ripple to the image I couldn't account for—bad chemicals? bad light?—but I was pretty sure I could make something out of this shot. I reset the enlarger to its highest magnification and arranged everything how I wanted, then printed another copy, and another.

It took me four tries, but I finally managed to get the damn thing sharp enough to use, and I could clearly make out the detail I thought I'd seen in the regular-sized print: Mr. Dapper's face was turned toward the ladies on his left, but his eyes looked straight into the camera. His gaze was raw hatred carved in obsidian.

All a bunch of coincidence, I knew. There was no way he'd seen me, or my little spy camera, I'd happened to catch him as his eyes shifted. But the illusion was damned convincing—that icy stare might have been meant just for me. The glow of the safety light made the whites of his eyes look like he'd burst some blood vessels, like a prizefighter I'd once seen after an especially brutal bout, and I couldn't shake the feeling they were watching me, as if he could see right through that picture and into my skull.

Who the hell was this man, and why was my Miss Gray mixed up with him?

I snapped the photo up on the line to dry and got the hell out of the darkroom.

In the outer office I stopped a minute, lingering over Cass's desk, not sure why I was doing it. Her workspace was immaculate, as always—everything lined up just so, pens standing at attention in their brass fixtures, tidily-typed invoices stacked up neat as could be in her OUT basket. That one picture standing alone at the corner, her mother all silver hair and pearls, a subtle hint of a smile on her lips. I wondered for a minute what Cass was doing right then. Maybe just putting a coffee pot on the stove, fixing herself some breakfast before getting ready to come in to work. I tried to picture her place—something small, given what I could afford to pay her, but cozy, and every bit as shipshape as her desk, chintz curtains and lace doilies on the tables. It was funny —all the time we'd worked together, I couldn't think of a single time I'd ever seen her outside the office. That one lone framed picture could've belonged to anyone—or no one.

Still, some part of me couldn't help asking those questions I'd never bothered to ask before. Who was Cass O'Clare, after she left suite number five-thirteen in the Cain Building? Did she have a fella? Did she even want one? And—why would I find myself asking now, after all this time? I kept seeing her expression when she told me there was something different about this case, kept recalling the hint of a shadow in those always-bright eyes, a tiny suggestion of what I'd seen in the mysterious Miss Gray's eyes. Something about it …

I sighed, raked a hand through my hair. It was too damn early and I'd had enough of shadows. I thought about the wrinkled sheets on my shut-up Murphy bed, twenty blocks uptown. If I could catch a cab at this hour, I could get home in time to catch half an hour's sleep before I had to come back and open the office for the day.

Then I remembered the fifth of bourbon stashed away in my bottom desk drawer. A minute later I was slumped in the hard wooden chair behind my desk with the bottle in my hand and a fire burning its way down my throat to my gut. For a while after that I didn't think about funny pictures or too-dark bars or Miss Gray or Cass O'Clare or much of anything else.

FOUR
BUSINESS HOURS

A h, Frank. Again?"
I struggled to open my eyes to that voice, but my
eyelids were pasted shut. I rubbed at them with fingertips on
hands that weighed ten pounds each and tried again. They went
up slowly, in fits and starts. The light falling in through the slats
in the blinds came at a sharper angle now, muted behind a gauzy
gray layer of clouds, but it still pricked at my vision for a second
or two.

Cass stood just inside the door marked Private, shaking her
head at me and frowning at the empty bottle at my elbow.

"I had a feeling I was gonna findya here," she said, "I really
did. You gotta stop treating yourself that way. You aren't a
sponge, you know. Now here, put this on," she said, holding up
a hanger with a freshly-pressed shirt on it. "Make yourself look
professional."

"You keep that handy, do you?" I said, taking the shirt.

"Someone's gotta look out for you," she said, stepping out
and closing the door so I could change, as if catching a glimpse
of me in my undershirt might cause a scandal. Once I put my
coat and tie back on, I'd at least be presentable. Well, apart from
the bags I could feel under my eyes, and the five o'clock shadow.

"Do we *have* any clients today?" I asked, poking my head out into reception area while I straightened my tie.

Cass pulled a clipboard out of a drawer and gave a quick glance at the single page it held. She gave a sour little frown she clearly didn't want me to see.

"Only Miss Gray this morning. If she shows."

"Mm," I grunted. "Better give the hotel a call, see if she ever checked in. Anyone else?"

"A coupl'a fellas after lunch—salesmen, I think."

"Cancel 'em," I said, with a wave of my hand. "I don't wanna see anyone today who isn't payin' for my time."

Cass gave a little sigh. "Yeah, I bet."

I answered her sigh with a glare that she ignored by busying herself straightening the pencils in her pencil cup. Smiling in spite of myself, I closed the office door and settled back into my chair.

I sat back a minute, letting my fingers wander over the eighty-eight keys I sometimes imagined running along my desk, plinking out a few measures of "Aria da capo" from Bach's *Goldberg Variations*. I rarely got to play a legitimate piano, and music was something I pretty much kept to myself. But even letting my fingers wander through the motions tended to help me think. I suppose a lot of people listen to music for pretty much the same reason.

My fingers strolled over invisible keys; my mind drifted free. I'm not sure if my eyes slipped closed or not.

All of last night wafted through my thoughts again, like a dream, its substance unraveling under scrutiny. The mysterious Miss Gray, the west-side dive with its half-baked efforts at opulence, the music that made my skull ache, the pallid strangers inhabiting the smoke-fogged chambers. The fella staring out of the picture at me, Mr. Dapper, sultan of that cock-eyed harem. Who the hell was he? I got the sense he mattered, or some people thought he did, anyway. Some instinct tugging at my gut insisted this fella was in the middle of everything, that when I figured him out, the rest of the pieces would snap into place pronto.

I hefted myself out of the chair, went into the darkroom, plucked the three good prints off the line, and slipped back out into my office. I dropped the things on my desk with a twinge of revulsion, then sat down and forced myself to study them.

If I'd expected the close up to look less unsettling in the flat light of the overcast morning, I was disappointed. Mr. Dapper's eyes still seemed to pierce the glossy surface of the photo and dare me to meet his gaze. If I'd been a smoking man, I would've put those paper eyes out with a nice hot cigarette, for sheer spite. The scar on my brow itched something fierce.

I dropped the picture again, pushed the stack aside and sat back, gazing out through the blinds at nothing in particular. Outside, the mist had coalesced into something a shade thicker, and a somber rain had begun to fall.

The buzz of the intercom shocked me out of my brown study.

I sat up and tapped the respond key. "What's the word, Cass?"

"I just got off the phone with the day manager at the Chandler. Miss Gray never showed at the hotel. You want me to check around with the cops?"

I thought about the flicker of fear in Miss Gray's eyes when I'd suggested going to the police. Made me wonder about a few things. Might be calling in the boys in blue wasn't such a bad idea at that; I could at least find out if there was a missing persons report matching my client's description.

Even so, I hesitated. I had this strange and powerful feeling in my gut that if I opened the door to the cops, I'd have a mighty hard time shoving it closed again—at least not before something bad slipped through. At best, police came with all sorts of rules and protocols and paperwork. I'd left all of that behind for a reason.

And I couldn't quite bring myself to betray those dark, haunted eyes.

"Uh, hold off on that, willya, Cass?"

I could hear the doubt in her voice, even over the coughing static of the intercom. "Sure thing, Frank. If that's what you want."

I let that go, too.

Then another thought occurred to me. "There is something else you can do for me," I told Cass. "Get on the phone with the City Register's office and see if you can track down who owns the buildings on Cocytus Street between Canal and Sunset?"

"Sure thing, Frank."

Cass clicked off and I tipped back in my chair, tugging at my chin like maybe I could massage a few useful thoughts out of it somehow. I wanted to chase down the name of the fella in the picture. More than a few of the city's lowlifes owed me favors, and a couple seemed the types who might recognize Mr. Dapper if they got a look.

But that would have to wait. For the moment, I didn't want to leave the office, in case Miss Gray decided to put in an appearance. Some part of me knew it was foolishness—hell, I wouldn't have bet even money I'd ever see her again—but the mere possibility of digging a little deeper into the mystery of her, of looking into those gorgeous, haunted eyes again, kept me rooted to my chair. Even that empty rumble in my stomach couldn't move me just then.

I pulled the rest of the pictures out of the darkroom and pretended to study them, even though they were, every last one of them, useless, all the faces blurred or running like wet ink, unrecognizable. But even those distorted inkblot images had a creepy quality to them that made me squirm, as though they were somehow obscene, visions snatched from a twisted mind. It was crazy, sure, but I felt it all the same. After a few minutes I stuffed them all in my desk drawer and tried to pretend I'd never looked at them. I wouldn't even let myself think how different those two prints were from what I'd thought was the same nega-tive had turned out, or what the hell it might mean. Then I went to shuffling around some of my own paperwork I'd been putting off, and made a couple of basically pointless phone calls to some city desk and crime beat editors I knew in case anything useful had slipped past me in the papers lately. There'd been nothing.

Mostly, I tapped out soundless symphonies on my desktop, and waited.

It turned into a wasted day, but I was more anxious than angry.

I hadn't had a trace of the erstwhile Miss Gray, and no new clients had wandered in, either. Even Cass's hunt for the owner of Club Erebus had led to nothing but dead-ends—somehow no one held the deed, no one paid the taxes, no one even paid to keep the lights on. It was about enough to make me wonder if I'd dreamed up the whole crazy night. But the photos in my desk and the negatives in the darkroom made a pretty convincing argument otherwise.

The sun had just settled behind the jagged line of buildings to the west when I tapped the intercom and told Cass to take off.

"But—it ain't closin' time yet," she said. "Still forty minutes—"

"Never mind," I said. "I don't think we're getting anyone else in here today. You go on home." For a minute I found myself wondering again what Cass did, away from the office. I couldn't imagine it.

"If you say so," she said, but didn't click off. After a static-filled pause, she went on, "You ain't gonna sleep in the office again, are you, Frank?"

"Nope," I promised. "All outta hooch here anyhow. Think I'll probably call it an early night myself."

"I hope so." She sounded relieved, but also maybe a little

dubious. I'm not sure myself if I knew I was lying to her when I said it, but I think she guessed. Still, she went on, "And make sure you eat a real dinner. You gotta take better care of yourself, you know that? I ain't always gonna be around to remind you."

"You're a first-class gal, Cass," I told her. "Go home."

"G'night, Frank."

She clicked off.

I slouched in my chair and watched that sign on the flophouse across the way wink on and off while I listened to Cass moving around in the outer office, her chair rolling back on the rough hardwood floor, footsteps and noises I couldn't place, then finally the front door—the one with Orpheus Investigation Agency painted in neat white letters across the frosted glass—rattling shut.

I sat back and waited some more.

I'd started giving serious thought to getting a quick bite somewhere, or maybe just picking up a bottle of bourbon and heading home, when the phone in the outer office rang, shrill as a fire alarm. I stepped into the outer office and plucked the handset out of its cradle.

"Orpheus Investigations."

"Miss O'Clare?" asked the befuddled voice on the other end, obviously clued in to the fact he wasn't talking to my secretary.

"This is Mister Orpheus, what can I do for you?"

"Uh, well, Mister Orpheus," the fella on the other end of the line said, "this is Arthur Geiger, the day manager at the Chandler Hotel. Miss O'Clare said to call if a, uh, certain lady came to check in here."

I clutched the phone a little extra-tight.

"Yeah? Well?"

"She just came to the desk, sir. She seemed, uh, a little … well, confused, if I may say so."

"She still there?"

"Uh ..." I could almost hear him craning over the desk to scout the lobby for her, "just on her way out, I think."

"Well don't let her go. Keep her right there—I'll be there in ten minutes."

He started to say he'd do what he could, but I hung up before he could finish, and was still tugging my coat on as I slipped out the door.

FIVE
ROOM SERVICE

I grabbed the first cab I could and told the kid behind the wheel to get me uptown posthaste. I hadn't thought too much about the cash I'd blown on this job last night, but I'd be a liar if I said it never crossed my mind that if I wanted to recoup my costs I'd have to make sure I still had a client. Beyond that I can't say exactly why I kept badgering the kid to step on it, already, forget that light, it's still yellow … Yeah, the erstwhile Miss Gray was a fine looking woman, and any fella with a little bit of fire in his veins would shove his own mother for another gander at her. But I've run across plenty of lookers in my day and none of them got me worked up the way I was now. I itched to push a few more of the pieces of this weird puzzle into place and I couldn't do it without a client … but that wasn't all and I knew it. It was more than curiosity, more than desire or even money. Somehow, in one night, Miss Gray had set her hooks in me like no one had in a long time. Maybe ever.

I climbed out of the taxi where the gilded Chandler Hotel towered over Elm Avenue, paid the cabbie, pushed my hat down on my head, and went inside.

Miss Gray sat in a high-backed velvet chair, sipping tea from a china cup. She had a tired, nervous air about her—her right hand trembled as she lifted the cup to her lips, and those haunted eyes seemed to stare blankly into oblivion. A slender man with a bald dome and a dark suit stood over her, looking from the door to her and to the door again. My friend Mr. Geiger, I figured.

When he spotted me he wrinkled his brow and glared, then nodded. I nodded back.

"Mister Orpheus?" he asked. He had a voice like gossamer, slick and thin and flimsy.

"The same," I said. "I'll take it from here. Thanks."

Geiger nodded and wandered away, looking a bit lost, and more than a bit relieved.

I dropped my coat and hat on the brass stand beside the low glass table and sat down across from my client. She was every bit as well-dressed as when I'd met her, but this outfit looked fresh and clean, a svelte white dress with a frilly red lace collar. Her smoldering hair hung immaculate over one shoulder, as fine as the silk of her skirt.

"It's nice to see you," I said, settling back. "I was beginning to wonder if I was ever going to again."

She studied me for a moment as if I were a complex equation, then frowned and drew back some. "Do I know you?"

I heard a lilt of hope in her voice, but it was a hope as pale as her ghostly face.

"*I* thought so," I said. "You certainly look like the woman who came into my office yesterday afternoon, asking me to find a name for her. That red hair is pretty hard to miss. That *was* you, wasn't it?"

She pinched her pink lips together until they were nearly white. "I ..." She paused, stared at me. "I don't remember. I'm not sure of anything just now. I ... you'll think I'm crazy, Mister —Orpheus, wasn't it? I might *be* crazy. You see I—I'm not even sure who I am ... My name, where I live ... It's like it's all just out of reach at the very back of my mind ... I found myself walking along the street tonight and didn't have any idea where I was going, or why … I felt through my pockets because … I don't know, I felt as if there was something there I needed. I found money—quite a lot of money, to be honest—and this."

She held up the business card I'd given her, then turned it around so I could see where Cass had written the name and address of the Chandler Hotel on the back.

"I figured someone who knew me might've written that … or maybe *I* wrote it myself … so I might as well come here and see if …" She trailed off, dropping the hand holding the card into her lap. "So, you're Mister Orpheus."

"As advertised," I said. "You really don't recall hiring me last night?"

"I—" She looked at me, cocked her head, frowned. "I remember something … almost like a dream. Something I dreamed a long time ago, and forgot all about …"

"Until I came along to remind you."

She nodded. I resisted the urge to lean across the table and take her slender hand in mine and promise her it would all be okay. She looked like she needed that kind of reassurance and I sure as hell itched to be the one giving it, but I was a complete stranger to this woman. If she was telling the truth, she'd known me for all of three minutes. And anyway, I had no idea if it'd all be okay or not. I certainly had my doubts.

"Well, you're not dressed the same way you were when we met the first time, so it could be you found your way home between then and now. And some part of you thought to keep my card on you, otherwise it would still be in the gray suit you were wearing when you came to my office."

"Gray …" she murmured, and I wondered if she half-remembered the sobriquet I'd given her. "That's all I have for memories—gray. A fog I can't see through and can't look past. It's a dreadful feeling, Mister Orpheus. Like standing on the ledge of a high building, with nothing to catch you if you fall." Her hands pulled and twisted at one another. "Tell me—please, Mister Orpheus. Tell me whatever you know about me."

"It's not much," I said, "but …" I told her all about how she'd showed up at my office and made that strange request, about the stack of cash she'd dropped on me, and the rest of our chat. I didn't mention following her over the bridge into the unsavory part of town, or anything about the strangely sinister Club Erebus and Mr. Dapper and his entourage. No point bringing any of that up just yet.

"I had my secretary book you into a room here," I finished. "I'm glad you finally showed up." I looked into her haunted eyes, watched them closely. "Any of this ringing any bells with you?"

She dropped her gaze and stared into her cup like she was trying to read the answers in the dregs. For a minute, she didn't say anything.

"I remember … Not all of it, but … enough, I think. It all feels like something that happened to someone else, that I watched from outside. Like a movie. But I can remember … most of what you told me."

"I take it your identity is still a mystery to you?"

"Apart from what you've just told me, all the rest is … vague, meaningless images. Impressions floating around my mind … They don't mean anything to me. I feel as if they aren't even my own thoughts."

"Can you tell me about any of them?" I asked, hoping I still sounded casual. I didn't want her to figure just how much I wanted to know about those images. No need to make her nervous, after all. And no need to clue her in to the fact that I knew more than I was saying.

But it didn't matter, because she just shook her head.

"No, it's all too … foggy …"

I saw that same dark glimmer in her eyes as she said it, and thought I heard her wanting to say something other than "foggy." Now she was the one keeping something from me, and it wasn't making my job any easier. But pumping her for her secrets wouldn't get me anywhere, either. She'd only clam up or get mad, and neither option would buy me anything.

So I asked, "You still want to employ my services?"

Finally she looked up at me, *into* me, with those dangerous, haunted eyes of hers. "You seem to be the only reliable part of my life right now," she answered, and again I hurt for her a little. "I'd be crazy to turn you away. Perhaps I am crazy. Perhaps *that's* my problem."

"You're not crazy," I told her, sounding, I hoped, several shades more confident than I felt.

She sighed and looked again into her empty teacup. I could see by her face that those leaves weren't telling her anything.

"If this isn't what it feels like to be crazy, I can't imagine how awful craziness must actually be," she murmured.

The helplessness in her voice broke through my resolve.

"I've got some information for you, but I'd rather not talk about it here. Can you come back to the office with me for a few minutes?"

She hesitated again, her hands shaking. Something about her whole look and demeanor reminded me a little of … But I put it out of my mind. I couldn't bring myself to think such unkind thoughts about the woman across from me. I couldn't attribute ugliness of any kind to that face.

The woman I'd spotted in Club Erebus the night before seemed that much more a stranger to me. Then again, so was the version of my client on the other side of the table.

At last she nodded, just a little.

"Let's go," she said.

We went.

The cab dropped us off under the dirty brown canopy of the Cain Building and we rode the clattering cage elevator up to the fifth floor in silence.

I led her into my office and she settled into the good chair, the red glow from the Hotel Moira sign splashing across her hair, red on red, over and over, like a warning. Part of me still wanted to hold back about the club, but I couldn't spin up a rational reason for it, and the potential benefits were clear as clean glass.

"The bad news," I said, taking my own seat on the other side of the desk, "is that I don't know who you are—yet. The good news is that I've gotten a look at what you've been doing with your nights—last night, in any case."

I tugged the drawer open and produced the close up I'd made of Mr. Dapper from my little photo session at Club Erebus. I dropped it on the desktop and pushed it across to her.

"You recognize that man in the center there?"

She picked up the photo and immediately sucked in a breath, like someone who'd just burned her finger. Her face lost the last of its color and the print dropped out of her hand and flopped back onto the desk like a dead moth. She drew back, eyes closed, and didn't say a thing.

"I gather you remember that face. You ought to—you were in his company last night, along with a half-dozen other women and another man I didn't get a good shot of. You know who that fella is, by any chance?"

Without opening her eyes, she said, "I don't know that man." Her voice sounded thin and brittle as old paper.

"Really?" I said, raising an eyebrow at her, though she couldn't see it. I don't think either of us bought her line.

"Only ... in my nightmares ..."

"And last night, at a place called Club Erebus on the west side, just past the Narrows Bridge," I added for her. "Ring any bells now?"

Miss Gray shook her head slightly. She shivered as she answered. "No."

That I believed, even if it didn't especially seem to make any sense.

Miss Gray opened her eyes and stared out the window, at the muttering city night.

"When I handed you that photo, you looked like you'd seen a ghost, maybe even the devil himself. I think some part of you remembers him. Why don't you take another look and see if that face jars anything loose—"

"No." Her voice was low but solid as granite. She plucked at her fingers as if trying to tug off a pair of over-tight gloves.

I studied her face, let a minute pass between us in silence.

"So," she said, very quietly, still pulling at her hands, "what do we do next?"

The tone of her voice let me know she didn't expect much of an answer. I considered taking it personally, but I could read her face, too, and I knew it wasn't me she didn't believe in. She didn't think *anyone* could help her. And whatever I might have seen the night before, it wasn't an act. Or if it was, she was the best actress I'd ever seen.

And maybe she was right.

"I'm gonna take you back to the Chandler and make sure you stay put all night. Then we'll see how you're doing in the morning. Meantime, I've got a few other things I want to follow up."

She nodded slightly, but her eyes had gone someplace else and her fingers went on working each other over. I thought again of the way she'd acted in the lobby at the hotel, overlapped that with the way she was acting now, and knew I'd seen something like it before, and dammit, I should've recognized it immediately. But maybe her high-class clothes and that strange quality of innocence about her had gotten my mental gears jammed, because I didn't place that behavior until later, when things had totally slipped out of my hands without me even knowing it.

Rather than making the connection that would've told me so much, I got lost again in her eyes, in that air of hopelessness about her. I wanted to take her in my arms and try to convince her with my touch that all was not lost, that she could still be saved from whatever dark shadows haunted her life.

Instead, I said, "There is, uh, the small matter of my retainer. Don't be offended, but I'm gonna need some operating cash here, and since you may disappear tomorrow and forget you ever hired me ..."

Talking money helped push those tricky feelings down where they belonged, turned her into a client again.

Miss Gray nodded, reached into a deep pocket and produced more of those much-used greenbacks. She peeled a few of them off and pushed them across the desk to me. I tucked them away without bothering to count them.

We cabbed it back to the Chandler and I took her up to her room myself, stepped inside to give the place the once-over. Not large, but plenty nice enough, all dressed up in art deco from the pearly-glass light fixtures to the flare-backed bedframe to the polished wood nightstands—phone on one, sleek little Bakelite radio on the other. Two narrow windows looked down on a dirty cobbled alley and the fire escape clinging to the rough brick wall of the building across the way. Well, it couldn't all be luxury, I supposed. Even my client's impressive bankroll would only stretch so far.

"Will this do?" I asked my client.

She looked around the place like maybe she hadn't noticed anything about it when we first walked in. "Yes, I'm sure," she said, sounding anything but.

I checked those windows. The panes only slid up a few inches, not nearly enough for anyone to slip in or out—and in any case, the eight-story drop seemed pretty likely to discourage a person from taking that particular exit. The lock on the door looked sturdy enough—sturdy enough to keep someone *out*, anyway. Not as good for keeping a person *in*.

"Best keep your door locked all night," I told Miss Gray, "just in case someone without my good intentions comes looking for you. I'm not saying anyone will, but … well, we really don't know what we're dealing with here, do we? So let's play it safe. Don't open the door until morning, and don't open it for anyone who isn't me. Even the charming Mister Geiger. If he's got any problems, tell him he can work them out with me. Understand?"

She nodded, but her gaze had wandered off out the window somewhere, back into the night again.

"Call my office at eight sharp," I said, lingering near the door. I had work to do out there but couldn't quite bring myself to leave her, not the way she looked right now. Scared, uncertain, seeking any kind of solace. Those lips begged for a comforting kiss, that finely-appointed shape ached for a reassuring embrace.

I stuffed my hands into my coat pockets. Bad enough I'd allowed myself to feel anything for her. I couldn't compound my mistake by acting on those foolish impulses.

She went on gazing out into the dull electric glow of the nighttime city, the lights all haloed with fog, and trembled again, her hands working to rub a little warmth into her soft white skin.

"You alright?"

She hugged herself like she felt a cold draft.

"I feel like … like …"

She stopped, and shook her head. I let it go, but I think we both knew what she meant. *I feel like there's someplace I'm supposed to go …*

"Will you come by in the morning?" she asked, turning those haunted eyes on me. "Before eight, I mean?"

I try to stay cool when I'm on a case—hell, even when I'm not—but that beautiful, helpless face melted me a little.

"Sure, if that's what you'd like."

Did I see a tiny spark of hope in those eyes? I thought so—
and that about finished me. I forced myself to open the door.

"Are you … are you sure you have to leave now?"

I was sure I wanted to close that door behind me with the
two of us on the same side and not open it again until sometime
well after the sun climbed up over the bar-graph skyline to the
east. Just looking at those porcelain features, those black-opal
eyes, stirred a fire in me that I hadn't fed in longer than I cared
to think about. But giving in to that heat would be wading
neck-deep in muddy water, the kind a fella could sink in
without a trace.

A little voice at the back of my head whispered that the only
way I could be sure she didn't wander off again was if I stayed
right there in her room … and if something else happened to
help the night pass a bit quicker, well, so it goes.

It almost seemed like a chance worth taking. That voice
made a good point—damn near talked me into the kind of
mistake a fella with as many years' experience as I had should
never even think of making.

Looking at her, I knew she wouldn't object if I put my arms
around her.

But I said, "Yeah, I better go. There's a fella I wanna talk to."

She said nothing, only nodded slightly and went back to
staring out the window. I wanted to go draw the white curtains
closed, as if any prying eyes might spot Miss Gray eight floors
up, but thought better. If I went back into that room, I was
pretty sure I wouldn't walk out until daybreak.

"You stay put," I told her. "Right?"

"I hope so," she whispered.

I gave the door another look. No latch on the inside, just a
keyhole.

"Alright, let's up the odds, shall we? The second I'm out this
door, you lock it, then slip the key out under the door. I'll hold
onto it until I come back by tomorrow morning. You'll be

locked in, but at least we'll both know where I can find you when the sun comes up."

She gave a shuddering sigh, and nodded.

Again, I started out the door. Again, she managed to stop me.

"Mister Orpheus ... thank you. I owe you more than mere money can repay."

"Only when the case is closed. And believe me, I'll be happy to settle for mere money."

It was a nice line, but not exactly the truth. I wanted to solve this case if only for the chance of chasing the ghosts from her eyes.

On that, I stepped out.

A moment later I heard her lock the door behind me, and a few seconds after that the key slipped out from under the heavy wooden door.

I plucked it up, tucked it in my inner jacket pocket, then I walked away, fast.

Once she was out of sight it was a bit easier to forget what I'd passed up, what I'd left in that room on the eighth floor. I stepped into the cage elevator and the old fella in the black-billed cap and white gloves rattled the gate closed and asked what floor. I said, "Lobby," and he nodded and set the clattering thing in motion.

"I want you to do me a favor," I said as we sank toward the ground floor. "The lady I came in with, you remember her?"

The little fella grinned. "I may be a might long in the tooth, but I ain't dead. And my eyes still work plenty good."

"That's good news for both of us," I said. "Make sure she doesn't wander off, got it?"

"My *eyes* work good, but could be my *hearin'* ain't what it useta be," the old fella said, grinding the cage to a stop and shoving the brass lever that locked it in place.

I'd expected as much. The last few days plus a decade's experience had taught me that nobody does a man any favors.

I found a couple of the bills my mystery woman had given me and pressed them into a gloved hand. They disappeared into the operator's pocket without a trace.

"If she happens t'ask," he said, with a sly, rubbery smile, "the elevator's broke, and the stairs don't work neither."

"Good man," I said, and he slid the door open and ushered me out with a pleasant—and maybe slightly more honest than usual—"Have a *good* night, sir."

I gave the same speech to the concierge, greased that wheel too, then went outside and had the doorman flag down a taxi for me. I had to trust my precautions to keep Miss Gray safe for the night, much as I hated to let her out of my sight. I wanted to find out Mr. Dapper's real name, and I was pretty sure I knew where to start asking.

SIX

SNITCH

The fella I needed to find was a mole named Hally Thersis. In his younger days, Hally had his hand in just about every game on the West Side. He carried the bag for a number of small-time bosses, broke a few fingers and a few windows when little shows of force were called for, and generally hooked lowlifes up with whatever they might be looking for. Strictly two-bit stuff, but the kind of thing that gets a man's name known with a certain element. Hally was climbing up there in years these days so the rats that slunk around the canal neighborhood took him for harmless. I guess that made him easy to talk to because they seemed to drop secrets on him most of those fellas wouldn't have trusted their own mothers with. Which was fine with me because Hally, in my experience, never minded making a few extra bucks selling an earful of gossip now and then.

I had the cabbie wait for me outside the Cain Building while I grabbed the pictures off my desk, the enlargement of Mr. Dapper and the two other decent prints, for good measure. I settled into the back seat and told the driver I wanted Parnassus Street. The fella raised his eyebrows at me in the mirror but pointed the taxi in the right direction anyway.

He didn't bother with the usual cabbie chitchat and that suited me fine. I busied myself studying the photos again in the islands of light the streetlamps threw down between rivers of dark. Yellow light spilled through the cab's windows and I saw Mr. Dapper's ice-cool gaze, pointed right at the camera like he'd known I was snapping his picture, and wanted me to know he knew. Even now I didn't like looking into those dead black eyes —not haunted, like my client's, just cold and hard and mean. A shark's eyes, soulless and predatory. I shuffled the photo back under the stack while we sank into darkness. When we emerged again, I was looking at one of the blurred images, the unrecognizable women clustered around the sharper shape of Mr. Dapper. I could tell the form on the far left belonged to the sallow gent who'd reminded me of an undertaker, sitting there mostly ignored by the strange harem. Rumbling into the next oasis of light, I looked at the last picture in the stack, the one that showed the girls most clearly and Mr. Dapper hardly at all. And there ... I waited out another plunge into darkness, and rise into street light glow ... I saw my client, entangled in the moment, a butterfly in a spider's web. Something about the image stuck in my mind, something I could *almost* cull even from that shadowy image. I felt it as strongly as I'd felt that other instinct while I watched my client in the hotel ... And both things dangled there just outside my mind's grasp. I was letting other thoughts distract me, letting my feelings tangle up my thinking and it was getting in the way of doing my job.

I thought again of Cass, warning me not to touch this case, but pushed the memory aside. Cass was sweet, and a damn fine secretary, but she tended to get a little carried away with that "sixth sense" she claimed to have. Still, I got the feeling that the sooner I put the mysterious Miss Gray and all the rest of it behind me, the better for everyone.

I reached up to claw away the itch that'd suddenly sprung up in that scar of mine, but it wouldn't go. I opted to try ignoring it.

Shadows washed over the photos in my hands then ebbed away again like an over-eager tide. What the hell was it about those shots, anyway? I knew some secret sat there in plain sight for me, but I couldn't grasp it. If I could just catch hold of that loose strand of detail, who knew what I'd unravel? But I groped and plucked and came up empty-handed. I figured I might as well stash the damn things away and let it go for now, think about other things awhile. Instead, I went right on staring at those photos until the cab nosed up against a garbage-strewn curb and the cabbie mumbled, "Here y'are."

I stuffed a couple of bills in the hand he flopped back toward me and told him to keep the change, then climbed out and slammed the door behind me. The damp gray stink of the canal mixed with a belch of exhaust as the cab roared away. Apart from the retreating rumble of the taxi, the place was quiet as a tomb. I ambled down Parnassus—hardly a street, really, more of an unglorified alley with a name and a couple of three-stool coffee counters tucked away here and there.

I found Hally right where I expected to, in a dingy little automat called the Delfy Café, as if the name could class the place up. The old fella sat slouched in a corner booth, steaming up the window with his sour breath. He hardly bothered to look up when I slipped onto the patched-up vinyl bench across from him, just went on prodding at a flat and soggy-looking wedge of cherry pie. He dragged one pulped fruit out of the mess, leaving a sticky red snail-trail behind it, then poked it into his mouth and chewed a minute, like an old dog with a chunk of rawhide.

"I still don't know why you like this place so much, Hally," I said, by way of greeting. "The food here makes army slop look like dinner at the Ritz."

He chewed a minute more, swallowed pointedly, then tipped back his little brown pork pie hat and nodded at me.

"Long time no see, F. O." Hally referred to nearly everyone by their initials. Guess it was left over from his numbers-running days and all the accounts in the black books. "I'm guessing you didn't come here to catch up on old times, huh? I'm guessing on accounta you never do."

"You see right through me, Hally."

Hally grinned at that, showing uneven teeth the color of old newsprint, now caulked together with muddy red-black cherry sludge.

"You want ... lemme see, you want ..." He rolled his eyes up like the answer might be scribbled on the water-stained ceiling, poked his pink tongue out the side of his mouth. "You want ol' Hally to maybe name a name for you, huh? Am I right?"

"Yeah," I said. He always was.

"I always am," he said, and dropped me a wink, his face a crumpled-paper mess of wrinkles.

"You have a gift, Hally."

He nodded as he excavated another cherry-corpse from the ruin of his dessert and sucked it off his fork and chewed.

"Let's see just how gifted you are," I said, shuffling the enlargement of Mr. Dapper to the top of the stack. "Can you put a name to this face?"

I slipped the photo onto the table next to his half-empty coffee cup.

Hally dropped his fork.

He looked up at me, all hints of joviality erased from his features, his face the color of pigeon's feathers. He pushed the picture back at me without looking at it again.

"No. I dunno that man. You maybe should ask someone else. Or maybe don't ask anyone, you wanna be smart."

"Don't try to play me, Hally. You don't have the touch anymore."

Hally glowered at me. "I mean it, F.O. Let it go before it burns ya."

The man was genuinely scared, which struck me as both unsettling and distinctly interesting.

"I'll make it worth your time if you give me a name. Say—double my usual contribution ..."

"I dunno this fella's name, and you don't wanna know it either. So take a hike."

"I have to track him down, Hally. There's a lot at stake here."

He'd forgotten all about his pie and coffee. "You go deaf, F.O.? Walk away from this and don't sneak no peeks over your shoulder as you go. 'Cause otherwise I'm sayin' this could get ugly for you, I mean like you ain't seen ugly."

I leaned back, draped an arm along the back of the bench.

"Didn't I see you cutting cards with Nikki Scoda down at the Dark Horse the other night?"

Nikki "Six-fingers" Scoda was another small-time hoodlum leftover from Hally's day, but unlike Hally, he'd never gotten out of the life, at least not as far as I knew.

"You must be thinkin' of some other fella," Hally said, his face set like old plaster.

"Associating with known felons, gambling ... those are both violations of your parole, aren't they?"

"The cops ain't gonna bust me for nothin' like that. Look at me, I'm an old man."

"Say I happen to mention what I saw the other night—"

"You didn't see nothin' on accounta I wasn't there," Hally broke in.

I ignored him. "—to my friend Detective Snider in the vice squad, he'll have you back behind bars before you can finish that coffee there."

"Like hell," Hally said, but all the bluster had gone right out of his voice.

"A fella your age," I went on, "won't do too well in the clink. So the way I see it, it's pretty easy for you. You give me a name and maybe a little direction and walk away a some-what richer man, and I keep my mouth shut next time I see Detective Snider. *Or*, you keep your mouth shut, and I give my pal a call and you wind up back in the hoosegow for a while, scraping to make bail—if you last that long. Your choice."

Hally picked up his fork, tapped it loudly on his plate, then dropped it again. He looked out the window, looked at the half-dozen other booths around us, all dead-empty. A vague shape moved somewhere behind the wall of food-slots, dropping an egg salad sandwich into one nook, a slab of chocolate cake into another. Apart from that we were alone.

Hands shaking, Hally picked up the prints and flipped through them, wincing.

"You didn't hear this from me, no matter who asks," he whispered, glowering at me.

"I was never even here," I assured him.

"That man," he jabbed a finger in Mr. Dapper's direction, "he's real bad news. They call him Mister Radamanthus—always Mister. He ain't a fella you wanna get feelin' insulted, you hear what I'm sayin'? I hear he's a lieutenant in the Tartarus Syndicate. The tall fella with him," now he indicated the undertaker, "is Myles Ferryman, I think. He ain't nobody, just Mister R's favorite lapdog. I don't know who them girls are, but that fella, he's always got a bunch of 'em flocking around him. If he ain't too busy to be bothered, I mean."

"Mmm," I said, nodding. "And you know all this how?"

"Could be a did a few things for the Tartarus crowd, back in my youth. Odd jobs, is all, ya know. Radamanthus was already making his bones, even though he was hardly more than a kid."

"You're saying he's older than you?" I asked, not able to keep the doubt out of my voice, and not particularly trying.

Hally scowled at me, then dropped his skinny shoulders in a shrug.

"Some folks get old graceful, and some of us don't," he said.

I thought of Mr. Dapper's good looks—mature, but also strangely ageless—and cold fingers crept up and down my spine. "It's obviously not clean living," I said.

Hally snorted. "Next to him, I'm clean as hospital sheets."

"Oh, you're an angel," I said. "So, tell me about this Tartarus Syndicate. I can't say I've ever heard of 'em."

"Nobody knows squat about 'em," Hally said. "Not even me, F.O. Only that they been around a while and even the bosses are nervous about 'em."

"You said Radamanthus is a lieutenant. So who *runs* the show?"

Now I saw Hally get tense all over again. His eyes kept taking inventory of the automat. Checking for flies on the walls, I guess. When he didn't find any, he said, "I only hear whispers, okay, so don't quote me on nothin', but the way I hear it, the big man is someone they call Mister Menace. Don't ask his other names, I don't know 'em. Just Menace. I ain't ever seen him or heard what he looks like, so don't ask that either. All I know is his name makes some pretty mean fellas break out in a cold sweat, you know what I'm sayin'?"

"What's their game, this Tartarus bunch? Numbers, booze? Girls?"

"Maybe all them things. Maybe none."

The idea that this Tartarus crew might be running call girls made sense for a second, then didn't. At least three of the women draping themselves all over Mr. Dapper in those pictures weren't working girls. Too well coiffed and dressed and made up. Too much life in their eyes.

"Anyone who knows is too scared to say," Hally went on, "and anyone who says don't really know. Way I hear it, Mister M's muscle don't use guns 'cause bullets get the job done too quick. He likes 'em to use knives … likes to make his enemies bleed. It's sorta how his goons sign their work, I guess you could say."

"Thanks Hally," I said, sliding out of the sticky booth. "You've been a real help."

"Walk away from this one, F.O.," Hally said again, but softly now. "I'm tellin' you.…"

"Thanks for the advice." I tucked the photos away inside my

coat and tossed a few more bills on the table next to his coffee cup, then pushed through the door and into the dark of Parnassus Street.

Last I saw him, Hally was sitting in the automat, staring at his thumbs, his coffee and pie completely forgotten on the table in front of him.

SEVEN
UNINVITED

I was drifting into sleep on an amber ebb tide of bourbon when a realization hit me like a prizefighter's right-hook. I flopped out of my Murphy bed, yanked my clothes on, and jumped into my shoes. Eleven minutes later I was climbing out of a cab and making my way into the Cain Building, up to my office. It was late, but with that thought buzzing around inside my skull, sleep was no longer an option.

I had to look at those pictures again. I had to see if I was right.

My key had just touched the lock on my office door when the subtle sounds of movement coming to me through the open transom stopped me still as a department store mannequin. Whoever had been moving around on the other side of the door with the frosted glass window must've heard my footsteps on the creaky hardwood floor, because he stopped as quickly as I did. I wasn't fool enough to let myself think I'd imagined the whole thing. Someone had gotten in all right, and by the continued silence I gathered he was still trying to decide whether or not I'd noticed.

Or maybe I'd jumped to the wrong conclusion—maybe my self-invited guest wasn't a "he" at all.

In the drawn-out quiet, I took a good look at the lock. No signs that it'd been jimmied. I wished for the cool potent weight of my piece, but the damn thing was locked up in a desk drawer in the inner office; I never carried it unless I was on the job and had a good reason to expect trouble. I sure as hell hadn't expected any tonight.

My mistake.

Slow as I could, I reached out and gave the knob a twist—or tried to, anyway. Locked.

Damn.

That meant I'd have to use my key after all, and the fella on the other side of that door couldn't miss hearing the tumblers rattle as they turned back the bolt. I'd give away the last of whatever surprise I had left on my side.

For a second I held back. I thought about getting the cops down here to take care of things, a few of the boys in blue with badges and guns to wave around. But there was no telling what might happen in the time that would take—the nearest phone, other than the one in my office, was a payphone in the lobby. By the time I got down there and made the call and the dispatcher got some patrolmen on the scene, my visitor could easily finish whatever ransacking and robbing he'd come to do and make his getaway down the fire escape. In any case, I had strict orders from my client not to bring the cops into this, and as long as she kept footing the bill, I'd play by her rules. She'd seemed so damned earnest about it, like calling in the regular law might tear open a hole in her life she couldn't ever patch up again. Hers just wasn't a trust I could betray, even when common sense said I ought to know better.

I gave myself another second to figure how to proceed. Whoever was on the wrong side of my office door knew I was there, or would know as soon as I slipped the key into the lock. Neither of us was fooling the other one, so I went with the direct approach.

"Okay, friend," I said, loud, hoping my voice masked the

sound of my unbolting the door, "I know you're inside. I'm gonna count five and then open this door. Then you and I are gonna have a little talk about what you're doing in my office. Understand?"

I cocked an ear up at the slanting transom, but there was only silence from the other side.

"One," I said loudly, "two—"

I threw the door open before I ever got to three, slamming myself back against the wall beside the doorframe in case my guest had been waiting for a nicely framed shape to take a few plugs at. No way of knowing if the fella had come packing heat, or if he'd gotten into my desk and was in the mood to get in a little target practice before he went home from this party. The last thing I wanted tonight was to wind up full of holes from my own damn weapon.

But rather than muzzle flash and thundercracks, dead silence rang out from inside.

The fella was either real patient, or gone.

Damn again.

I waited half a minute in the hall, listening. Silence. A full minute passed. Silence. If the fella even had to breathe, I didn't hear him doing it. Maybe he'd slipped out whatever window he'd crawled in through while I'd been shouting nonsense, hoping to distract him. And maybe not.

There was no way I could avoid making myself a target as I went through the door, but I didn't see I had any choice. I went in low and fast and flattened myself against a wall, my gaze skittering madly across the darkness, hoping to catch any hint of movement, any out of place shadows framed against the crimson glow winking in the window.

The quiet held, deep and black. I could just about hear my heart beating too hard, and that was all.

I gave a moment's thought to clicking on the light, but if the fella did have a gun, I'd only make his shot that much easier for him.

Slowly, I straightened up, my vision adjusting to the gloom now. I could make out all the prosaic details of the outer office —Cass's desk and the battleship-gray filing cabinets standing against the wall, the wooden coat rack in the corner, naked for the moment. The chairs standing where they belonged. And the door to my inner office, standing open on three narrow inches of total black. Which it shouldn't have been.

I frowned, and felt my hand wander up to scratch that scar, which had come awake itching again.

I waited what must've been five minutes—I could just about count it up by the ticking of the clock on the wall beside Cass's desk. The fella had obviously gone the same way he'd gotten in; nobody could hold still that long without making a single sound.

I turned on the light in the main office, and looked around.

If anything was out of place, I couldn't spot it. Cass would know for sure, but I figured I could wait until morning to bother her with it. Right then, I was more concerned about what might've been done to the inner office.

I slipped inside and turned on the light.

If I'd expected the place to be tossed, I was disappointed. In fact, for a minute I thought my visitor hadn't touched anything at all, that maybe I'd scared him off before he could get started with whatever fun he'd been planning.

Then I saw the drawers hanging open on my desk like sprung jaws, and the scraps of paper littering the floor. I circled the desk and looked down—and muttered a few choice curses under my breath.

The photos. My visitor had gotten to them and turned them into confetti. I could see a bit of shadow here, a curve of face there, something that might've been a hand, something that was probably a bottle.

I gave a grunting laugh. I couldn't help myself. I'd made a point of stopping by here on the way back from my tête-á-tête with Hally to stash the snapshots away in my desk. Where they would be safe. Now the proof I'd come back at this ungodly hour to get lay at my feet, shredded. I'd delivered it right into the intruder's hands.

Except—

I stooped, looking closer. A few of the pieces were larger, and one photo had only been torn into rough quarters. Seemed maybe I *had* interrupted the vandal before he'd had a chance to make good on the job.

I dropped the four corners onto my desk and arranged them like a cheap jigsaw puzzle. It wasn't one of the better shots, just a collaboration of blurs whose shapes I could only half make out. It was enough, though, to make me feel pretty confident about that insight that'd chased my sleep away for the night.

Still, I had to make sure, so I bent and started sifting through the bigger shreds of the other photos, looking for a scrap of confirmation.

I'd just caught sight of a delicate hand cradling a half-full wineglass, a black stripe on the ring finger, when the lights went out and the door slammed shut behind me. I whirled to face it, blinded by the sudden dark.

The fella hit me from behind.

I never saw him coming, never even heard him. But at least I understood, as I hit the deck, why he'd left the pieces in my trashcan instead of taking them with him. He'd baited a little trap for me and I'd gone and stuck my big foot right in it.

Or maybe the fella was just an idiot who got lucky.

I'm still not sure what the hell he clobbered me with—a sap, a baseball bat, a fist the size of a Christmas ham, could've been any of those. All I know is his first shot caught me across the back of the head and set off blazing green fireworks in my skull. I flopped forward onto my knees, struggling to maintain even a scintilla of balance, knowing that if the fella got me down, I might never get up again.

I wobbled, trying to turn to face the man, to at least get a look at him in case I ever had the chance to go hunting for him.

Somehow, he hit me from the other side, another brutal, crashing blow. This time he got me right across the orbit of my eye, knocking all the color and most of the light out of the world, bashing my nose with his follow-through for good measure.

Still trying to get up, I flopped onto my back, as if this fella couldn't finish me off at his convenience. I managed to half-sit, and was rewarded for my effort with a bash to the mouth that snapped my head back against the hardwood. My body went on struggling to get up, but my brain had taken about enough—my consciousness was draining out of my skull in a steady trickle of blood, the darkness becoming uniform and featureless.

Something heavy slammed my ribcage and shoved me hard to the floor. I managed to open my left eye a slit and gaze up at the goon standing on my chest. He stood about sixty feet tall and was made entirely of shadows. And yet I thought I saw something distantly familiar in that fading outline. I couldn't be sure, though. Under those circumstances, I couldn't even be sure of my own name.

"You wanna watch where you go stickin' that fat nose of yours, pal."

The voice drifting through the haze in my brain sounded thick and dull, with a low animal snarl under the words, like static on a poorly tuned radio station. If I'd ever heard it before, I sure couldn't place it then. It was hard enough just catching a breath with his solid-granite foot on my ribs.

I think I tried to say something back at him, or maybe I twitched, or inhaled too deep—anyway, I did something that didn't sit right with him because he lifted that massive foot off my chest and delivered a kick to the soft part of my midsection that sent pain blazing through me all the way to my teeth. I lay there groaning, not able to do much of anything else.

Now the giant crouched down over me, filling the world above me like a towering thunderhead. For an instant, I had the sense someone was there with him, some phantom hovering over his shoulder in the background, a shadow that didn't belong, and I had the crazy thought, *So that's how he got in*—whatever the hell *that* was supposed to mean. But I only had a second to try to make sense of any of it, then a thick hand grabbed my collar and hauled me up into a reclining position, my arms hanging at my sides as useless as broken twigs. I wished this idiot would finish me off and get it over with, or leave me there to writhe in peace.

No such luck.

"You gonna remember what I said?"

I managed to make a thick gurgling sound neither of us could make any sense of. My guest chose to take it as a negation.

"Maybe I better oughtta leave you a reminder then, huh?" he said, and I saw a sharp metal wink in the bloody neon glow from the sign across the street. When the blade descended toward my half-open left eye, I let go of consciousness and sank into blessed black oblivion.

PART II: ORPHEUS DESCENDING

EIGHT
HOUSE CALL

I came awake to a feeling like angry hornets crawling around in my face, trapped between the skin and the muscle and not real happy about it. I tried to express my unhappiness at this situation through a properly piercing scream, but my lips were mashed shut and my jaw really didn't care to cooperate. Hot-lead pain blazed up through my skull every time my heart pounded, so that my head and heart throbbed in a dizzying syncopated rhythm.

"God, Frank, oh my God!"

The voice floated down to me out of the black, senseless sky behind my eyelids, but I didn't have to see her to know that voice. I struggled a second to open my eyes, but the effort rumbled thunder-like through my brainpan and I gave it up for a while.

Eyes.

I tried to count them, even through the mask of pain somebody had put in place of my face. I thought I got to two, but counted again to be sure. Two. So the goon had only wanted to scare me and work me over a little. I can't say I was exactly ecstatic with relief right then, but knowing I might still have some depth perception didn't bother me any.

"Just stay still, Frank, I'll call an ambulance … oh my God
—" Cass stammered from somewhere above me.

"No," I managed to say, "ambulance."

"Hush, now, Frank," Cass whispered sweetly. "Just lie still."

"No ambulance."

I amazed myself by putting some force behind the words.

"Frank! Your face is … I mean, God, Frank. I'm *calling* an
ambulance."

I couldn't allow it. An ambulance meant a hospital. A
hospital meant sooner or later someone would call the cops.
Cops meant people asking questions I couldn't answer, or didn't
intend to. I wasn't having any of that.

"No damn ambulance," I muttered. "Call Doc Ambrus."

I managed to tilt my head, ignoring the avalanche of pain in
my skull, and opened one eye—the one not puffed-shut—as far
as it would go, which was just about nowhere.

"Frank—"

"Doc … Ambrus."

"Okay," Cass relented. "But if he ain't in, I'm calling Mercy
Hospital and have 'em send an ambulance."

I settled back onto the comforting hardwood floor and let
the lead weights in my eyelid drag it closed again. I tried to call a
phrase or two of music into my mind—a whisper of Mozart or
Strauss to salve the pain some—but my hands didn't feel up to
the task of moving over the ivories, imaginary or otherwise, and
I never can make the music come to life without tickling it
awake with my fingers. Funny how the notes seem to live in my
fingertips and nowhere in my gray matter.

I heard Cass pick up the phone, heard her exchange hurried
pleasantries with the Doc … and then for a while I didn't hear
much of anything. And that was fine by me.

Next thing I remember, someone yanked my right eye open and blazed a white light straight into my brain.

"Knock it off, Doc," I muttered, surprised at how well my mouth worked given how mashed my lips felt. "I already had one fella try 'n blind me."

Doctor Jayr Ambrus was a retired GP who'd had a family practice sometime back, though there was still some dispute about precisely which Family he'd practiced for. I'd done some work for him a few years ago when he'd suspected his wife—a pretty, empty-headed strawberry blond twenty years his junior—had gotten involved with a fella closer to her own generation. I'd gotten pictures of the wife with the interloper, and the interloper had gotten dead—though not by me, to be sure. Doc promised me he hadn't asked anyone in his Family to rub the poor slob out, but he'd gotten his wife back, and plenty contrite, and he couldn't say he felt real sorry for the boy with the great big hole in his skull. For my help, Doc had offered his whenever I needed it. I had to say he was a gracious sort, for someone who didn't put too much stock in the Hippocratic oath.

"Gotta check for concussion," Doc said, letting my left eye go and prying the right one open without much regard for the fact that it was blown up like an innertube. "For all I know you could be in a coma right now. Hell, the way you look, you might be dead."

"You're a real riot, Doc," I said through lips that felt like jellyfish, all soft and puffed up and full of poison. Still, thinking of that shadow I thought I'd seen behind my attacker, I had to wonder how badly rattled my brain might be.

"Hush, now," Cass said, nearby. "Let the man do his work."

"Smart girl," Doc said, prodding my face with what felt like red-hot knitting needles but may've just been his fingers. "You should listen to her."

"Like when I said this case felt all wrong," Cass said. "I told you there'd be trouble, didn't I tell you?" Her tone didn't have a hint of gloating in it, only a kind of giddiness I took for nerves and shock. Must've been a fun time for her, finding me sprawled out and broken on the floor of my office, my face looking like a tomato someone had peeled, pureed, then stomped on for good measure. Maybe it wasn't as bad as it felt, but knowing how a shaving cut bleeds I figured it must've been hell to look at.

"Yeah, you told me," I agreed from inside my halo of agony.

"He gonna be okay, Doc?"

"If he were in anyone else's hands, he'd be coffin stuffing," Doc said, working my face over with acid-soaked steel wool, or maybe only cotton gauze. "Fortunately I specialize in putting the meat back together after it comes out of the grinder, so I think I should be able to make this lump of hamburger into a face again."

"Thanks loads," I said.

"You got much pain?" he asked, prodding, making sure I had plenty.

"Never been better," I said. The hurt in my flesh tried to shove me back into the dark of unconsciousness, but I fought it. I thought of the revelation that'd brought me down here in the dead middle of the night, and the photograph tatters on the floor, the wreckage of the only tangible evidence I'd gotten so far in this case. A nasty thought occurred to me then.

"Cass … the dark room …Check the negatives.…"

"Huh?" she said, forgetting in all the fun that she still worked for whatever was left of me. "Oh, sure Frank. Right."

I heard her low-heeled shoes shuffle across the floor.

"Nasty business ya got here, Frank," Doc Ambrus observed.

"You're one to talk," I muttered. The sounds continued to come out enough like words for him to make some sense of them.

"Now, no point dwelling on the ugly past. We've both got skeletons in our closets, huh?"

I didn't think he had anything specific on me, but the general principle was sound enough. I offered agreement by way of silence.

"There ain't no negatives in the dark room, Frank," Cass reported. "Sorry."

That figured. I doubted the goon who'd broken my face had much by way of brains, but even dumb hired muscle like him would have strict instructions to make sure the negatives got destroyed. Thinking that, I finally placed that odor in the air.

"Look in the trashcan," I told Cass.

A half-second's quiet.

"Hm," she said. "Buncha ashes and, uh … melted lookin' stuff."

The remains of the pictures and the negatives, I guessed. Torched in the trashcan and left here to make sure I understood what my guest had dropped in to take care of. Pounding me to within an inch of my life had been the added bonus, his good luck.

"How …" I managed, slipping, trying to yank my senses back into place by force of will. "How did he … get in?"

That queer thought I'd had when I imagined my attacker had brought a friend echoed in my mind right then—*So that's how he got in* … But it made even less sense now than it had then.

"I," Cass started, then stopped. I could just about hear her looking around the room, inspecting windows, doors. "I can't figure. Wasn't through the front door?"

"Locked when I got here," I said, while Doc went on about whatever he was doing. "Not jimmied."

"Coulda been picked," Doc ventured. He'd started prodding at other parts of my battered body, but that didn't matter so much. The pain wrapped around my skull washed out any other aches and bruises.

I thought about Doc's comment, but lock-picking didn't seem like my midnight visitor's style. He struck me—so to speak—more as the type who took the "breaking" part of "breaking and entering" pretty literally.

And yet there didn't seem to be any sign of that, not from

what Cass said and not in what I remembered from my interrupted inspection of the place last night. If I could have
managed it, I would've frowned at the apparent contradictions
in all this.

Doc said, "You're gonna need to be sewn up. I'll give you
something for the pain—or would ya rather just bite on a
bullet?"

"Just hold your horses, Doc," I said, fending him off with a
hand that shook badly. "Cass, call the Chandler and have them
ring Miss Gray's room. If she doesn't answer, have the day
manager go pound on her door. Tell him to use his passkey if he
has to. I wanna know if our client slipped away again."

She went into the outer office to make the call. I waited
while Doc went about pulling various instruments of medical
torture out of his little black bag. The call lasted a long time, and
much of it was silence. That couldn't mean anything good.

When Cass came back, I knew what she was going to say.
Not that I liked it any better for that.

"She's gone, Frank," Cass said. "The fella said her bed didn't
even look slept in."

I sighed. More legwork ahead, and no knowing if it would
lead to a paycheck.

I tried not to think about how much it bothered me to
imagine the erstwhile Miss Gray out there lost, alone, hurting,
or maybe just hurt.

"Okay, Doc, your magic potions all ready to go?"

He tapped the syringe and smiled entirely too broadly.
"Always," he said.

"Great," I said. "Fix me up, and fix me up."

I hardly even felt the needle as it pushed a dose of morphine
into my blood. And then for a while I didn't feel anything at all.

NINE
ITEM

S omewhere in that opiate sleep, I found dreams. Maybe there was one, maybe several washed together, swimming in and out of one another. I can't recall any of it clearly anymore. I vaguely remember walking empty, rain-slicked streets, the air ripe with decay. Seeing myself from somewhere outside my own eyes, in a dark place, but not alone. My mystery lady rises from a shadow; she wears a smile that casts no light in her haunted eyes, a smile that chills me. But when she comes to kiss me, I respond in kind. Of course I do. There's a chill to her embrace that makes me try to squirm away, but I can't, don't really want to after all. I feel eyes on us, but can't see who's watching, and don't care. Let them watch, let them ogle, if it gives them even a tiny taste of what I'm feeling, that crazy dark thrill ...

I drifted out of my haze, my head bobbing like a balloon on a long string above my neck. Cass and the Doc had deposited me on the battered sofa that Cass always urged me to replace because it was an eyesore and didn't do much by way of impressing clients. I told her my clientele wasn't typically all that concerned with furnishings and the thing did just fine thanks. It was lumpy as hell but in the lingering cocoon of the morphine it felt great. I silently thanked a God I didn't much believe in for Doc's tendency to play a little loose with the pharmaceuticals. I supposed the men he usually patched up didn't have many scruples when it came to those kinds of things. I wondered how many of his "patients" got this kind of treatment just by asking for it, probably with cash.

Then something broke the surface of the murky waters that filled the back of my brain, and I sat up and nearly flopped onto the floor. I knew why Miss Gray's behavior the other night had looked so maddeningly familiar—my profession had taken me into enough opium dens and drug alleys to recognize a junkie who needed a fix.

I rubbed my eyes, my face tingling wherever my hands touched, and tried to piece it all together—thoughts and face both. My nameless client didn't strike me as a user—not that pricey clothes and nice manners meant anything there; rich folks get hooked the same as anyone else, just on more expensive junk. Still, something in those eyes made it hard for me to think of her as the type. But I couldn't ignore the evidence my *own* eyes had already found—the pale skin, the strange way she'd acted, the dubious company she kept in bad parts of town. I thought maybe I'd stumbled across an answer to at least a few of the questions that had dragged me into all of this.

As it turns out, I was a lot more wrong than right—and wrong in ways I could never have dreamed, not in a year of nightmares.

"Welcome back to the world."

Cass's voice swam to me through the lingering mist of blunt force and swirling morphine.

"Thanks."

"How you feelin'?"

"Not," I said. "Not much, anyway. Thanks to Doc."

"I don't like that man, Frank. I don't trust him as far as I could throw him, which ain't too far if you haven't guessed."

"Me either, but I know he won't get the cops involved in any of this. That's what matters for now."

Cass sighed with unmistakable reproof. She wanted to say again how she'd warned me this case would be trouble, and remind me what a thick-headed fool I was, not getting the cops in on this, but she was nice enough to let it go.

"Frank, I been wonderin' … What were you doing here so late, anyhow?"

I hadn't thought about that much since that truck had hit me last night, but now I saw those tattered pictures again, and the details I'd managed to salvage before it all went bad—the evidence that proved the midnight insight that had dragged me here in the first place. There had been that shadow on her ring finger, for one thing. Not enough detail for me to say for certain, but I would've been willing to bet good cash it was that strange ring with the red vein running through it. But that intrigued me a lot less than the main attraction—the trend I caught running through the images that had come out at all. My client hoisting a wine glass in the one clear picture, taking a drag on a long cigarette in one of the blurred shots—always with her left hand. I'd watched her in my office, at the hotel, watched her take my card, watched her sip her tea and handle the photo of Radaman-thus, and do it all with her right hand. I supposed she might be ambidextrous, but that didn't really wash either, since I'd only seen her use one hand at a time. I wondered a minute if maybe I'd flipped the negatives when I printed them … but no, I remembered seeing the other fella, the gaunt lackey Hally'd called Ferryman, sitting on the same side of things in the picture as he had been in the club. The photos had been all right. It was my client who was all wrong.

I considered sharing some of this with Cass—I generally found it to be good policy to keep her informed—but dismissed the thought without asking myself why.

"Just catching up on business," I told her. Not a lie, exactly, just a good deal less than what she deserved of the truth.

She sighed again, to say she wasn't happy with me playing coy—but I also sensed something else in that sound, something that made me pick up my head a bit.

"Something on your mind, Cass?"

"Well …" She hesitated, and I managed to open my eyes and give her what I hoped was a hard-edged glare. "It'll wait until you're feelin' a bit better."

"I think I can handle it now."

"If you say so," she said. "This was in the evenin' paper. I just saw it a few minutes ago, while you were still out."

I winced, stared at the window. Sure enough, it was evening already, and swiftly darkening toward night—the Hotel Moira sign was flashing its crimson smile again, like a cheerful warning. Cass handed me a copy of the news, folded open to the story she meant.

Small Time Crook Murdered

the headline said.

I shook my head, knowing well enough what was next.

Police went to Melinoe Street late last night responding to a call reporting a murder. There they discovered the body of Harold "Hally" Thersis, obviously the victim of foul play …

The story didn't say what "obviously the victim of foul play" meant, but it did go on to mention that Hally had been associated with any number of disreputable people and businesses in his younger days, and said the cops hadn't picked up on any suspects yet. I figured Hally's past being what it was, the police wouldn't exactly be working overtime to nab whoever'd put him on the slab.

The story, I saw, had been interred on page sixteen. Buried in obscurity just as Hally was likely to be. Somehow I doubted he'd mind.

I dropped the paper on the sofa beside me and watched the red neon splash across the office windows and vanish, splash and vanish. It was almost hypnotic.

So: I was a mess, and Hally had finished up dead. A sudden queasiness went through me as I put the pieces together and asked a question I'd never know the answer to but had to ponder anyway: had he given me up before his killer started pounding on him, or did the goon beat my name out of him before finishing him off? I hoped for Hally's sake he'd coughed up my name at the first hint of trouble, and that things had proceeded quickly from there. That the end had at least been quick.

I'd taken Hally's paranoia for the jitters of an old man with a rough past, but clearly I had to rethink that now, had to consider what I was tangling with in this Tartarus Syndicate, and this Mr. Menace.

All I know is his name makes some pretty mean fellas break out in a cold sweat, Hally'd told me. And within a few hours, he was dead and I was in danger of following him to the morgue.

It made me wonder why they hadn't killed me, too. But I suspected I knew. After all, it was one thing to rub out a nobody like Hally who'd lived his whole life on the wrong side of the law and didn't have a real friend in the world. But a fella like me ... I may walk that line sometimes, maybe I even tripped over it once or twice, but I'm a mostly-respectable businessman in a decent part of town, and if I wound up "the victim of foul play" the way Hally had, the police might take it a bit more seriously. I felt pretty confident Cass would make sure they did. The Tartarus Syndicate could take Hally out without calling any real attention to themselves, but that wouldn't be quite as easy with me. Better just to clean me out of evidence and scare me off if they could. And I had to say—at that minute, sitting there thinking of poor Hally and of that blade sweeping down toward my eye, I was plenty scared. Ready to throw in the towel kind of scared. Miss Gray fascinated me, and I felt for her, a bit too deeply. And she paid well, thanks. But none of those things matter to a fella who gets what Hally got.

Still, if they could get to Hally that quick, and end him so fast, what might they do to Miss Gray? I was a sap and I knew it, but the thought of anyone marring those perfect features in even the slightest fashion made me furious enough to punch a bull between the eyes.

Taking a few long, deep breaths to steady myself, I perused the article again, thinking mostly about what it didn't say. Hally's remains had been found on the West Side, just beyond the river. That put the whole thing in the one-three precinct.

I tried to stand, but my legs weren't having any of it. They felt like two sausage-casings stuffed with clay. My whole body felt as dull and heavy as a damp sandbag.

"Dial a number for me, will you, Cass?"

"Yeah, of course. What number?"

It took me a minute to dredge it up from the murk of my brain, but at last I rattled off a string of digits that sounded about right. Cass handed me the receiver and I stuck it up against an ear that was numb as a clump of cauliflower. The phone felt like about twenty pounds of cold dead weight in my hand. It rang twice at the other end before someone snatched it up. A voice told me I'd reached the Homicide Division. I told the voice my name was Ernest and I wanted to talk to Sergeant Angelo. A minute later, Angelo's gravel-rough baritone sounded in my ear.

"What's the story, Ernie?" Ernest was the name I used when I didn't want to advertise the fact I was plucking fruit from Angelo's grapevine. Sometime back I'd done him a couple of big favors and he still owed me a few small ones.

"I hoped you could tell me," I said. "You see the little item on page sixteen, about our old friend Hally Thersis? I figured your boys caught that one."

"Yup," Angelo agreed in a dead-flat voice.

"So what's the dirt, Angelo?"

"You have a personal interest in this one?"

"You could say. I need to know the stuff that didn't make the papers."

"Nan's," Angelo said. "Three hours."

"Sure," I said, and Angelo, never a man to mince words, hung up.

TEN

DISH

The face that glowered at me from Cass's compact mirror a few minutes later looked like something from a mad scientist movie, one where the crazy fella in the lab coat has sewn a monster together from spare parts. The ache had started gnawing again as Doc's magic shot wore off, but I could live with it. Not that I had much choice in the matter.

"You sure you're up to this, Frank? Jeez, that fella practically killed you."

"I'm going to Nan's, Cass, not the Black Hole of Calcutta."

"In your shape, it's about the same thing. Anyway, you don't exactly look too good."

"I'd noticed."

"Don't know why that cop friend of yours can't come to the office," Cass said, taking her compact back and snapping it closed.

"We try not to advertise our association," I said. "Some cop on the beat sees him come into this building, maybe somebody catches on. No cop with any self-respect would show his face in Nan's, so it's the perfect rendezvous."

Cass sighed, that old familiar sound. "I oughtta know better than to try to talk any sense into you."

"Yeah," I said, shrugging on my coat and pushing my hat down to shadow my face, "you oughtta."

I left.

The rain coming down on the twilight streets was that sullen gray kind that gathers from the mist and falls in slow motion, the kind that can hang there over the asphalt for days. I tugged my collar up and tipped my hat forward and plunged in, the drizzle embracing me coldly. My .38, all cozied up in my shoulder holster, nudged me in the ribs with every step. I rarely carried it unless I knew I was walking into a dicey situation— but lately my entire situation seemed fairly dicey.

Even as I walked those couple of blocks to the back-alley diner called Nan's, I couldn't help wondering just what I was really going after. What did it matter how Hally Thersis had died, anyway? Dead was dead whether you got shot or knifed, and I couldn't say I'd ever had any personal feelings for the man. Still, something itched at me, some instinct that whispered that Hally's death—and especially the stuff that hadn't shown up in black and white—was another big piece in this whole twisted puzzle. So I followed that instinct down Cora Street and around the corner into Nan's.

The place smelled of grease and cigarette smoke, and if the tiled floor and walls had ever been white, their current jaundice-yellow made it hard to believe. Angelo perched vulture-like on a stool at the counter, his beige coat bunched up under him in a lazy clump of wrinkles. A cup of coffee sat steaming on the yellowed countertop in front of him, but he hadn't touched it. No wonder—Nan's had the worst coffee in town.

Angelo raised an eyebrow at me as I sat down beside him and ordered the obligatory cup myself. The stubble-faced man behind the counter offered me something that was either a smile or a sneer and tipped a cupful of black liquid into a dirty cup.

"You've looked better," Angelo offered.

"Nice of you to notice," I answered. "But we're here to talk about our late lamented friend."

"Real piece of work, that fella," Angelo said.

"Mmm. So what's the scoop, Angelo? What happened that the papers aren't saying?"

"Messy business," Angelo said, dumping cream into his coffee and letting it hang there like a cloud, not bothering to stir it. "Some poor chambermaid found him in a room at a by-the-hour hotel on Melinoe Street."

I knew the area—west side, on the wrong side of the river. Same as Club Erebus. "Any record who rented the room?"

"According to the clerk, nobody did. He claims the room should've been empty."

I nodded. It all sounded entirely too much like the club nobody owned.

Angelo lit up a cigarette, took a long drag then puffed gray smoke into the greasy air, a thick-bodied dragon with a leather hide and a receding hairline.

"Poor girl who found him got herself quite a shock. Old Hally was sliced up good. Looks like they pounded on him to tenderize him some, then started in with ... whatever they used. Something nasty-sharp."

The words hit me like a body blow. I could almost hear Hally talking about Mr. Menace's hired muscle. *He likes 'em to use knives,* Hally'd said. *Likes to make his enemies bleed.*

"Far as we can tell, they started with his wrists," Angelo went on, the same way he might talk about the weather. "Opened 'em nice and wide." He put his right pointer finger to his wrist and drew lines back and forth across it, in a long shark-tooth zigzag. "Nothing neat and tidy. Then they opened his throat. Looks like ol' Hally put up a fight. Blood everywhere. Except ..."

"Except?"

"The coroner says not enough of it. Blood at the scene, blood in the body ... all comes up damn near two pints short."

"So he bled someplace else," I said. "They started him somewhere and finished him off in the room."

Angelo sighed out more smoke, shook his head in the cloud.

"Doesn't play that way. No sign that the body was moved, and no trace of blood anywhere but in that room. Can't see how anyone could've dragged him there in that shape and not left some kinda trail, no matter how careful they were being."

I stared at the food-spattered menu board beyond the counter without especially seeing the words scrawled there in hasty chalk scratches.

"So someone ... what? Removed some of the blood from the scene? Why?"

"Yeah," Angelo agreed, absently tapping his cigarette butt into his still-full coffee cup. The ashes wandered in lazy circles across the surface of the brown liquid.

I sat back and gazed at nothing. My face had started to itch again, but it wasn't the stitches Doc had put in a few hours back, it was that old scar over my left eye, nagging. I chose to ignore it.

Angelo sat equally silent beside me.

"Any thoughts on what the weapon was?" I asked at last.

"His wounds weren't all that deep—just deep enough. Something short and sharp. Can't say beyond that. Maybe the coroner will come up with something more definite."

The obvious question rose to my tongue, but I chewed on it a minute before asking. I guessed I already knew the answer, but had to be sure.

"Any idea who did this?" I asked. "Or why?"

Angelo took a quick tug on his smoke, spat out an acrid fog.

"Nope. With Hally's record, could be a hundred fellas for a hundred reasons," Angelo said. "There was one peculiar thing, though. Seems someone painted a big red circle on the wall over Hally's body. I imagine you can guess the artist's pigment of choice."

"I imagine I can."

"You have any idea what that's about?" Angelo asked, tapping more ash into his coffee.

I could clearly picture the rings with the strangely fluid red bands, the crimson circle on the secret door at Club Erebus.

"No clue," I said.

Angelo nodded like that was all he'd expected, and all he'd wanted. He shrugged. "Don't suppose we'll ever crack this one." Meaning the police precinct had written Harold "Hally" Thersis off already, foul play notwithstanding. They'd poke around enough to seem like they were doing their job, then let the matter drop so they could spend their time on more important matters—on this side of the river.

I felt my broken lips perk up in some aching version of a low-wattage smile. I couldn't help it. Fact was, I had a better idea who'd killed Hally Thersis than the cops, and I was keeping it tucked away under my felt fedora, even if the evidence was written all over my face—or carved there, as the case might be.

My smile turned into a frown, which I directed at my own coffee cup.

If I was right, the dotted lines connected me, the photos, the shadowy Tartarus Syndicate, and Hally Thersis. In one night, Hally had been slaughtered, I'd been attacked, and the photos had been destroyed—all within a few hours after I'd pried the names Radamanthus and Menace from Hally's lips. Fast work— scary-fast. This Mr. Menace character must've had ears all over town to have gotten word of what I'd been up to as quick as he had, and muscle enough to flex at a moment's notice.

I'd wandered too deep into the dark, brushed up against powers big enough to swallow me whole. Cass had been right from the start.

It was time I got out of this game.

I dropped a fistful of change on the yellow, peeling-at-the-edges Formica counter.

"It's on me," I told Angelo, and slipped out into that sullen rain.

ELEVEN
STIFF

I probably should have expected what happened next.

Closing time had slipped past thirty-odd minutes ago but the office lights shone through the frosted glass and the door wasn't locked.

I opened it slowly, just in case my late-night visitor had come back and was in the mood to finish me off after all, but didn't feel too surprised when Cass nodded at me from behind her desk.

"She's back," Cass said, pointing to the inner office with a slight nod. "I thought I oughtta stick around until you got here."

"Thanks."

"Maybe I better stay 'til we're ready to close."

"I'll handle it," I said.

Cass questioned me with her eyes. I dropped my hat onto the rack by the door and went into my office, giving Cass a look I hoped put her question to rest. A moment later I thought I heard her chair rattle across the floor as she got ready to leave.

My attention fell entirely on the woman seated before my desk.

She wore what I took for expensive silk, dove-gray trimmed with red, red piping on the lapels, red pockets, red buttons, red gauze tied around her wide-brimmed hat. Her skirt rose almost to her elegantly-stockinged knees, the deep V-neck of her fine jacket disclosed a glimpse of a nicely draped silk blouse. My heart thumped a shade too hard in my chest. The erstwhile Miss Gray had impressed me with her loveliness before, but something about the figure she cut just sitting there made her seem an entirely new person, more beautiful than any woman I'd ever set eyes on.

That old familiar plea glimmered in her dark eyes, along with what I took to be a hint of alarm at the sight of me.

"Glad to see you found your way back," I said, dropping into my chair, ignoring the crawling pains in my face, and that clawing itch.

"You're hurt," she said, sounding more perplexed than worried, much to my chagrin.

"It looks worse than it is," I said. "You do remember who I am?"

"Yes," she said, softly, her ripe red lips creasing into a vague frown. "I remember … coming here … I hired you to find out who I am."

"Anything else?"

"I remember you took care of me." She paused, let out a sigh that defined the word *forlorn*. "I remember knowing I didn't have anywhere else to go."

I tried to ignore the ache in my chest, too.

"I was hoping for something a bit more useful," I told her, trying to keep my voice flat, businesslike. "Your name would've been good."

"If I could remember that, I wouldn't be here."

That stung a little, too, but all I said was, "At this point, I'd take it anyway."

She studied my battered mug, and that frown deepened.

"Does that have anything to do with me?"

"I don't know." That, strictly speaking, was true. I had my suspicions, of course—strong, deep, wide suspicions—but I didn't really *know*. Nothing that would've stood up in court, to be sure ... though I had the feeling that wherever all this ended up, it wouldn't be in court.

My client fell quiet a moment. I waited, unable to keep from gazing at her porcelain features, so pale and perfect, but cool, distant.

"How much of what I told you last night do you remember?" I prodded.

She looked into her lap and studied her lace-gloved hands. I couldn't help wondering if she still wore that peculiar ring I'd spotted in the photos, but somehow I doubted it.

"Very little ..." she answered. "I recall ... there was a picture. I don't remember the face ... But ... it frightened me. That much I remember perfectly."

"The picture was of a man called Radamanthus. Does that name mean anything to you?"

I knew it did—I saw her flinch, just a little, when I said it.

"No," she whispered, but I could see in her eyes that something deeper inside knew better. I thought for a minute of what those other pictures had shown—Miss Gray using her left hand, to drink, to pour ... I thought of those anxious twitches and ticks. They'd all vanished now, but I had the feeling they lurked just under that porcelain surface.

I nodded, ready to play my hole card.

"What about someone called Mister Menace?"

The very last of the color in her face vanished, as if her features had been evenly covered under a sudden snow, and her haunted eyes shaded away into utter darkness. She winced without twitching a muscle and went granite-rigid. A breathless gasp fell from her ashen lips—two tiny, bottomless words. I thought they were *Oh, God*.

I let silence hang over the room for a minute, leaving the two of us alone with the grumbles and honks from the traffic in the streets below.

"I take it you know the name," I prompted at last.

"Yes."

I waited.

Miss Gray said nothing at all. She seemed completely lost somewhere deep inside herself, like a child in a dark mirror-maze at some cheap roadside carnival.

"How do you know that name?" I asked.

The question fell away around her like so much dust, not touching her at all.

I leaned over the desk, clutched one of her gloved hands, squeezed as tight as I could while still being gentle. That shook her out of her daze, a bit. Her dark, dark eyes focused on me, but the expression I saw in them reminded me of someone gazing at a half-familiar stranger.

"How do you know that name?" I repeated.

Her answer came in a whisper so low and breathless it might have been a dying gasp.

"He ... I think he murdered me."

An arctic chill gusted through me, but I managed to resist the urge to drop her hand and pull away from her, back to the safe side of my desk.

"You're looking pretty good for a stiff," I told her when I could get any words out. "If this mysterious Mister M tried to murder you, I'd have to say he didn't do a very good job of it."

My client didn't respond. She'd gotten lost in that interior maze again. It left me wondering what she saw in those mirrors in her mind.

I pressed on. "Help me out here. It's one thing to lose track of your own name. It's another thing for a living woman to tell me she's been murdered and not explain what she means."

She shook her head, helpless. "I don't know. I feel like ... like a ghost, trying to remember how I died. I know that doesn't make any sense."

In some crazy way it did, but I didn't care to say as much. No reason to push her any deeper into that darkness.

"I remember pain ... Not exactly physical pain, but ...

something even worse, somehow. Like he was tearing out everything that makes me who I am. Tearing it up roots and all. Tearing apart my future, too. Erasing me. What's that if not murder?" Again she cast those eyes on me, and again I understood what *haunted* really meant. "And it's more than that. I can't explain it to you, Mister Orpheus. I don't understand it myself. But it's true. He murdered me. I may walk and speak, but I'm dead, Mister Orpheus. I died by his hand."

I hunched my shoulders against another shiver and thought about the hooch in my desk drawer.

"You're not making much sense," I told her.

And yet something deep inside that tangle of words seemed to make *perfect* sense, almost like I'd felt it all along, but hadn't caught a glimpse of it until now.

"Nothing makes sense anymore," Miss Gray said, in that same strengthless voice.

I decided to try another route.

"What did he look like, this murderer?" I couldn't quite bring myself to utter the name again.

"I remember his eyes," Miss Gray murmured. "They were black—like two empty wells. As if … as if there was nothing human behind them." She gave a laugh, tiny and brittle and about as cheerful as a funeral dirge. "Every time I talk to you I sound like a madwoman, don't I?"

"No, you sound like a sane woman caught up in something mad." My voice was smooth enough I half believed it myself. "You remember anything else?"

She shook her head slightly, hardly enough to alter the shadows falling across her ivory features.

"Only those eyes," she said.

I let go of her hand and settled back in my chair, ran my fingers through my hair. My eye went on itching, but I refused to scratch. The aches in my face had died away to a low throb, but I couldn't wait to anesthetize myself with a glass or four of bourbon once my client was out the door. Maybe sooner.

I sat silent a minute, listening to the muttering traffic and the insect-buzzing neon and waiting for everything my client had said to sink in. Only it didn't sink in, just lay there on my mind, too dense, too dark to absorb. I had the distant sense that if anything, rather than absorbing those thoughts, they might absorb me.

That decided it.

I tugged open the bottom drawer, planted the bourbon bottle in the middle of the green desk blotter like a graveyard monument, then put glasses on either side of it. I always kept a couple of extras around for whatever occasion might arise.

"You sound like a person who could stand a stiff drink. I know I could."

Miss Gray didn't answer, but after I tipped two fingers of amber liquid into one glass and pushed it her way, she wrapped her hand around it. I put three fingers in my own glass.

"*Skol,*" I said, lifting my glass to her, then half-emptying it in one swallow. She raised her own glass, regarded it a moment, watching the golden poison roll around and around, then put it to her red silk lips and took a sip. I'd swear that was all it was—a sip. But when she put the glass down a second later, it was empty.

I refilled hers and freshened my own.

After a couple more glasses for each of us I felt my innards starting to go loose and warm and my brain and mouth relaxing a bit. Even the aches and itches that made up my face seemed far away and unimportant.

Miss Gray rose out of her chair and drifted to the window, as if something in the dark had whispered her name and she'd recognized it instinctively. A moment later she turned, eyes downcast, hands folded in front of her, low, where her jacket buttoned. Even with the booze casting its pleasant yellow fog over my brain, I could see her laced-together fingers squirming, tugging at one another.

"I should go," she said. Her voice had found a bit of volume and assertiveness, and I didn't think it'd come out of that bottle growing empty on my desk.

"Oh? You have somewhere to be?"

"Yes."

"Yeah? Where's that?"

I said it as fast-but-casual as I could manage, thinking maybe if I caught her unaware, whatever deep-buried defenses in her brain kept the truth hidden might not have time to stop the answer from spilling out. Hoping the booze had lubricated the gears enough.

"I don't know," she said, smashing that hope. She moved swiftly toward the door, walking without seeming to walk at all, as if she'd stayed put and the whole world had shifted to accommodate her. "But I have to go."

I rose, caught her as she tried to slide by, like a father catching his kid in mid-swing on a playground. I had one arm around her waist, cupping her elbow, the other around her back, my hand gripping her shoulder—again, gentle but firm.

"I can't let you do that," I told her. Our faces were very close, side-by-side so our profiles must've matched up like the ones in those pictures that look like two faces or a vase, depending on how you choose to see them. I could smell a distinct but subtle perfume on her cool silk skin. For an instant I thought I caught a whiff of something else, too, something raw and base but not entirely unpleasant. But probably it was only the smell of the worn wooden floors and the old plaster walls and that endless drizzle creeping in from off the streets. It didn't matter half as much as those devastating eyes or those bitter-cherry lips. She turned away from me like something had embarrassed her.

I held her there firm and frozen and for a minute neither of us spoke.

"An hour ago I was ready to drop this whole case," I told her, talking slowly. "Figured I was going someplace I shouldn't and oughtta get out before I got lost for good. Now you come back and tell me you're a murder victim and for some crazy reason I believe you. So let me ask you—what do you think I should do now?"

I felt her make a less than half-hearted attempt to move, maybe away from me or maybe toward me. Now she turned those dark, dark eyes on me again, black as polished obsidian. "Please," she murmured. I wasn't sure if she meant *please let go* or *please* don't *let go*, but I held on either way. Even with her stiff and tight in my arms, she felt exactly right there, as if she'd belonged all the time.

So I told myself then, anyway.

"I can't walk away, can I?" I asked, not really meaning for it to be a question at all. "And it's not because of any Mister Radamanthus and not because of any Mister Menace. It's because I couldn't live with myself if I let you go into the darkness out there all alone."

Her steady gaze faltered. She closed her eyes and I saw a subtle touch of color rise back into her cheeks for the first time since I'd dropped Mr. Menace's unlikely name on her.

"You don't owe me anything," she said.

"True," I said, "but at this point I guess I owe *myself* something. And maybe that'll work out best for both of us."

Now at last she moved again, shifted into my arms and nestled her head against my shoulder. I held her close and ran a hand through that long spun-silk hair. Her whole narrow body felt cool against mine, like a fresh sheet on a summer night. Without another word between us, she lifted her lips to mine and kissed me, long and deep, and deeper, deeper than I'd ever been kissed. Any pain left in my battered features faded out of existence entirely.

And somewhere in all that, I faded, too. Darkness slipped in from the shadowed corners of my office and blotted out time. I thought I heard someone say, "I have to go," but that might be something I only told myself later, trying to fill in the gap with anything halfway meaningful.

After that, the black took over completely.

TWELVE
SONATA

W hen I came back to myself sometime later, I stood alone in the middle of the office, as out of place there as an igloo in the Sahara. The clouds had broken wide open sometime while I drifted in the dark, and now the rain fell hard and heavy, washing over the windows in thick dirty beads. The red light splashing from the Hotel Moira sign turned the rain into runners of bright blood.

It wasn't like waking up. I didn't feel anything like a fella who's been asleep, groggy and somewhat disheveled. My head was as clear as a good autumn day—even the last of the bourbon haze had burned away. I'd just gotten … lost somewhere. Lost in Miss Gray's strange embrace, her insatiable kisses. I could still taste her on my lips, a bitter memory with a sharp edge to it, but not unpleasant. Not in the least.

I couldn't help patting myself down, feeling for my wallet, my latchkey, the other random detritus a man gathers in his pockets … my Harpe .38. Everything I could think of was where it should've been, but that didn't chase away my feeling that I was missing something, that my client had stolen something small but important from me before she'd slipped away into the night.

I wandered to the window and stared through the bead curtain of neon-stained rain as if I might catch a glimpse of her drifting away down the sidewalk five stories below. I saw cars prowling the asphalt like huge steel beetles, spotted a few pedestrians hurrying along under the batwing silhouettes of businesslike umbrellas. No trace of my client, of course. I had a good enough idea where she'd gone—back to that dark neighborhood beyond the river, back to Club Erebus and whatever waited beyond the door with the red circle painted on it. But there was no point in trying to follow. Even if I was right, and even if I went with enough green in my pocket to grease the hinges on a few dozen doors, I'd never get past that last one. And in my current state, I didn't much feel like trying. Seemed like a good idea not to show my face—or whatever was left of it—around that part of town right now.

The itch and the aches had calmed down a bit, enough that I could ignore them without working at it too much, so I dropped into my desk chair and let my mind idle a bit.

What exactly was I dealing with in this Mr. Menace character? The mere mention of the name seemed to strike notes of terror in people, and maybe not without reason. I wouldn't soon forget the shadow of fear that had darkened Hally's face when I'd coaxed the name out of him; the bright panic in Miss Gray's eyes when I'd said it to her. I also considered the fact that within hours of my getting that name from Hally, he was dead—*slaughtered*, if you wanted to be forthright about it—and I was wearing a roadmap of scars on my face. Whoever this smartly-named Mr. Menace was, he had good ears, and long arms.

But who the hell was he? Boss of the so-called Tartarus Syndicate, Hally'd said—thugs, pimps and racketeers of the West Side, I figured, the typical lowlifes from the wrong end of the Narrows Bridge. So how come I'd never heard of him, or them? Not that I knew every mobster in town, but I'd been in the business long enough to know most of the bigwigs by reputation, at least. And Miss Gray's description was basically worthless. Empty black eyes. Could be anybody, or nobody. Not much chance I'd recognize the fella if I bumped into him on the street.

All at once, despite everything—despite the pain in my face, and the fear knotted tight in my gut, and the futility of the idea —I wanted to go after her. I wanted to find her and drag her out of whatever snake pit she was in right now. I wanted to rescue her from Radamanthus, from Menace. From herself. Hell, I didn't just want it—I ached for it, like I hadn't ached for anything in a good long time. That needle in my chest went a lot deeper than all the ones in my face. It didn't even matter what she'd taken from me, I wasn't looking to get anything back. Actually, I wanted to give her more. Any excuse for one more taste of those red-as-wine lips. It didn't make any sense and I knew it, but that didn't make the need any less real. I wanted to be near her and keep her safe, and there wasn't anything else to it.

But that dark labyrinth of the West End stretched out between us, and the black door. And there was whoever had attacked me, and whoever had murdered Hally. Plenty to make a fella think twice.

I frowned out at the night, then turned my back on it.

What I saw when I looked back into my office was that bottle sitting three-quarters empty in the dead-center of the green blotter on my desk. I wanted it, wanted to rinse my mind clean with booze. Maybe I could wash away that gnawing desire to chase after Miss Gray. The amber liquid called to me in a sweet, subtle voice, but it wasn't loud enough to blot out the pangs tempting me into a fruitless search of the mean streets beyond the canal.

But I thought I knew what *could* muffle that siren song, at least for a few minutes. Long enough to unfog my sopped-in mind and allow me the luxury of some clear thinking. I left the bottle to itself and headed out into the city, in the opposite direction of the West River Narrows Bridge and everything beyond it.

In the gloomy lounge at the Highsmith Hotel there was an old baby grand piano tucked away in a corner most of the regulars had forgotten about. No doubt some slinky girl in a fringe-covered dress had perched on its black enamel top, singing torch songs to indifferent crowds back when the Highsmith had been a classier place, but these days I was pretty sure no one tickled those ivories but the occasional drunken businessman, and me.

I walked past Johnny O, the bushy-eyebrowed fella who'd been behind the bar there for as long as I'd been coming in. I gave him the customary nod, he shot me a not-so-customary frown.

Whathahell happened t' yer face? that look asked.

I caught a glimpse of myself in the backbar mirror and wished I hadn't. All that wavery blue-green light playing up from the four-dozen bottles ranged along the shelf made the whole bar look like it was under water. It cast the scars and swelling and darkening bruises in a sickly glow, making them look that much more ghastly.

I gave Johnny O a look back, one that I hoped said, *Don't ask, pal.*

Guess it got the point across because Johnny O shrugged and went back to wiping down highball glasses with a white towel. He didn't bother asking what I wanted because he already knew.

I settled onto the bench in that shunned corner and put my fingers to the ivories. The pseudo-lacquer finish had chipped and peeled in places, the polish was permanently ringed with the ghost circles of beer mugs past, and the D above middle C was sour as spoiled milk, but in a joint like this nobody much cared. The thing sounded pretty good when I started coaxing Mozart's Piano Sonata number eleven out of it. A bit highbrow for the Highsmith, sure, but neither of the rumpled suits slouched against the brass rail of the bar even looked my way. Long as their glasses magically filled up each time they emptied them, those fellas didn't have a thing to say.

Sometime while I played, Johnny O left a glass of soda water with a twist of lime on the piano in front of me. It was a deal we had. I came to the Highsmith when I wanted *not* to drink. It was just as well—the hooch here was cheap, real rotgut stuff, the dregs of the dying months of the eighteenth amendment.

I wandered through the sonata, letting the notes waft through me, stilling all the things moving around in my skull. The itching around my left eye faded, and so did the hurt in the rest of my head. Even that ache of longing after the missing Miss Gray subsided, like a jagged rock slipping quietly under the surface of an incoming tide. Another soda and lime came along and I downed it to the strains of Bach's "Invention no. 4 in D Minor," unhurried, letting the music live at its own pace.

Somewhere inside the subtle complexities of the Bach piece, it occurred to me that looking for Miss Gray tonight was every bit as pointless as I'd told myself—but that hardly meant I couldn't find her. If my little inspiration played out, I could maybe track her down in a much more real, much more important way. And wasn't that exactly what she'd hired me to do? If I could put a name to that captivating face, it might be worth more than a hundred nights spent wandering the bleak back alleys of the West Side. And for all I'd found out so far—things someone obviously wasn't happy I knew—I couldn't see how it took me any nearer to closing the case. I'd resisted poking my nose into any of the missing persons noise going on around the police precincts in town because Miss Gray had all but sworn me to keep this away from the cops, and for some crazy reason I trusted her instinct there. Still, other options weren't exactly dropping at my feet.

But then I should have spent less time looking at my feet and more time looking at Cass's desk. A whole stack of possible leads landed there every morning, and every evening an hour before closing. The same package that had brought along that tidbit about good old Small Time Crook Hally Thersis. Not that there'd been anything in the newspapers lately—if there had been, from the news to the crossword puzzle, Cass would've spotted it. She hadn't, so it hadn't been there.

But what if we looked back a few weeks, or months? My Miss Gray was an uptown lady, the moneyed type, probably from a line of moneyed types. If you wanted to find someone like that in the paper, you skipped the news and browsed the society pages. If Miss Gray was what I figured, she'd be in there somewhere—her face in a snapshot from some charity gala or self-congratulation shindig, or maybe among the debutantes at a not-too-long-ago cotillion ball. There were three major papers in town, all of them eager to splash the faces of the rich and well-groomed in as much ink as they could spare. And all three archived their old issues going back years. It was a long shot—a helluva long shot, which was maybe why I hadn't come up with it already. But sitting there coaxing that elegant music out of those yellowed keys, it was the best I could come up with.

Another notion crossed my mind then, a much darker notion.

Maybe I ought to check the obituaries.

But that was foolishness. Whatever she might have said about Menace murdering her—and however much I might have somehow believed her—she pretty clearly still hadn't ended up in a morgue somewhere. And in any case, whose obit would I look for?

I shut the lid on the black-and-whites, dropped enough cash on the bar to cover the bubbly water and still leave Johnny O smiling, and headed home.

Sleep that night came in broken-up pieces shot through with vividly convoluted dreams of fiery hair and crimson lips and dark, haunted eyes.

THIRTEEN
MORGUE

I waited until nine the next morning on the off chance Miss Gray might show up at the office the way she'd shown up in my dreams, but no dice. I hadn't expected much, but that tight knot of want in my gut kept me there, just in case. At nine-o-one, Cass and I closed up the place and headed off on the chore I'd set. I wasn't crazy about abandoning the office, but this was definitely a two-person job.

I had an old pal in the archives at the *Tribune*, so we went there first.

Cora led us down into the low brick walled basement, the place the newspaper fellas charmingly called The Morgue. The name fit. The place was grim, dusty lightbulbs shining feebly under even dustier tin hoods, row upon row of tall wooden shelves bearing long lines of canvas-wrapped binders turning the basement into a shadow-stuffed maze. Ordinarily I would've spent a few minutes bumping gums with Cora, making nice while she chattered away in that bubbly voice of hers. It never hurt to make a source feel appreciated, and in any case I liked her sense of humor. Today, though, my mind was someplace else. I said "sure" and "uh-huh" at all the right breaks in Cora's prattle and after a minute she left like a breeze, saying, "Good luck, hon."

"Yeah," I muttered, looking around at all the binders lined up on the metal shelves like good soldiers, "we'll need it. It's like we're looking for a needle in a whole room full of haystacks."

Cass put a finger to her bottom lip and cocked her head a little, then led me down a certain row and pointed at a particular shelf.

"Well, guessin' Miss Gray's age, I figure this is about when she'd have her coming-out party," Cass said, tapping the paper label that identified the dates covered by the papers archived on that shelf. "Cotillion season around here is November, December, so we should start there. Of course, we may hafta work back or ahead a year, but it's a place to start."

I nodded, impressed at how fast she'd worked it out— impressed but not especially surprised. Together we dragged a couple of the binders to a stout wooden table in one corner of the chilly room. We sat down in a pool of light from one of those tin-hooded bulbs and started scouring the society pages from back around the time an angry, cursing young wife wearing nothing but a bedsheet tried to scoop my left eye out with her pretty red fingernails.

Cass and I thumbed our way through page after page, binder after binder, month after month until they grew into a year. After a time, Cora brought down coffee, and that helped get us through another year worth of binders. We broke for lunch at quarter till one without having found a trace of Miss Gray anywhere in those yellowed pages.

"I still don't know why we're bothering," Cass said as we sat chomping chicken salad sandwiches from the *Trib*'s commissary. "Your face never woulda got messed up like that if you'd let go of this one like I said. And poor Hally might still be alive."

That one stung a little, and she meant it to. I raised an eyebrow at her, feeling my wounds tug some, but not too bad.

Only my eye bothered me really, still puffy and tender, and that old scar itching a little for good measure.

Cass chose not to read the look I'd given her.

"That woman spooks me, Frank," she went on, shaking her head, making her hair bounce. "But that ain't the most of it."

Now she hesitated, looking down at her sandwich, poking it as if its shape didn't please her. "Can I be honest a second?"

I'd never known her to be anything less. It was a big part of why I liked to have her around. "Why stop now?"

"It's you, Frank. The way you're acting lately. Not taking new cases, locking yourself up in your office ... drinking all the time. ..."

I was tempted to remind her that no one had come in since Miss Gray, that the door marked Private had been closed but not locked, and that I'd been a hard drinker since before I could knot a tie. But I sensed that underneath all that, she might have a point, and I didn't want to let on, so I kept my mouth shut.

"It worries me a little, Frank," she said, not quite meeting my eyes. "You know what a wreck I'd be if anything really bad happened to you. I hardly got a wink of sleep last night thinkin' about you all crumpled up on the floor in the office and blood everywhere and your face. And if you go and get yourself killed, I'm out of a job. That ain't nothin' these days. I've got a mother to take care of, you know."

I grinned. Cass's fingers stopped poking at the sandwich and her hand started toward me and I knew she wanted to reach out and grab my hand and give it a squeeze but didn't quite dare. I didn't ask myself if I wanted her to. For all the years I'd known her, my relationship with Cass had been almost entirely professional—within the weird boundaries of my strange business, in any case. I'd always thought it best to keep it that way; anything else could only complicate matters. Truth was I'd never let myself think too much on how I actually felt about her, and now I realized I didn't even know. I found myself wondering again about her life outside the office and whether or not there was a fella in it, some clean-cut type who would marry her away from me one day. I guess I'd always counted on her to be the spinster type, but that was pure selfishness. I had to face the fact that Cassandra O'Clare was a catch—a bit plain at work, maybe, but I bet she dolled up nicely, and she had plenty of moxie and brains to boot. How long could it be before some smooth-talker came along and hooked her? I found myself looking at her now as if I hadn't ever seen her before.

"I just wish you'd be more careful, is all," Cass finished, taking her hand back.

"I can take care of myself," I said by way of comforting her some. If I'd responded to that note of concern in her voice, gone all soft, Cass would really have started to worry, and maybe with good reason.

Anyway, someone else was too much on my mind.

I can't help wondering how different—how much *better*—everything would've been if I'd only put my hand out for her to take. A question like that can damn a man, I think, assuming he isn't already damned. I try not to ask it too often, but I can't help wondering.

Cass simply nodded at me, gave me a half smile that had a kind of lost quality to it. Not lost like my client's haunted eyes, but ... well, it was like Cass knew some important decision had just been made, that things were subtly different now and always would be.

"Sure, Frank," she said, and ate her sandwich.

We'd managed to kill off a hefty chunk of the afternoon in that dank-smelling but somehow still dusty basement when Cass finally said, "Hey ... Hey! Take a look at this, Frank!"

I sidled up next to her and looked down over her shoulder at the picture she tapped with her varnished nail. The grainy black photo on the jaundice-yellow paper showed a group of smiling girls in expensive clothes gathered around a linen-covered table. I gathered from the candles burning in crystal fixtures and the etched-glass windows behind the crowd that the scene was an expensive restaurant somewhere uptown. The girls, all in their early twenties, held up fizzy champagne flutes, grinning madly and mugging for the camera—all but one. One girl hung back some, her smile pleasant enough but rather bored, her gaze wandering away somewhere beyond the camera like she was maybe searching for a discrete escape route.

I could hardly imagine those bright, wandering eyes coming to look so hopeless and haunted, but I knew that face. Even with a few years shaved off it I knew it instantly.

Cass read the caption beneath the picture aloud. "'Miss Damia Nyx, Miss Elenore Duncan, Miss Evelyn Night, Miss Valerie Alder, and Miss Nicolette Morgen cry "Cheers" to the opening of Ambrosia, the city's newest, hottest hideaway.'"

My client, the erstwhile Miss Gray, was the one looking politely disinterested right in the middle of the group.

So there it was. After three days that felt like about as many months, I had her name.

"Evelyn Night," Cass said, whispering the words as if they had some kind of magic power. I guess in a way they did.

My heart thumped double time in my chest and my face started to ache, but I pushed it all aside. I jotted down the name in my leather-bound notebook—not that I'd forget it. One look and it was etched into my brain for good. But habit took over and I wrote it anyway, and the names of the other girls, and the date at the top of the newspaper page, and the name of the place. I'd heard of Ambrosia—swanky dinner joint overlooking the park, the part of town where rents ran as high as the big steel buildings. The kind of place with fingerbowls on the tables and at least four different forks at each setting, where the waiters are all old men with accents.

"Good work, Cass," I said. I resisted the urge to give her a little peck on the cheek. Instead, I started away, saying, "Keep looking for anything else you can find. I'll be right be back."

"Where you goin'?"

"Make a phone call," I said.

"You watch yourself, okay?" she said. "I'm not callin' Doc Ambrus again."

That gave me pause. Not that I was too worried for myself, with the .38 snug in its holster under my arm, but I suddenly didn't like the idea of Cass alone down here among the shadows.

"Tell you what," I said. "Why don't you take the rest of the day, go spend some time with your mother. I figure you deserve it—you're the one who cracked the case, after all."

"Huh," Cass said with a nod. "I guess I did at that. Well whatta ya know?"

I waited until Cass's cab pulled away from the curb, then found a phonebooth in the *Trib's* big marble lobby. I raked the glass-and-wood door shut behind me, then dialed the number from memory. A minute later someone answered, "Chandler Hotel."

Just the voice I wanted to hear.

"It's Frank Orpheus," I told Arthur Geiger. "Just wondering if my client's been in at all in the last twenty-four hours."

"Er, no, sir, Mister Orpheus," the day manager said. "Her key's still in the box. Do you want me to continue holding the room?"

"Yeah, you do that," I said. "And if you happen to see her, tell her she'd best call me right away. And if she says she can't remember me, you dial the number for her and hand her the phone. Got it?"

"Yes, sir." I could tell by the waver in his voice this whole thing made him nervous. I wondered if he even knew why he felt that way, but I didn't bother to ask.

"Good man," I said, and hung up.

I hadn't expected her to be there, but had to give it a try. Here I had the answer, the vital piece of information she'd come to me to find, and I might never see her again to tell her. The thought of it pulled the knot in my gut that much tighter. I wanted—hell, *needed*—to see her face when I said that name to her. I guess I hoped it would undo what that other name—Mr. Menace—had done. I hoped it would give some color back to those cheeks, some hope back to those eyes.

But even then, the case wasn't exactly closed. I had a name, sure, but what was that really? My client wanted to know who she was, and who a person is is a lot more than a name. What I really had here was a good place to start.

I figured Evelyn Night couldn't have much by way of family or close friends, or any steady man in her forgotten life. A kept lady or a rich kid with family would've been missed by now. It would've made the paper, and the cops would be poking around —it would be a whole big mess. Girls who sipped champagne at openings of places like Ambrosia didn't disappear for three days or more without causing a fuss unless there was nobody to make a fuss. Still, I supposed it was possible she hadn't been missed because whoever—boyfriend, husband, parents—thought she was somewhere else. A trip to Paris or Nice or some little Greek island. Wasn't that what rich girls did with their free time? Or maybe someone *had* filed a missing persons report, but it'd been hushed up to the press for some reason. I wondered how I could check on that without waking the cops up to what I was doing. In any case, my gut told me it didn't matter: Evelyn Night was a rich loner and the only one looking for her was me. I couldn't even be sure she was still looking for herself.

Time to take another long shot, I guessed. I picked up the receiver and dialed the operator. When she answered I gave her a fake name and a phony badge number and asked her for the number and address of a Miss Evelyn Night, N-I-G-H-T, like what came after dusk. The operator's tinny voice went away for a minute and then came back and rattled off the information I'd asked for, which I jotted in my book. The operator went on, "It ain't listed, but I figure it's okay, you bein' a cop and all." She paused, wanting me to fill her ear with a few grisly details about why I wanted Miss Night's number. I said "Thanks" and dropped the handset back into its cradle.

The address I'd scribbled under the info cribbed from the old society page was on Elysian Avenue out in Asphodel Meadows, way uptown. Not the priciest part of the city, but getting there. I took a glance at my watch and figured I still had time to make a trip north, if I pushed it. I hurried out into the rain and waved down a cab, then headed off to have a look at the life Evelyn Night had left behind.

FOURTEEN
TWENTY-TWO

Number twenty-two Elysian Avenue turned out to be a three-story brownstone shaded by wide green maples. The carved-oak door with the polished brass fixtures and the beveled glass windows hung with white lace curtains all said *money* in a fine, full-throated voice. The operator hadn't given me an apartment number or any such thing, and anyway the curtains were the same all the way up, so I figured the whole place belonged to Miss Night. Pretty swanky digs for a single young woman, if it was all hers.

I stepped off the curb and up the wide steps, businesslike, and gave three solid knocks on the door. Waited. Knocked three more times, and waited again.

Nothing.

I stole a quick look up and down the wide sidewalk, decided the coast was as clear as it would ever be, and crouched down. I poked open the brass mail-slot and peeked inside. I could just make out a heap of neglected envelopes on the polished cherry-wood floor. A good bet no one had been home in days, maybe quite a few of them in a row.

I straightened up and walked quickly around to the side of the place. Sure enough, I spotted a narrow alley cutting into the block between the buildings, no more than a rough brick passage lined with rusty trashcans. I slipped along it, thinking how rich people's trash stinks as much as anyone's, maybe worse. Finally I came to the low back stoop. My luck was in— the back door had a nice mullioned window with four rectangular panes. One last glance up the alley assured me no one had noticed what I was up to. I slipped my hat over my elbow, turned my back on the door, and gave a sharp jab of my arm. One of the lower panes shattered with a secretive plinking of glass. I swept the last razor-y shards out of the frame with my hat, shook the slivers away and dropped the old fedora back onto my head, then reached through and unlatched the door.

The kitchen I found myself in was big but didn't look like it'd seen much use. Copper pots hung from wooden pegs on the wall over the spotless gas stove, and the only dirty things in the large sink were a flock of crystal glasses with rusty wine stains in the bottoms. Not much of a cook, my Miss Night, but a real party girl. No domestic help, either—none that had been by lately, anyway.

Beyond the kitchen was a well-appointed dining room— large table dressed in lace, crystal chandelier dangling above, silk flowers in china vases in the corners, antique felt-patterned paper on the walls. More for show, I guessed. I wondered how long it had been since anyone had actually eaten a meal in this room. At least as long as it'd been since anyone cooked in that kitchen.

I bypassed the living room and headed upstairs where I figured I had the best chance of finding what I'd come looking for. People who entertain the way Miss Night did clearly don't put their lives on display in their kitchens and living rooms— not their real lives.

Bedrooms are another matter.

The first one I found looked to be the master bedroom, but I could tell right away it wasn't Miss Night's, and never had been. Pictures stood in heirloom frames, the king-sized four-poster bed was all made up with dark velvet covers. There was a primness to the place that spoke of much older occupants.

I took a gander at some of the photos in the silver filigree frames. Some were society shots—a good-looking couple at various points in the second half of their lives, rubbing elbows with folks who came from money or had big names, or both. I recognized at least one former mayor, a couple of state senators. The other shots were family stuff and pretty soon I confirmed what I'd guessed. This was mother and dad's room. I found several pictures showing the elder couple with the lovely Miss Night, everything from her christening to what looked a lot like the debutante ball I'd been searching for. Best I could tell, the photographic excursion down memory lane stopped around five years back—around the time that picture we'd found in the paper had been taken. And I noticed something else, too. A subtle layer of dust coated every horizontal surface in the room. The whole thing had the feel of a museum display. That set me to thinking, but I wanted to dig a little more before I put my notion to the test, so I abandoned the old folks' room and tried to track down Miss Night's.

Evelyn Night's bedroom—it couldn't have belonged to anyone else, I was pretty damn sure of that—was on the third floor. A tad more modest than the master bedroom, but still bigger than my whole digs. Somewhere between midtown and here the rain had let up and now the afternoon sunshine streamed white and bright through the two large windows. It shone on walls the color of eggshells, walls hung with a dozen or more photos, all in shades of gray, most in smart silver frames that wanted polishing. The bed was dressed up in satin and silk with tasteful trims of lace and looked like no one had slept in it for a good long time. Across from it sat a polished wood dressing table dominated by a tall oval mirror, ivory-handled hairbrushes and whalebone combs sitting neglected like shells on a beach. But two items particularly grabbed my attention. One was a large wedding picture—the old couple from the master bedroom

—in a solid black border, with stubby votive candles on either side. A silver plate fixed to it glinted with two engraved names, and a date.

The other object that'd snagged my eye was a long porcelain pipe engraved with pretty oriental designs and sporting a little brass bowl near one end. I'd never spent much time with the hop heads who haunted the southwest side near the bad part of Chinatown, but I knew an opium pipe when I saw one.

So dope was her thing after all—or one of her things, anyway. But if she'd abandoned this expensive toy here whenever she'd abandoned the house, maybe she'd moved on to something else. In any case, the puzzle was coming together in my head and it made a sorry kind of sense.

I forgot about the black frame and the pipe and took a look at some of the other pictures. Some showed that older couple, or them with the girl my client had been. They looked like holiday snaps, shots from the boardwalk on the shore and various other all-American resorts, but also photos from more exotic locales, Paris and Tuscany, Venice and Crete. The rest were a lot like the one in the paper, the one that'd sent me this way in the first place—Miss Night with various other moneyed girls, and swank young men in pricey suits. A couple of the girls turned up over and over, and so did one of the fellas. Something about him snagged my attention, and I found myself looking back over all of the images he'd shown up in. In every picture he gave an over-enthusiastic grin that was more of a leer, and in every picture where he turned up he had a long arm draped around Miss Night's shoulders, or wound around her waist like a boa constrictor. Like he wanted the world to know he owned her. I didn't recognize the kid, but there was a glint in his dark eyes, a certain set to his sharp jaw, a severity to his widow's peak, that had a familiar stink to it. Even if I'd still had that one clear shot of Mister Dapper, I knew the clown in the photos wouldn't look like him in any blood-relation kind of way. The attitude this kid radiated ... it wasn't the same as Radamanthus's, but he sure as hell wanted it to be. Ditto the pinstripe suit, cut to be a cheaper imitation of Mister Dapper's high-toned duds.

I took one of the photos off the wall and tucked it under my arm. I didn't figure anyone would miss it anytime soon.

After a quick glance around, I spotted what I needed—a phone crouched on the nightstand. I picked it up and dialed Cora's number at the *Trib*.

"Well hello, detective. Missing me already?"

"Every minute," I answered. "Look, can you do me a favor when you have some time?"

"It'll cost you lunch."

Another time, I might have chuckled at that, but just then I wasn't feeling all that jovial.

"I need you to look for an obit for me," I said, and gave her the names and the date I'd seen engraved in silver on that black frame. "When you get it for me, can you give me a call at my office? I guess I'll be back in an hour so. Better make it two. You still got my card?"

"Right in my pocket book," Cora said.

I hefted the picture I'd pilfered from the wall, thinking about the laughing girls, the leering man. "Thanks, Cora. You're a pal."

"And don't forget it," Cora said, and hung up.

Five minutes later I had the picture out of its frame and tucked under my coat and was out on the street a few blocks from twenty-two Elysian Avenue, hailing a cab.

FIFTEEN

TOMBS

The central post office huddled at the intersection of Forty-First and Elmore Streets, long and low and dark. All the white globe lights outside and in couldn't seem to chase away the ashen shadows hanging between the big yellow stone columns, couldn't fight off the gloom that choked the marble-floored halls. I walked inside, not bothering to take off my hat, and wandered past the long bank of mail boxes, their polished wood faces all scratched and gouged by a couple of decades of poorly-aimed keys. I ignored the crowd shuffling through the labyrinth of velvet ropes and walked straight into the enormous foyer of the main entrance. The crowd looked like the usual sort, house-wives and secretaries, a few businessmen and kids running errands for their folks, but I kept my eyes peeled all the same—searching out sixty-foot-tall goons and their shadowy companions, I guess.

There were maybe three dozen faces tacked to the corkboard wall between the big doors, almost all of them grim, angry men scowling at the cameras that'd captured them. Lots of them were doubled up with themselves—front shots and profiles—and quite a few had numbers under their chins. All of them had the word WANTED hanging over their heads in thick black print you just couldn't argue with.

I was playing another long shot, but maybe not quite as long as the one that had paid off with the newspaper photos. That other face had looked a little familiar, and not only because of the subject's cheap effort to look like Mister Dapper's illegitimate son. I thought maybe I'd seen it once or twice before. Here. In my business, it never hurts to take a gander at the wanted board once in a while, just to know who's blowing in the wind.

It took a minute but then I spotted him, stuck in among all the other crooks and thugs. The fella in the picture stared straight at the camera. He was trying to look mean and dangerous, the way a lot of career criminals do in their first mugshots, but mostly he looked bored. The rap sheet at the bottom said the fella was wanted on charges of assault, larceny, extortion, and conspiracy. Great start to a promising life of crime. And, I thought, the sort of résumé a fella doesn't get without connections. The kid had *half-rate gangster* written all over his sheet.

I checked the picture on the board against the one I'd copped from Evelyn Night's place, but I didn't really need to. I knew I had my man.

Junior Dapper's name was Maurice Guilio, a.k.a. Marcus Giles, a.k.a. Gerry Martin.

I jotted the particulars down in my notebook, tucked that and the photo away, and strolled out of the building. I was shaking some but it didn't have anything to do with that clammy rain coming down again, spilling out of the downspouts all along the sidewalk. I figured I knew how all this came together, but I needed to pick up a few more threads to tie it up. That meant going and sticking my nose where I'd been told to leave things well enough alone. And I could have. I could've turned my back on all of it and walked away, easy as that. Even now I wasn't in too deep to pull myself out. But if I took the next step, I'd be out of the shadows and into the dark, and it might be a long time till I saw the light on the other side.

Then I thought of Evelyn Night's eyes, the feel of her body up against mine, the touch of her lips. I thought of how all the information I'd collected today could maybe set her free, could maybe chase the ghosts out of those eyes ...

I hailed another cab and told the driver to take me to the Tombs.

The cabbie let me out on the rain-slicked curb outside the nondescript brick building behind the neoclassical edifice of the City Police Headquarters and I took the wide stone steps two at a time and pushed inside. Cops milled and chatted, public defenders rushed in and out, a man I recognized as a Deputy Assistant DA drifted through, chatting with a couple of plain-clothes detectives. The place had a real name—the Metropolitan Criminal Detention Center—but nobody bothered calling it that. The Tombs said it better. A dark, stinking catacomb, blank concrete and naked light bulbs hidden away behind thick wire mesh, except in the entryway and offices where a few rough jabs had been taken at making the place presentable. It was a lot closer to the cops than I'd wanted to come with this case, but I was pretty sure nobody here knew my face. Probably none of them even knew my name. Being small-time has its plusses once in a while.

I strolled up to the desk sergeant like I belonged there and showed him the forged credentials I carried for circumstances like as these.

"Fred O'Mera, with the PD's office," I said. "For Ander Farris."

I remembered seeing in the papers that Farris had been busted a week or so ago. I didn't think he was in the middle of anything, but he was the only fella I knew who might have his ear to the ground.

The cop looked like he'd been on that desk most of his career. He frowned at me and my broken face from beneath bushy gray eyebrows, frowned at my ID, frowned down at the register book at his elbow.

"What happened to your face?"

"I cut myself shaving," I said, hoping the tone would shut down that line of questioning.

The cop grunted, looked at his book again.

"Nothin' about a Fred O'Mera here," he mumbled.

I rolled my eyes in fake disgust. "The clerk at the office said he'd talked to you people, told 'em I was on my way about the Farris case."

"Sorry pal," the desk sergeant said with a shrug of his meaty shoulders.

"Look, Mac," I said, "I got ten other cases I gotta work today, I don't have time to stand here gabbing with you just 'cause some pencil-pusher forgot to write down a phone message. Why don't you give 'em a call and see if you can find anyone who knows I'm here so I can get on with my work, huh?"

I'd have some pretty explaining to do if he called my bluff and found out nobody named Fred O'Mera worked at the public defender's office, but I guess my attitude and the phony credentials sold him, or else he was too damn lazy to care. "Sign in," he said, and tapped a black line on a yellowed page.

I signed Fred O'Mera's name left-handed. It had taken me a month of practice to get good at it and it was all I could do with my south paw, but it came in handy at times like this, when I needed to be someone else.

The sergeant frowned at my scrawl, his bushy eyebrows knitting together like mating caterpillars. Then, with a snort, he shoved a visitor's pass across the desk at me.

I hooked it to my coat and walked away without giving the desk sergeant so much as a nod.

The guards scrutinized my ID again, and the pass, and made me check my piece, and patted me down to make sure I wasn't packing anything else. They didn't think twice about why a PD might be carrying—disgruntled former clients, angry family members of clients, angry family members of victims, whatever, PDs had damn good reason to tote some self-defense.

A minute later a big guard in a sharp blue uniform led me to a grungy interrogation room, and five minutes after that they brought in Farris. He stared at me thickly when he saw me, checking out my busted face, but wasn't quite dumb enough to say I wasn't really his lawyer. The guards locked Farris's cuffs to the concrete-slab table then locked us in together.

"How ya doin', Andy?" I asked when we were alone.

"Better than you, huh?" Farris said. "Whatta you want, Orpheus?"

He said it without the "e"—*Orfus*—but I was past being perturbed by things like that.

"Just some polite conversation," I said, taking off my hat, crimping the brim into a sharper shape. "You like polite conversation, dontcha? About our mutual friends?"

Farris scowled.

"You want I should name a few names, that it? What's in it for me?"

I leaned back in my chair and laced my fingers together behind my head to remind him I could move away from the table and he couldn't. "You'll see in a minute," I promised.

Farris glowered, those beady eyes shadowed under that granite-boulder forehead.

"You know a fella named Maurice Guilio? Or Marcus Giles?"

His glower turned into a pale frown, his gaze fell away into the far corner of the room.

"I don't think I wanna talk after all," he said.

"Then just nod your head. You know him?"

Farris's big head went up and down a couple of times, almost like he couldn't help himself.

"Who's he in with?"

Farris went white as bleached linen. "Huh-uh," he muttered, "Nope. I go shootin' my mouth about that, they're gonna find me with my head on backward."

"No one knows I'm here but you," I said. "You just say a couple words I wanna hear and I go away and no one ever finds out we had this little chat. Otherwise maybe I start shooting off *my* mouth about how you blabbed it all to me, and maybe someone with big ears hears. And I'm pretty sure you know who I mean."

"You lookin' ta get me killed, Orfus?" I heard real strain in his voice. "That whatcher after?"

"I'll make it easy for you," I said. "I'll say it so you don't have to. He reports to a fancy-dressed fella called Radamanthus. Yes or no?"

Again, Farris's head bobbed like it wasn't plugged in to his will. That frown dug in deeper. I was just glad the big Bruno didn't have the sense to call the guards and get me tossed. Best to keep him rattled and hope for the best.

"So he's a soldier for the Tartarus Syndicate. One of Menace's men."

If Farris could've flung himself back from the table, he would've, but the handcuffs made it impossible.

"Don't."

"Don't what?"

"Say that name. The 'M' name. Don't. That man ... hears things. You didn't get them bruises slippin' in the bathtub, did ya?"

I felt another chill, thinking about how fast Menace's catspaws had gotten to me, and Hally. Seeing a big dumb thug like Ander Farris squirm like a child at nothing more than the sound that name made in the interview room tempted me to think twice about what I was involved in. Seemed more and more likely Cass had gotten it right from the start.

I shoved the thought out of my mind.

"What is it about this fella?" I asked, leaning over the table toward Farris like a conspirator, pretending the line about my face hadn't shaken me good. "Why does his name get a big gorilla like you shaking in his shoes?"

Farris went on frowning, shook his head, but spilled his guts anyway. "He—he finds things out. Like if you say his name he can hear it ten miles away. And they say he can, he can be in two places at the same time. Like he's ... I dunno, a spook ... somethin'."

"Or the Devil himself," I said, as much to myself as to the thug sitting across from me. All my scars ached and itched, the one over my left eye especially.

Farris snorted, tugged at his fingers. "If you're lookin' for that Guilio kid, don't bother. I hear he got himself disappeared about a week ago. Permanent like. What I hear is they made it real slow so's people around the Tartarus neighborhood could hear the screams for hours and hours, so's they'd remember not to cross up ... that man. So's none of the other fellas in the group would make the same mistakes Guilio made."

"What mistakes are those?"

"Got too big for his britches, 's what I hear. Thinkin' he could start givin' orders. Thinkin' he could muscle in on Radamanthus's action. Not playin' by the rules."

I thought of the young fella in those pictures, trying too hard to look more important than he was. Didn't seem hard to believe he could step on a few toes and end up paying a heavy price for having two left feet.

"Dumb bastard shoulda knowed better. Everyone knows you don't go against ... Everyone knows, you just don't." He shook his head in disgusted disbelief. "Anyway, I'm through talkin'." Farris sat up straighter now, like he'd just come to his senses.

I nodded, got out of my chair and went to the door. I gave three loud knocks for the guard.

Farris's face twisted up all of the sudden, a pretty nervous look on such a big man.

"You won't say—"

"I was never here," I promised. The same line I'd given Hally Thersis, for all the good it had done.

The door screeched open and I slipped out.

SIXTEEN
SHUTEYE

I was wonderin' if you were gonna make it in before I went home for the night," Cass said as I dropped my hat on the stand. Her tone was breezy enough but I thought I read a little relief in those baby blues of hers, like she was happy to have me back no worse off than when we parted ways.

"Weren't you headed to your mother's house?"

"I got halfway there before I remembered she's visiting my aunt up in Smyrna. So I figured I'd come into work ... you know, just in case."

Just in case Miss Night came in, she meant, and I liked her a lot for that. I guessed it told me something about her life outside of work, too.

"Good thing I did, too," Cass continued, "'cause you got a call I figure was pretty important."

"Cora from the *Trib*?"

Cass nodded. "She got that information you asked for." She flipped open her memo pad, reading. "Mister and Missus Danaus Night. Died in an automobile accident on ..." She scanned her notes and gave me a date a few years back. "Only surviving relative, Miss Evelyn Night, their daughter." Cass looked back at me with real sorrow in her eyes. "Tough break, huh?"

I nodded, thinking of my client suddenly orphaned at the very beginning of her adult life. Being left alone in that big, empty museum-piece house. "Yeah, tough."

"She inherited their whole estate—a house in the city, a summer place, stocks, bonds, and plenty of cash. At least she doesn't have to worry about keepin' the lights on."

The whole picture was coming into focus for me now. The lady loses all the family she has in one smash and ends up in an empty mansion with more cash than she can figure out what to do with. She's like a luxury yacht cut loose from its moorings with no one at the helm. She starts looking for some diversion, a little adventure, why not? Take a few risks because you're feeling like you've got nothing important to lose, only money. Plus the booze and the opium and … whatever else … helps her forget about what happened to mother and dad. She meets Junior Dapper at some ritzy club where he plays Mister Big by throwing the Tartarus Syndicate's money around. And he's got that vaguely dangerous edge she's been looking for, even if she didn't know she was. He likes the looks of her—and hell, who wouldn't?—and they make some time for each other. Pretty soon she's mixing with some of the bigger fish in that scummy pond, swimming with sharks like Radamanthus and too turned around to realize how deep the water's getting, or that the big fish have big teeth and big appetites. Or maybe in her pain she just doesn't care. Junior makes a few wrong moves and ends up feeding the guppies in the West River or who the hell knows where, but by now Miss Night's in up to her neck, there's no getting out.

But right about there the yarn started to unravel. What happened next? What could've blotted out her mind, left her leading a double life and not even knowing it? I'd seen rotgut and dope wreck people's brains, but never like that. What the hell did she mean when she said that this man Menace was her murderer, had already killed her? It had a dark, seductive kind of logic that I couldn't untangle.

"Has she called, Cass?" I tried to keep my tone businesslike, but judging by the resignation in Cass's eyes, I guess she heard my feelings creeping in.

"Not yet, Frank. Sorry."

"Mmm," I grunted, and went into my office to think things over, and wait.

🔫

"Y'ain't gonna stay here all night again, are you, Frank?"

I looked up from the glass of bourbon I'd been contemplating as Cass poked her face in the door. Her smile looked tight, a bit forced.

"I don't know when she might come in, Cass. I should be here, now that I've got a name to give her."

"Well shoot, why don't you just put a cot in here? At least you'd get some sleep once in a while."

Because if I put a cot in here I'd never go home, I thought, *and I'm not ready to sink that low in life. Not yet.*

"I'll be fine."

"Mmm," Cass said, maybe imitating me. "I tried the Chandler again for ya. No sign of her there, either. Fella on the desk said he'll call if she comes in."

I nodded.

Cass lingered.

"How's your face?"

"Hanging in there," I said. Most of the cuts and bruises had quieted down to a dull ache that I could ignore easily enough, especially from inside an amber cloud of booze.

"You scared me pretty bad there, Frank," Cass said, hardly more than a whisper.

"Thanks for picking up the pieces."

"Sure." A note of disdain crept into her voice. "It's what I do, ain't it?"

She hesitated in the door a minute longer, silent, lips pursed like she had something to say but couldn't quite figure how to start.

I helped her out. "'Night, Cass," I said.

Her pursed pink lips twitched into a mild frown. "Okay. Good night, Frank."

She left.

By 8:00 PM it was pretty damn obvious that my client wasn't going to turn up. I couldn't help wondering if I would ever see her again, or if the deep darkness on the bad side of the river had claimed her for good, the way it had claimed Hally Thersis and that Guilio kid.

But no. I wasn't about to let it happen, not if I could possibly stop it. Right there in my shirt pocket I had all the secrets she'd come looking for—her name, her home, her past. I was itching to give it back to her at last, and now I couldn't even be sure I'd ever get the chance. Hell, I couldn't even make odds on whether or not she was still alive. Not that I had any reason in the world to think she might've been killed, but ... I kept hearing her telling me that this Mr. Menace was her murderer. The bourbon hadn't done much to soothe that itch or quiet those fears.

Bottle in hand I paced my office, as if walking around while I drank could erode away the hours faster. I listened to the traffic and watched the Hotel Moira sign wink its bloodshot neon eyes at me. Evelyn Night was out there somewhere, lost in the labyrinth of the city, maybe forgetting the last of who she was. I felt just about sick, not being able to do anything, not being able to even give her back her name. I wondered what the hell Radamanthus made those girls do, once they got on the other side of that door with the red circle. The thought of it stirred things up deep down inside me, things I don't like to think about too much. I took another swallow.

I went to the desk, pulled my piece out of the drawer, and hefted its cold, lethal weight, thinking maybe it'd make me feel not quite so powerless, maybe even give me the foolish bravado to go looking for Evelyn despite the impossibility of it. But the killing iron only made me feel strangely hopeless, so I tucked it away and sank down into my chair and closed my eyes for a few minutes.

Those few minutes unfurled into a few hours, but it didn't matter. I woke up around midnight, clear-headed enough to start drinking again—and maybe start thinking some, too.

I pulled out my notebook and flipped to the scribbles from that day's investigations. I ignored the stuff I'd already checked up on, and went back to the page with the names of all the girls in the caption.

Ms. Damia Nyx
Ms. Elenore Duncan
Ms. Evelyn Night
Ms. Valerie Alder
Ms. Nicolette Morgen

I'd circled Miss Night's name, but right now it was the others that interested me. I got the phone book out of Cass's desk and started riffling through. None of the girls from the picture were listed. I wasn't surprised. These society types always felt more important if their numbers weren't in the book where any old rabble could find them and call them up. I wondered if my cop routine would work twice in one day. I'd already wandered pretty far over the line, lying to get Evelyn Night's address, using fake credentials to sneak into the Tombs, threatening a prisoner … Might as well make a clean sweep of it, I figured.

I dialed the operator and gave my phony name and badge number, then told her the information I wanted. She rattled the information off with the gravel-rough voice of a three-pack-a-day smoker. Numbers and addresses for Nyx, Duncan, and Alder. There was no listing for Miss Morgen. The operator, every bit as helpful to the boys in blue as the last one I'd chatted with, offered the suggestion that Miss Morgen had maybe gotten married and might be listed under her husband's name. I supposed I could get that information from one of the other girls if I managed to contact any of them, or send Cass to hunt down marriage records at City Hall. I thanked the operator for her help, said what a good citizen she was, helping out the cops like this, and dropped the phone back in its Bakelite bed.

It was past too late to do anything with the information tonight, but at least it gave me somewhere to go tomorrow morning. I looked at my watch and remembered that it already *was* tomorrow morning, had been for about half an hour now. Probably, I thought, I should just call it a night, grab some sleep in something like a real bed, and start fresh on the new leads once the sun had been up a while—if it ever broke through the sodden blanket of clouds that still hung dripping over the whole city. All of this crossed my mind even as I put my head back down on the desk and let sleep take me right where I was.

I dreamed I was playing the elderly baby grand in that dark corner of the lounge in the Highsmith, Johnny O polishing glasses behind the bar, the regulars hunched over their drinks, all of them rendered anonymous, shadows blotting out their features. For some reason I dropped the classical stuff and started in on some old torch song. As I did, an invisible crooner joined in, providing the lyrics in a voice as dark and rich and smooth as the smoke from a fifty-dollar cigar. I turned away from the piano but somehow kept right on playing, and looked at the figure slouched on the nearest stool. I hadn't seen her at first but she'd been there all along, I knew that somehow. She wore that same elegant gray suit I'd first seen her in, those same pearls. Her wide-brimmed hat draped a veil of darkness across her face, leaving only her fine mouth and delicate chin uncovered. Her skin was white as talc, her lips red and moist so that I couldn't help thinking of fresh-spilled blood. She smiled a tiny, devastating smile, the kind people in the pulps call a "come-hither" smile.

I went thither. The torch song went right on playing itself on the piano without me. I didn't mind.

Neither of us spoke because there wasn't anything to say. I took her with rough arms and tugged her off her stool and crushed my face to hers and we kissed again, kissed deeper than before, deeper than I'd ever kissed any woman, deeper than I'd ever been kissed. Deeper than it's possible to kiss. We might've been trying to drink one another in and swallow one another whole, like two ravenous pythons. I wanted it to last forever.

In the shadow of her hat brim, I couldn't see if her eyes were open or closed. Mine were closed. I didn't think to wonder how that could be since I was seeing everything. Maybe I was standing outside myself, watching all of this. I can't remember, if I even knew. Dreams aren't obligated to make sense.

Then again, neither is reality. I know now, better than anyone, that logic and order are manmade boxes, and sometimes reality is the wrong shape and size to fit in. And for that we can only blame the box makers. There's no point at all in blaming the world.

I caught a glimpse of us in the tall backbar mirror, me and Miss Gray-Night—and it was like a late-autumn wind had blown through me. There was nothing in my arms but shadows. No—there were no arms, either. Just darkness. Johnny O was gone, and the nameless regulars. We had the place to ourselves. Neither of us moved our hands but somehow I was undressing her or maybe she was undressing herself, that expensive jacket sliding away, that fine blouse slipping off feather-soft flesh, all pale curves and cool expanses, and I was utterly lost in her then, helpless. And I didn't care.

Then I noticed the reason I couldn't see the rest of her face was because there wasn't anything there. Only mouth, and shadows. Something warm and wet ran over my cheek, down my throat and chest.

Darkness rolled over everything, obliterated the dream, or what I can remember of it.

I woke up I don't know how much later with my face in a pool of spilled bourbon. Guess I knocked the bottle over in my sleep. I stood it up to save what I could, then went to change into one of the spare shirts Cass kept handy. I found them folded up in a big filing cabinet beside her desk, along with two extra ties, trousers, and a pair of socks.

I tugged the shirt on, looking at my back-up wardrobe. I shook my head some, thinking about Cass's "cot" comment. I wasn't all that short of living here already.

I used my handkerchief to wipe up the rest of the spilled booze, wrung it out in one of the darkroom sinks, then sat back down. The sky outside was showing hints of dawn, pale blue streaks visible through the clouds and beyond the sawtooth skyline. Cass would arrive in a couple of hours, and then I could start chasing down the girls from that old society page picture and see if they knew anything about the life and times of their old gal-pal Evelyn Night. Until then, I figured I might as well go searching for another dream or two. Dark as the last ones had been, I found myself hungering for a few more.

I'd just closed my eyes and settled my head on my bourbon-smelling desk when the phone jarred me to wide-eyed alertness. I grabbed it before it could ring again.

"Hello," I said, forgetting the formal business hours manner of answering the phone by naming the agency.

"Mister Orpheus?" said a voice, distant as the sky, and much more beautiful. "Frank?"

"Where are you?" I asked. A dozen revelations banged around my brain, furious to escape, but I held back. This was information to be delivered face to face.

"I ... don't know ..."

"Can you find your way back to the office?"

"Tonight ... I'll try ... I can't talk now. I'm scared."

"You'll be okay. I have some—"

The phone went dead in my hand.

SEVENTEEN
SOCIETY

D id you get any sleep at all, Frank?"
      Not much sun managed to burn through the morning clouds, but somehow a stray beam shone straight down on Cass, making her shine like an angel. And she was that, I thought, white and bright and pure. Maybe a little too pure for a business like this—for a man like me.

"Sure," I told her.

It wasn't exactly a lie, but she nodded like she didn't believe it.

"There's a client in the outer office," she said. I figured she'd skipped the intercom and come in to tell me so she could make sure I was put together enough to deal with the public. I must've perked up a bit too much at what she said, because Cass hurried on, "No, not her. A man. A Mister Edward Mars."

I sighed to myself, but got up and walked out into the other room, not bothering with a fresh tie.

The man was tall and scarecrow-skinny, dressed in a plain brown suit that hung on him like the drapes in a cheap hotel room. His eyes were big and full of worry and he kept crushing his straw Panama hat between his long fingers.

"It's my fiancée, see," he said, like I'd already asked. "I think she might have someone, you know, on the side. I mean I hate to suspect her, I love Patsy or I wouldn't be marrying her, right? But I gotta know ..."

"Mister ... Mars is it?"

"Huh?" he asked, then, "Oh. Yeah. But Eddie's good."

"Eddie," I said, patting his shoulder. "I'm sorry, pal, I can't take your case. The agency's booked solid at the moment."

The fella looked crestfallen. I didn't glance Cass's way, but I could damn near feel her consternation boring into the back of my head.

"I can recommend another private eye I know, former associate of mine. He'll do a good job for you and won't break your bank account."

I jotted down Dick Foley's number and his office address and handed it to the nervous fella. He looked it over like it might be written in code, then tucked it in his pocket with a twitchy shrug.

"Uh," he said from the threshold, frowning, "thanks."

I nodded, and closed the door behind him.

"What's the idea, Frank?" Cass said, shaking her head at me as I turned around. "We ain't booked! We only got that one active case right now, and that one's just about done anyway, right? So why are you throwing good money out the door? You may not need the money, but I—"

"—got a mother to take care of, I know. Have I ever shorted you before, Cass? Even when times were tougher than this?"

"Well ... no."

"Then don't get your stockings in a knot. As for Mister Mars there, it's *my* business what cases I take and what cases I don't. Unless that's *your* name on the door."

It was a bit rougher than I'd meant it to be, but I couldn't exactly un-say it.

Cass scowled, the way a mother might scowl at a kid who'd just told an obvious fib. "I don't get you, Frank," she said from behind her desk, shaking her head some more. "The way you been lately, it's not you. I feel like I don't hardly know who I'm workin' for these days. I said don't take this case. I said that woman was gonna be a buncha bad news. Now look how you're acting. It's not good, Frank." She sighed.

I wanted to tell her my mother died when I was twelve and I wasn't looking for anyone to fill the job, but I swallowed my temper as best I could. I knew Cass was only trying to look after me, and probably I needed some looking after. But right then I didn't especially care to be treated like a kid.

"I've got some leads to follow up on," I said, going into my office for my notebook, my gun, and a fresh tie. Didn't really figure I'd need the piece considering the day's agenda, but lately I didn't want to go any further than the bathroom without some kind of protection. I strapped on the shoulder holster and tucked the .38 in against my ribs where it wouldn't show much through my jacket or my topcoat. I stashed the notebook away, knotted my tie, grabbed my coat and hat and got out, shutting the door on Cass's frowning eyes.

I started at the top of the list but got no answer at Damia Nyx's number when I called it from an uptown payphone. When I tried the next number, someone I took to be Elenore Duncan's maid explained that Miss Duncan was spending the season in Spain and couldn't be reached for several weeks. I told the maid it must be nice to be rich and not have to work for it. She made a soft sound I took for agreement, and hung up.

Miss Valerie Alder answered her own phone.

I introduced myself as a reporter with the *Tribune*. "You know a Miss Evelyn Night?"

"Evvie?" the voice asked. "Sure, I know her!"

"Mind if I come by, ask you a few things about her? Background on a little feature I'm working on?"

"I haven't seen Evvie in months—years!" Valerie Alder cried.

"I'll only take a few minutes of your time," I promised.
She said sure again, and gave me directions.

Five minutes in a cab and I found myself deposited outside a
nice looking Greek revival place with its wide back to the park. I
rang the bell, heard it chime inside, very musical. The woman
answered her own door, too, and did an admirable job of
pretending not to notice my mangled face.

"Hi!" she said, bright as sunshine. "Come in!"

The place was nice, fresh-cut flowers in antique vases on
fluted marble pillars, ferns in the corners, big windows looking
out on trees and hedges. All of it much more alive than Miss
Night's forgotten dwelling.

"So whatta you wanna know?" Miss Alder said, ushering me
into what I think people with money call a sitting room. More
large windows let in the sun that had finally burned through the
rain for a few minutes. I sat in a needlework chair that looked
like it cost more than most automobiles.

"Oh, just your general impression of Miss Night," I said,
nonchalant. "My editor figures she'll make a nice feature for the
society pages. Wealthy orphan girl and all."

"I don't know how much I can tell you," Miss Alder said,
settling onto a snow-white chaise lounge, the sort of thing you
only ever found in houses with sitting rooms.

"Like I say, it's been ages since I saw Evvie last. We used to
be thick as thieves, oh, sure. Going to all the best parties, eating
in all the fine restaurants. Oh, we had a glorious time!"

"So what happened?"

Miss Alder shrugged. "Nothing really. We saw less and less of
each other, that's all. Honestly, I got the feeling Evvie had gotten
bored with all that, the country clubs and charity balls and
everything. I can't say I blame her. It's nice enough, oh sure, but
pretty bland after a while. Though I must say I still enjoy

rubbing elbows with movie stars and wealthy industrialists from time to time."

I liked this woman's open manner, that honest smile, never mind the "oh sure"s. I could almost believe money hadn't made her forget she was a person like the rest of us. But I also knew I'd gotten the useful information out of her already. Still, I asked a few more questions, mostly to pad out my cover story, things that would go in that piece I was writing for the *Trib*. I also managed to find out that the unaccounted-for Miss Morgen was now Mrs. Thomas Leigh and lived with her husband in a city far more prone to sunny days, and on the other side of the country. No help there.

After a few more essentially meaningless questions, I thanked Miss Alder and let myself out.

Seemed I was back to Damia Nyx or no one. I put another call to her number but again got no answer. I decided to cool my heels awhile at the lounge at the Highsmith, let my mind wander some while my fingers stumbled over the yellowed piano keys. Mostly my thoughts kept wandering back to that dream, and pretty soon I found myself tickling out that torch song from the deep of my mind. Without that smoky voice to accompany it, the notes all sounded lost and empty. Cheap sentimentality.

And it hit me then how right Cass had been, smacked me like a sucker punch. What the hell was I doing, sending clients away—sending them to that fool Foley, of all people? There was a damn good reason I'd cut out on my own, and now I was taking money out of my own pocket and putting it in his. I'd lost my good sense, it seemed. Lost my good sense over a bad woman—a woman who practically had "doomed" etched into the crystal of her lovely eyes.

No, I thought, arguing with myself again. *Not yet. I've got what she wanted. I've got her name. I can still give her back her life.*

I can still save her. I've got to.

I slapped the cover down over the piano keys, finished my soda and lime, and headed out to keep an eye on Damia Nyx's place.

It was dusk when I finally saw signs of life at the big Victorian house on the corner of G Street and Avenue E. I'm not sure why I decided to stay there all afternoon, pretending to read a newspaper on a bench across the street while I spied on the place. Playing a hunch, I suppose, answering some subtle instinct that promised I'd find answers here.

I tossed my paper in a trashcan and got up to pay Miss Nyx a visit, but paused a second. The fading light, all muted shades of blue smudged with shadows, had turned the charming house into something from a kid's ghost story, one of the ones that stays with you even after you grow up.

Scoffing at myself, I put my shoes in motion and ambled across the street, rang the bell. No answer. I waited. Rang the bell again. Waited some more. And the whole time I felt like a school boy acting on a dare.

At last the door opened on a pale round face, crimson makeup shadowing high, fine cheekbones. The girl's bleached-blonde locks clung to her head in a tight wavy 'do that looked about ten years out of style, little curlicue locks poking down over her ears, close to her skin. She offered me a smile that was all warmth, and didn't show a hint of surprise at seeing a scarred, disheveled stranger on her doorstep. Unlike her old pal Miss Alder, Damia Nyx wasn't pretending she hadn't seen how bad I looked. That should've tipped me off that something was wrong, but I guess her open expression took me in. Which probably is exactly what she wanted it to do.

"Hello there," she said, like she'd been expecting me.

I dropped the earlier pretense about the newspaper article

and introduced myself by name, handing her my card. "You know a Miss Evelyn Night?"

She cocked her head, thought a second, then said, "Why don't you come in?"

With the heavy claret-colored curtains drawn against the streetlamps, the place was all deep crimson gloom inside, like stepping into a velvet-lined coffin. Wooden furniture with dark varnish, expensive wallpaper in dark colors, dark art deco paintings in dark frames. Even the small brass chandeliers seemed barely able to hold back the shadows. It was a wonder I'd seen any hints of light at all through those velvet drapes.

She took me into a small room with a well-stocked bar on one side, all polished mahogany and gleaming brass fixtures. It was pretty apparent the 18th amendment had never reached the Nyx household. I sat on a bar stool while Damia Nyx poured herself a glass of wine that perfectly matched the curtains. "Care for anything, Mister Orpheus?" she asked. She had the breezy voice of someone who entertained guests just about every night.

I'd spotted a bottle of Prize Stallion Kentucky Bourbon—mighty pricey hooch, and well over a decade old now—standing among the other decanters, but managed to resist the temptation with a casual wave of my hand.

My hostess settled herself on a stool beside me, crossed her legs at the knee, and sipped her drink. "So, what brings you asking about Evvie? Is she in some kind of trouble?" Her burgundy-colored skirt showed off a lot of leg, long and twice as silky as her dress, a great shape hinting at greater things just out of sight. It was damn distracting and she knew it, but I managed to turn my attention to my notebook and my work, though all at once that old scar over my eye had started up on me again.

"Trouble?" I repeated. "You could say. She's missing." That was true enough, I supposed.

Damia Nyx laughed, a bubbly sound that made me think of champagne.

"Who told you that?"

She did, I thought.

"A concerned party."

She laughed, something between a scolding and a dismissal. "No, no. Evvie's not missing."

"How can you be so sure?"

"We move in the same circles," Miss Nyx said, her smile and her voice lighting up the dark room. "If something happened to Evvie I'd know."

We move in the same circles. I wondered if that was meant as some kind of taunt, but pretended I hadn't caught it.

"She hasn't been at her residence in at least a week," I pointed out.

"Evvie never was a homebody." Miss Nyx waved a small hand, sweeping the question away. "Drove her folks crazy, poor souls. Then after they, uh … after their terrible accident, she spent even less time in that dreary old place."

I thought about the grim decor all around me and marveled that Miss Nyx could call Evelyn Night's home dreary.

"You shouldn't worry about Evvie. I'm sure she's just found someone to keep her company."

I pretended that statement didn't sting me at all.

"Anyone in particular?" I asked.

Miss Nyx shrugged. "Evvie had a few boyfriends I knew of. No one steady. I don't think she wanted anything too serious. She and I are just good time girls, you know?"

I knew. All I had to do was look at her. Damia Nyx, with those long eyelashes and that blond hair and those slender legs, was the kind of girl who could drive a man crazy and he'd come back the next night and beg for more. She reminded me of … But I put that thought away before it could cut me. Another mistake.

"What about a fella named Maurice Guilio? Or Marcus Giles? Maybe Gerry Martin?"

"Sure, I knew Maury. He also called himself Martin Guiley sometimes. He was a kick. I met him at a club one night and just knew Evvie would flip for him. He was just the type she went for—dark, mysterious, kind of dangerous looking."

"Maybe it wasn't just a look."

Damia Nyx gave another dismissive wave, sipped her wine. "Maury was harmless. That tough fella stuff was all for show. He wanted to impress the girls and make himself feel important, that's all."

"*Was* harmless?" I asked. "Something happen to him?"

Best I knew Maurice Guilio's untimely demise was still no more than a rumor among the city's bad element, crooks and thugs like my pal Farris. What would a rich kid with the right breeding know about it?

"Haven't seen him in weeks," Damia said, splashing more Chablis into her glass. "I got the feeling he wasn't coming back."

There wasn't a hint of disingenuousness in her tone, not that I could hear. If she knew Guilio had gotten himself slaughtered like a prize pig, she wasn't showing it. Still, something about that phrase—*I got the feeling he wasn't coming back*—struck me as coolly final.

"When was the last time you saw Miss Night?"

"Oh I don't know," Damia Nyx shrugged her fine shoulders. "Maybe last week … two weeks ago … The nights all blend together, you know? All the parties, the clubs.…"

She shrugged again, then raised her glass in a toast to Miss Night or to me or maybe just to herself, and took a swallow of wine.

I nodded back at her, charmed despite myself, hoping it didn't show.

"I'm going to see Evvie tonight, actually," Damia Nyx said suddenly. "We're meeting for cocktails around nine. You can come with me, if you want. See for yourself that Evvie's not missing."

I had to get a good solid hold of myself to keep from jumping on the invitation like a half-starved dog on a soup bone.

"Sure," I said, casual as I could. Even as the word came out of my mouth, I knew it was another mistake, but I was helpless to yield to my better judgment. "Should I have the cab pick you up here?"

"Ah, who needs cabs? We'll take my car. I'll pick you up— say, quarter 'til nine?"

"Sure," I said again. And pretty well sealed my fate.

EIGHTEEN
RIDE

The long black Dashiell Falcon carrying Damia Nyx pulled up outside the Cain Building right on the dot of eight forty-five. I could just make out the driver as a silhouette behind the wheel, sharp nose under a flat-billed chauffer's cap. Something vaguely familiar about that profile, but I couldn't place it.

The back door swung open and a familiar, delicate hand waved me toward the car.

I knew even as I climbed into that wide backseat that something here didn't add up, that I might well be delivering myself up to the shadowy Mr. Menace like an early Christmas gift, but I yanked the door closed behind me anyway. I'd waited at the office all evening without a trace of my client, all my new information at the tip of my tongue and her nowhere around to tell it to. Risky a move as this was, it still figured to be my best shot at finding her. And, despite that nagging itch in the scar over my eye, I was keen to see exactly where Damia Nyx took me. I might finally get a look behind that door with the red circle. The big question was what it might cost me.

The driver pulled away from the curb without a word from Miss Nyx.

I couldn't help looking her up and down more than once.

She'd changed into another dress every bit as short as the earlier one, red with black fringe and a shiny black cord that pulled the bodice tight, the plunging neckline showing off her terrific figure. Gorgeous, but as out of date as her bob. She lit a cigarette on a long black holder and took a deep draw. A boxy little hat perched on that platinum blond coiffure. I figured she had to be the same age as my client, but with the bright twinkle in her eyes and that smile curled up on her dimple-framed ruby lips, Damia Nyx looked like the same debutante I'd seen in that old picture from the *Trib*. Even so—or maybe because of it—she seemed just right to fill up a man's arms and work a man's lips with hers and whisper breathless nonsense in his ear as his hands took her in. I couldn't help thinking her flesh must be smooth as silk and twice as soft under that dress. I didn't like the thought, but I couldn't chase it away any more than a man standing on a high balcony can chase off the thought of what it would be like to jump.

"Mind if I ask where we're going?" I said, trying to distract myself.

She tipped me a long-lashed wink. "You'll see. It's just a little place Evvie and I discovered a while back."

"Hope it's nothing too fancy," I said, pointing a thumb at my ravaged mug. "I left my formal bandages back at home."

"Oh, there'll be plenty of people there odder looking than you," Damia said, giggling smoke. "And anyway, they always keep the lights good and low." She gave me a vulpine smile and giggled again, but whatever the joke was I didn't get it. At least, not then.

Instead I nodded, trying not to stare at her. I'd worked my share of cases involving good-looking women—they're usually the first ones men suspect of cheating, though in my experience they don't play around anymore than their garden-variety sisters. And sure, a few of those lookers came on to me, either to get me to forget what I'd caught them at or because it was their nature to go after anyone with some stubble on his chin. But I'd never been much tempted by any of them—that kind of thing's bad for business, and any half-decent detective quickly develops the strength to brush that stuff off before it clings. I did my job and if they were beautiful or homely, bright or dim, guilty or innocent, it was all the same to me. They were the elements of my profession, that was all.

So why couldn't I keep my eyes off this bleached-blonde? Hell, why was I here at all? Why was I even still on this lousy case? I was letting something pretty low get the better of me, and even knowing that, and knowing it couldn't lead anywhere good, I had a hard time caring, much less pulling back.

I tore my gaze off those slender legs and that splendid décolletage and gazed out the window as the city rolled past. Faceless people huddled under batwing umbrellas, drifting the sidewalks, looking as lost as souls in perdition. Even with my back to her I could feel Damia Nyx's brilliant blue eyes on me. I wanted to turn and drink her in all over again, let my hands go wherever they chose. I knew dear sweet Damia wouldn't object a bit. Raw sensuality hung around her in a sly but intoxicating perfume.

I watched my breath fog the window.

"You simply must tell me," she said from behind me, "who on earth hired you to go looking for Evvie? Whoever thought she was missing? It's all so very bizarre!" She said the last part with all the great relish of a practiced gossip.

"I can't say, of course," I told her, still gazing into darkness.

"No, I of course you can't," she said, sounding only a little disappointed. "I suppose it's always that way in your line of work."

"Mmm," I agreed. Then we were quiet a minute or two. Finally the feeling of her behind me—so damn close—won out, and I leaned back to look at her.

It was like gazing at an angel, a creature of unearthly beauty. Or perhaps staring into the eyes of the deep's most seductive temptress. I could even almost forget about Evelyn Night, looking at that face.

Almost.

"How long have you and Miss Night been friends?"

I forced the question out of my mouth and felt it break the spell ... or at least dim it down some.

"Oh it seems like forever!" Damia Nyx said with a flourish of her cigarette. "I can hardly remember a time when I didn't know Evvie!"

I nodded, wondering which Evelyn Night she knew—the somber, haunted woman who'd visited my office, or the stranger who kept company with the likes of Radamanthus and Junior Dapper. Or was her Evvie some other woman entirely?

"You know any of Maurice Guilio's cohorts?"

"Oh, a few," Damia Nyx said, taking a drag and tapping ashes into a chrome tray in front of her. "He had us along to ... well, a few of the places where they liked to gather. I think he liked to show off his connections, as if Evvie or I had any idea who his pals were!"

"It didn't worry you, rubbing elbows with gangsters?"

"Why would it? What would fellas like that do to a couple of harmless girls like us?"

It was maybe a better question than Miss Nyx knew.

"I can think of a few things," I answered, raising an eyebrow.

Damia Nyx waved a hand at me, dismissing my little provocation. "We were just out for a good time," she said, as if that justified everything. I supposed for her it did.

My eyes had started wandering again, all on their own, taking full measure of that body, those lips ... I turned away and gazed out into the rain just in time to see the huge gray spiderweb cables of the West River Narrows Bridge flashing past us. No surprise there. I hadn't seen Miss Damia Nyx in that kinky harem that had fluttered around Radamanthus, but she looked the part. It was the same thought I'd shut out earlier, but now I couldn't ignore it so easily. I was starting to wish I'd strapped my little derringer to my calf as well as packing the .38. Still, if this was some kind of trap, I couldn't figure why they hadn't sprung it right here in the car. Maybe Miss Nyx cared too much about her upholstery.

In any case, crossing that bridge made her claim that she was meeting Evelyn Night a bit easier to buy. I felt pretty sure this was the part of town where my client had been spending all her lost evenings. I settled back in the Falcon's plush seat, feeling the cold press of my piece at my side. I wondered who else might be meeting us tonight, and whether or not I'd end up pulling the trigger. Maybe I'd get a chance to spit some lead in the face of whoever had tried to break mine, although I didn't relish the thought of bloodshed. This whole thing still had the stink of a set-up. And here I was, intentionally sticking my neck in the snare.

I tried to get a better look at our chauffeur, but in the dark he'd turned into a shadow. I shook my head at myself, kept my mouth shut for now. I even resisted the urge to scratch that tiresome scar.

The car plunged into the labyrinthine streets on the far side of the bridge, made a left and another left, wending its way deep into the brick maze, past empty bars and locked-down shops and lonely tenements.

"So what's a nice girl like you do in a place like this?" I asked. I couldn't resist.

The smile Damia Nyx gave me, chin down, eyebrows up, touched me like cool fingers tickling an especially sensitive spot.

"You'll see."

I bet, I thought, but I was keen to get to it. Right then I think I would've done anything Damia Nyx asked without a thought. That smile wasn't the kind a man could turn down, be he a priest or a president or a dollar-a-day gumshoe.

The car slipped up to a curb and Damia said, "Here we are!" and hopped out.

I got out after her.

The driver—I never had gotten a decent gander at his face, not even in the rearview mirror—pulled away. Then for a moment I stood all alone with that tantalizing woman on a dark street surrounded by dark buildings under a sky made of lead, and the safety of bright lights and other people felt a thousand miles away.

"Well, come on," Damia said gaily, not waiting for me.

Naturally, I went.

NINETEEN

NYX

If I'd expected Club Erebus again, I was disappointed. The street we'd stopped on seemed abandoned, almost forgotten. Nothing but low narrow buildings with blank soot-streaked stone faces, windows soaped over or barred or boarded shut entirely. I wished my gun wasn't under my coat where it'd be almost impossible to draw fast if I had to. Looking at Damia Nyx, I couldn't believe that bright smiling girl could be leading me into anything much more dangerous than a secret love-nest. But I also believed it completely.

Damia Nyx strolled over to a recessed door, hidden so deep in the shadows I hadn't even seen it at first, and knocked. Something rattled, something scraped, and the door yawned open on a darkness that was deeper yet. Damia Nyx gave me a smile and a tilt of her head and stepped inside.

I followed. And as I did, I couldn't help noticing the small red circle painted around the doorknob, like an outline.

Inside, a short narrow hallway led to a flight of stairs that descended to a small landing, then doubled back out of sight. Apart from me and Damia there was nobody around. I couldn't figure out where the fella who'd unlocked the door had disap-

peared to. As I watched Miss Nyx sashay down the stairs, hips
swinging like a bell, it hardly seemed to matter where he'd gone.

It seemed like we went down a long time after the landing,
but it couldn't have been more than twenty-five or thirty steps,
and then we were in another narrow corridor lined with wooden
doors and lit with dim electric sconces set into the rough brick
walls. I smelled something like perfume or incense on the air,
mingled with the smoke from expensive cigarettes, but another
scent lurked under that, a dank cellar smell, and something
almost ... Almost what? It was familiar but I couldn't name it
right then.

I couldn't help wondering if the man himself, Mr. Menace,
lurked down here somewhere, the monster at the center of the
maze—but hell, even if he did, I wouldn't know him if I saw
him, unless his eyes gave him away.

Damia Nyx picked a door and led me through, then closed
it behind us.

The room was small, low ceiling and close walls, red satin
pillows tossed around a sunken table. Along one wall stood a
long black sideboard set with a half-dozen highball glasses and
four times that many bottles. Silver tongs poked out of a black
ice bucket. The place had a kind of ragged elegance to it that
made me feel like a fly buzzing into a gilded web.

"Where's Miss Night?" I asked as we settled in, dangling our
legs into the well around the table.

"I'm sure she'll be along anytime," Damia Nyx said. She
plucked two glasses from the board and set them in front of us.
"What's your poison, Mister Detective?"

"Bourbon," I said, eyeing the expensive bottle among the
other waiting soldiers. "Neat."

She poured three fingers of the stuff for each of us, then
raised her glass and tipped it my way.

"Cheers," she said.

I touched my glass to hers and made the crystal chime. We
drank.

The booze flowed free and Damia Nyx made small talk and I listened and the room started to tilt and bob a bit, but that was just fine. When she slipped up beside me and dropped her arm behind my back so she could lean close, that was okay, too. I'm not really sure how my arms ended up around her, but even that was okay. More than okay, actually—it was damn nice. That strong supple body pressing mine, stretching me out on the pillows, sliding on top of me. It had been too long since I'd played this kind of game, the game a lot of men go on living for. Damia Nyx was all soft curves and wandering hands and full sweet lips. I tasted corruption every time her mouth pressed mine, something dark and fetid just beneath the flavor of booze, and it made me choke some even as I pulled her to me for more. Somewhere in the midst of our tangling I'd lost my coat and shirt—and my holster and the piece in it, too—and she'd lost her dress, and that silk-naked nymph body was all I wanted in the world. I'm not sure when she undid my belt but I let her do it and forgot all about my .38. Her fingers wandered and her lips worked and I slid in and out of boozy darkness, sinking into some grand oblivion, hoping she'd come along with me. I had the crazy idea those rough walls had closed in on us even as the lights got dimmer, redder, and the music made the place thump and pulse like we were inside a beating brick heart. It made me sick and urged me on all at once. Something warm and sticky ran over my hands and I saw my fingers leaving tacky red prints on her pale pale flesh and she went on exploring me with her tongue. She took my fingers in her mouth and sucked the slick crimson off them and smiled a wet red smile at me and her eyes looked black as coal. I heard myself moaning, saying a name— and realized it wasn't her name. I was saying *Evelyn*.

Evelyn.

All my thoughts slammed back into place and I went instantly sober. What in the name of anything decent was I doing here, half-undressed and twisted up with this naked girl, my defenses down, my job forgotten?

And where the hell was all the blood coming from?

I looked down at my hands. My palms were pooled and sticky and ragged, weeping wounds slashed into my wrists, cross-wise, the kind of wounds that would bleed and keep bleeding but wouldn't kill a man, probably.

I shoved Damia Nyx off me. She flopped across the table sending glasses flying, splashing expensive bourbon everywhere. Cat-quick, she rolled onto her hands and feet and smiled at me, that same bright smile that made my body ache for her, even now. Her mouth was painted with something other than lipstick.

Damia Nyx's smile broke open over slick red teeth.

"You're so sweet," she said, licking her lips, then made little mewling sounds at me that crawled over my skin like cock-roaches. I stared, not moving.

She uttered a glassy laugh and came at me. She struck with the whip-crack speed of a cobra, faster than I'd expected, and my grab for my gun came a split-instant too late. My hand closed on the cold metal even as her teeth closed on my throat. If I hadn't been twisted away toward my cast-aside piece, she would've gotten my jugular and I don't doubt for a second she would've torn it out. Instead she dug in but couldn't get purchase, dug again, teeth tearing, bringing more blood, even while her hands scrambled at my shoulder, my stomach. Something sliced my belly and slid down. I forgot the gun and grabbed her arm in both hands and pulled it away before she could cut something more vital. As I did I saw her weapon—a ring, black obsidian showing vaguely through a paint-job of blood, a barb like a fish-hook poking out of the underside. She hadn't been wearing it earlier but I'd seen its twin before of course, and I hated to think where.

I flung the girl aside again and made another play for my gun. She pounced back, all lithe speed, still laughing that hate-ful, glassy giggle. I felt the ring plunge its barb into the flesh of my shoulder. I flopped away, rolled over my outstretched arm, strained muscles screaming agony, shook the .38 out of its holster and came up firing. Two shots at almost no range in the tiny room. The first slammed Damia Nyx in the shoulder above her right breast and flopped her back away from me. The second caught her in the left thigh. Her whole body convulsed with the impact. I tugged my pants up and grabbed for my coat with my free hand, then scrambled to the door. Unless I missed my guess, all hell was about to break loose as Damia Nyx's hidden friends surged to her rescue. I hoped I'd have at least a shot at the stairs before they did.

I pushed out into the hall, tugging on my coat as best I could while I waved the gun around. Faces floated in the dark around me, seen and gone. I knew they had to be the occupants of those other rooms sneaking peeks out their doors, but in the dark they looked ghostly and detached, like old portraits hanging in a fog. I thought I read anger and consternation and cool amusement in those faces but I couldn't have seen that kind of detail in the brief, corner-of-the-eye glimpses I got. I stumbled, ran, staggered backwards into the stairwell, waved the gun at the shadows following me down the hall, then flopped onto the stairs and started clawing my way up. I had no idea how much blood I'd left in the room, in the corridor, but that and the booze and the thick stench of perfume and decay and whatever else were making me lightheaded. Like a man in the grip of a fever nightmare, I clambered up the splintery wooden stairs, glancing again and again into the gloom behind me, waiting for those faces to rise up after me, teeth bared in brutal scarlet grins. I fought back the urge to stop on the landing and rest, but paused just long enough to listen for sounds of pursuit. I didn't hear a thing, except—

I sucked in a ragged breath and held it—

Glassy black laughter bubbled up from the dark like an echo from the abyss. It had to be my frenzied imagination playing memory for reality. I'd shot the kid twice; she couldn't be laughing. Couldn't be.

I let my breath out and fumbled my way up the second flight of stairs.

At the top I paused one last time for a quick look back.

Damia Nyx, dressed only in blood, smiled up at me from the landing. She blew me a kiss.

I scrambled down the hallway, slammed into the door full force, pushed through and collapsed onto the rain-slick street.

PART III: THE RED CIRCLE

TWENTY

4F

I found myself a nice, private alley about two blocks from the black door with the red circle around the knob and slouched against the wall, not giving a damn about the stink of garbage in the air. It was only then I noticed the thing I clutched in my left hand—a little glassy black ring. The blood on it obscured the vein of red that ran through the black, but I didn't have to see it to know it was there. I must have pulled the thing off her in our little tussle … Or had that slap-happy dame slipped it to me like some kind of nasty calling card? There was no telling with a Mata Hari like that one, and just then I couldn't be troubled to care. I stuffed the ring into my pocket, fished out a handkerchief, and managed to stanch the flow of blood from my left wrist some. It looked like hell and my legs felt rubbery under me but I figured I'd live. My gut and my shoulder stung and bled but already the shallow slashes were starting to scab up. No question I was a bloody mess, but now that the panic and the intoxication were fading some, I started to get the impression that my injuries might not be as bad as I'd first thought, even if they stung like hell. I wasn't dead, anyway. I decided to count myself lucky that Damia Nyx's jaws hadn't torn my jugular right out of my neck.

For a minute or five, I huddled there, willing my heart to slow down, my breathing to stop coming out in rasps. Whatever she'd gotten into me—and I had a pretty good feeling it had been something more than plain old booze—had burned off fast when the adrenaline hit, but I still needed that pause to get my head back together. Already the whole scene had taken on the feeling of a fevered delusion; if it hadn't been for the cuts, I might've sold myself on the idea it had all happened in my head. Hell, now that I was out of it, I couldn't say for sure how much of it had been real. I wondered if I'd ever know.

I rubbed my temples and tried to make my brain work.

One thing was sure—a man in my state, half-dressed and sticky with his own claret, couldn't just flag down a cab to get himself wherever he might need to go for help—even if cabs came anywhere near this part of town. And I felt pretty certain I needed some help. Fortunately for me, among all the boarded-up shops and abandoned apartment buildings on the ugly side of the river, a fair number of pay-by-the-hour hotels clung to life, places where the clerks make it a policy not to ask questions, whatever the clientele looked like. I stumbled into one with no name and tossed some cash on the front desk, where an old fella sat smoking a fat cigar and playing solitaire with a deck of girlie-picture cards. He raised a bushy eyebrow when he got a good look at me, then put it back down when he saw the cash.

"Name?" he said, around the stogie.

"John Smith," I said.

"Amazing," the fella said, fishing something out of a cubby hole, tossing me a key on a brown plastic fob that had 4F printed on it, "third one tonight."

The room was cramped and dark, dirty sheets on the bed and yawning brown water stains on the ceiling. The air sat thick and stagnant, heavy with a smell I didn't want to think too much about. But it had running water and, amazingly, a working phone, and that would do for the time being.

I cleaned up, ruining the one dubious looking towel dangling on the hook by the yellow sink, then tore the towel to shreds and patched myself up as best I could. With that done, I grabbed the phone and made a quick call, then dropped onto the bed and let my eyes slide closed. Then for some time I meandered in and out of a ragged doze. I could hear that lunatic music from Club Erebus, clear one minute and garbled the next, like a badly tuned radio station, and once I thought I saw Damia Nyx smiling in the window at me, that same sinful-sweet expression, and even after everything that had happened I tried to get up and let her in, but my limbs weren't interested in the idea so I just stayed put and stared at her. And then she wasn't there anyway, and almost certainly never had been.

A light, urgent knocking shook me to groggy wakefulness, and I stared at the window a second or two before I realized the sound came from the door. Mustering my strength, I climbed to my feet and stumbled to it. I held my gun at my side, low and ready, then opened the door on its useless brass chain.

"You look like hell," Doc Ambrus said, by way of greeting.

"If I look good, I don't need you," I answered, closing the door so I could slip the chain off. "You sure you weren't followed?"

"Who's gonna follow me?" Doc said, looking back over his shoulder like he was challenging someone to pop out of the shadows behind him. I had a couple of thoughts on that matter, but didn't figure he'd care for them much. With a quick glance of my own up and down the hall, I let him in and closed the door behind us and locked it, put the chain back in place, for whatever it was worth.

"We've got to stop meeting like this," Doc said, dropping his black bag on the bed and pushing me down to sit beside it.

"I'm not exactly having fun here myself," I told him.

"So what was it this time? Some crazed vixen, couldn't get enough of you, tried to take your privates for a keepsake?"

"You sound like you were there."

He peeled away my makeshift bandages and daubed the cuts with boiling acid that came from a bottle cleverly disguised as disinfectant. I tried not to bite my tongue off, swallowing that pain. The weapon that had drawn those clever red lines hadn't hurt half that much and I think Doc knew it, too. I saw the amused smirk on his lips. The sadistic bastard.

"You need to find a gentler playmate," Doc said, now cleaning up my wrist, now stabbing me with a small needle full of something amber-colored. My arm went numb and he began to sew. "Take that secretary of yours, Miss ... what is it?"

"O'Clare," I said. "Cass. Short for Cassandra."

"Miss O'Clare, yes. The lovely Miss O'Clare. Why haven't you two given into one another's charms yet?"

"Cass is a nice girl. She deserves better than a lug like me." The truth of it stung about as much as any of my wounds.

"Can't argue with that," Doc grunted.

"Anyway, you know I'm married to my work. That's plenty. Too much, sometimes."

Doc raised an eyebrow, studied my still-swollen face. "Can't argue with that, either."

"What's it matter to you, anyway?"

He shrugged. "Am I your doctor or not? I'm only trying to keep you from going all to pieces."

"Just take care of my body. I'll worry about the rest."

Doc dropped scissors into his bag and snapped it shut.

"Your body's fine as it's gonna be. I don't think you lost too much blood. Probably looked like more than it was."

It looked like plenty, I thought, splashed all over her naked body, smeared around her mouth. I didn't say anything.

"Still, we probably ought to get some fluids in you."

"All I need's a lift to the office, thanks."

Doc shrugged again. "Your funeral," he said, and we left together.

Stepping into my office felt a bit like coming to my senses. Even in her absence, the reassuring sense of Cass's level-headed pragmatism calmed my nerves some.

All the same, when I got back behind the door marked Private, I watered down some of my remaining bourbon and made an attempt at filling my veins with that. The stuff burned going down and hit my head almost at once, making my eyes swim, but I didn't much care. It was a distraction from gashes and wounds old and new, and that was enough. And it helped me forget about the clock counting away the hours. Hours with no Evelyn.

I was sure I'd lost her for good, after whatever the hell had happened tonight. I'd finally got all the information she wanted and I'd never see her again to give it to her. Who knew, maybe she had a new name, wherever she was. Or maybe she'd ended up someplace where she didn't need a name anymore.

I sat, listening to the insect buzz of the hotel sign just outside my window, and tried again to reconstruct what had happened in that strange room buried away beneath the west side. But the whole thing seemed more and more like a crazy dream, passion and hunger twisting into giddy, clawing fear, and nothing making any sense. Only the gauze on my neck and stomach and the stitches in my wrist convinced me it had happened at all.

I swallowed some bourbon straight and let it wash me away for a time.

TWENTY-ONE
THE GOODS

For a second time during that endless night, a tapping at the door dragged me out of the inviting darkness of sleep and into a far less inviting one. This rat-a-tat-tat came much more faint, slow and distant, like it was too tired to be urgent. After putting together where I was—asleep at my desk again—I realized the sound came from the outer door. Not bothering with the one shirt I had left in my cabinet, I wandered out past Cass's desk and opened the glass door. If I'd been more in my right mind, I might have considered the possibility that it was my friend with the stone fists come to finish the job, but somehow the thought didn't cross my mind. Or maybe I was past giving a damn.

Then I saw who was standing in the hallway outside my office and figured I must be dreaming again, because no one on earth could've looked so good to me.

Evelyn Night stared, then frowned, cocked her head and pondered me.

"Mister ... Orpheus?"

I nodded and swung the door wide for her. "Just like it says on the glass," I told her. "But after all we've been through, you should really call me Frank."

That seemed to light something in her eyes.

"Frank," she said, as if it had just come to her. "Oh, Frank."

She fell against me and I held her, close and tight, kicking the door shut behind us. We kissed, and there was a bitter taste in it that I couldn't quite ignore, much though I wanted to. Then I tore my lips from hers and spoke into the shadowy silk cascade of her hair, close to her ear. "I'm pretty glad to see you, too."

"You—you're hurt again," she said, brushing my bandages with the tips of her fingers.

"Nothing to worry over," I said. "The good news is it sounds like you knew these bandages were fresh—which means you remembered they weren't there the last time you saw me. Which means you may remember more than you realize."

She smiled that hopeful, broken smile again, so unlike the predatory grin I'd seen on Damia Nyx's face.

"Yes, I think I do," she said, and I thought I almost heard tears in that voice, even though I hadn't seen any on her delicate pale cheeks.

"Now that we're both clear on my name," I said, softly, "you know yours yet?"

Whatever hint of joy had touched her eyes guttered out.

"I think ... it's lost, forever."

"No. It's not."

She leaned back from me then, to study my face—searching it for lies, I guess. Or maybe just trying to put the pieces back together.

"Maybe you better sit down," I said, and waved a hand at the sofa where I'd convalesced a few eternities ago.

She sat. I stood, still holding her hands, one in each of my own. Her fingers were ice.

"Your name is Evelyn Night. You live at twenty-two Elysian Avenue, uptown. Ring any bells?"

I had hoped for fireworks to go off in those haunted eyes, but the ghost-inhabited darkness lingered. My client simply stared away at nothing that was in the office with us, some middle distance between Now and Then.

"Like a dream," she said, "one I remember dreaming ... almost ... but it feels like it could never really have been my life."

"It was," I said. "I suppose it still is." Now I paused, trying to decide exactly how much I should drop on her all at once. My gut told me to go slow, especially with the really rough stuff. "I, ah, paid a visit to your home—I hope you don't mind. Nice place. Very ritzy. Remember anything about it?" *Like pictures in black frames*, I thought, not wanting to have to say it.

She looked blank as a fresh sheet of paper, but nodded slightly. "I remember ... empty rooms ... lonely nights ... I remember hurting, being ... brokenhearted." She shuddered then, and I thought she might even faint, but she kept herself upright and looked right into my eyes. "How could I forget? How could I ever forget something like that? My parents ..."

I held her.

"I think maybe forgetting that is how this all started," I said. I couldn't help thinking of the darkness I'd put behind me a few hours ago, all tinted red and echoing with Damia Nyx's glassy laughter. I'm not exactly the churchgoing type, but right then I had no doubt a person could lose his soul in the smoke and shadows of Mr. Menace's depraved pleasure dens, all those places behind the doors with the red circles. Losing your name and memories there seemed easy enough.

"You want me to take you home?"

Evelyn shook her head. "I—no. I can't face that yet. Not yet."

"Well, there's no hurry. The place will still be there when you're ready."

She nodded against my neck, didn't say anything.

"Do you remember where you were tonight?"

"No," she whispered, shaking her head so slightly I only half-saw it in the gloom. "I want to, I just ... can't."

She swiped an errant lock of hair back from her brow. With her right hand, I saw.

"Well, let me tell you where *I* was," I said, stepping away now. "I was with a young woman. Hot stuff—a real killer. Name of Damia Nyx. Mean anything to you?"

"Should it?"

"Oh, you and her go way back. At least that's what Miss Nyx told me, not long before she tried to kill me."

"Kill you?" Evelyn looked genuinely shocked, and maybe a shade guilty, as if it had been partly her fault.

"Tried to relieve me of my blood by ripping my throat out."

"Blood ..."

"Tried to do it with her bare teeth. Well, and a pretty ring of hers."

"Oh, God," Evelyn Night said, and crumpled in on herself like a house of cards collapsing.

I wanted to hold back, to keep that last little bit of distance between us, not least because I still didn't know how deep she was in this mess, or how much I could trust her. But I couldn't simply stand there and stare. I dropped down beside her and put my arms around her again, felt her shake against me. If she was crying, it was in silence.

Then she said, "I think I remember now. Not everything ... but enough. I remember what happened to me. I remember what *he* did to me."

The way she said the word, I knew "he" meant the invisible boss, the phantom with a thousand ears. The man they called Mr. Menace.

"Tell me," I said.

She told me.

It was Marcus Guilio—Junior Dapper—who introduced her to Radamanthus, and Mister Dapper himself who'd brought her into the Red Circle. It had all been fun at first—not innocent fun, but enough to take the edge off her grief, to push the pain away. There had been the gatherings at the club, and then other things, too, things she didn't remember, or chose not to. I got the idea: games like the one I'd played with Damia Nyx, women and men all tangled up together in the dark, plenty of booze and bare skin and maybe some other, more exotic substances as well, say, the kind of thing that might have made it possible for a girl to shake off a couple of bullet wounds for a while. Only these games usually had more than two players at a time. It had quickly gotten so the perverse sport they engaged in at night seemed more real than Evelyn's empty days in the lonely mansion on Elysian Avenue.

Then came the night Radamanthus decided she was ready to meet the big man. Aides Clymenus, known to those who knew him at all as Mr. Menace. Radamanthus played it up for a big deal, a great privilege. The other girls, the ones who hadn't had the pleasure yet, made like they might die of envy. The ones who'd already met the man himself exchanged knowing looks and offered her the smiles of the damned, which she took for more jealousy. You'd have thought she was a good Catholic girl who'd been granted an audience with the Pope himself.

Radamanthus had a car waiting for her someplace past Club Erebus, through the rabbit warren on the other side of the door with the red circle. The fella behind the wheel was Myles Ferryman, the same tall, gaunt undertaker I'd seen with the Red Circle crowd the night I'd bribed my way into the club—and, no doubt, the figure I'd seen behind the wheel of Damia Nyx's Dash Falcon. Seemed Ferryman was the only one Menace trusted to know all the ins and outs of the Tartarus Syndicate's territory, all those empty tenements and notorious hotels and warehouses with no owners, all those rats' nests of criminality and degeneracy on the bad side of the river.

Evelyn had no idea where Ferryman took her, doubted even Radamanthus knew for sure. Just someplace deep in that twisted labyrinth of streets, down a flight of mysterious stairs—not, I gathered, the ones I'd followed Damia Nyx down. After that it was all darkness, like a dream of drowning, lost in shadows and the haze of smoke and the wine they'd practically gulped down before they left the club. All the memories tangled up and got vague. There were people waiting down there in the dark—men, women, she couldn't tell. They touched her, stroked and groped, did things with their mouths, their tongues and teeth. Somewhere in the middle of it all she lost her shoes and her high-class dress and anything she'd had on under it, and along with her clothes went all sense of place and time. In the utter black of those tunnels there had been only that fondling, only those obscene kisses. And then all that had faded and she was drained past the point of exhaustion, and alone.

So she'd thought, at first.

I watched her eyes as she told it, and it was like staring into a dried-up well—just like she'd described Mr. Menace. She wasn't behind those eyes at all, not right then. She was adrift in that lost moment, or maybe someplace between Now and Then.

She didn't hear the man in the dark with her, didn't see anything, not at first. But she knew he was there, she said, because she felt him, the cold air that clung to him. Like he was some kind of ghost, I thought—some kind of boogeyman. Then she saw the black gleam of his eyes, and her heart froze. She heard him whisper terrible seductions to her that she couldn't remember, and then she felt his icy embrace.

"He kissed me," Evelyn Night murmured, staring at nothing. "That was all. But … it hurt … I remember it hurt, and I felt the life draining out of me … He was taking it, taking my life. He was murdering me. And I let him do it."

I thought of Hally, the cuts with not enough blood, and of the black rings with the red bands and their wicked barbs, of Damia Nyx's sanguine grin, and didn't like where any of it was headed.…

Evelyn uttered a jagged laugh that turned into a kind of sob, then shook her head to chase the sound away.

"I could've fought. I could have gotten away from him … but … I …"

She dropped her head and I saw her gaze swim back into focus, back into the here and now.

"But you didn't want to," I finished for her, remembering the carnal gaze Damia Nyx had nearly beaten me with. How I'd almost *wanted* her to beat me.

"No," Evelyn whispered. "I didn't."

I sat beside her, but at an angle so I could look her in the eyes. "What happened next?"

She was silent a long time, then shook her head. "I don't remember. Only finding you, asking you to help me. Perhaps I only remember that because you told me about it."

"Could be. Do you remember anything else about life before all this?"

"I'm not sure I ever was the person you talked about. Whoever she was … she died in the dark. I'm not her."

I stared into her face. I couldn't believe that this beautiful, haunted and frail woman in my office was completely ensnared in Menace's poisonous web. This shaken girl was still more Evelyn Night than Damia Nyx, no matter what her memories seemed to tell her.

"Maybe you can be that woman again," I said, slowly. "Maybe Evelyn Night's not really dead. Not yet."

"I don't believe that."

She said it, but I'd swear I caught a glimmer of hope in her dark eyes.

"Who came to see me all these nights?" I pressed. "Not whoever Mister Menace and his goons set loose, the woman who disappears every night. She wouldn't give a damn, and she sure as hell wouldn't pay some poor dumb gumshoe to chase down her old name. So it must've been that other woman, the one who knew she had a real life and wanted it back."

"Then why can't I remember her?" she asked, tears shining on her cheeks. "Why does it all feel like a made-up story someone told me ages ago?"

I sighed, wanting the bottle again, or at least a nice piano aria. Anything to clear my thoughts.

"Well, one thing's sure, we've got to get you out of this tangled web you're in. Then maybe that old life will come back to you. I'd bet money on it."

"I don't even know *what* I'm involved in," Evelyn said. "It's all like a dream I can never remember when I wake up. Except that I can never really wake up, either—not to that life you talked about. Only to this ... whatever this is. This purgatory."

I had no response for that. What could I say, when I more than half agreed with her?

Then she stood up and pulled some cash out of a pocket, dropped it on Cass's desk and headed for the exit.

"Thank you, Mister Orpheus," she said, opening the door.

I stepped to the door and shut it again.

"Now hold on there, sister," I said. "You're not walkin' out on me as easy as that. I've taken a fair amount of hurt for you— we're in this together now." I hoped my tone came across more kind than tough, even if it wasn't my usual mode.

She answered with a broken smile.

"You've done all you can for me. Thank you. But ... Frank, you should get out while you can. And you still can."

Like she'd heard Cass saying it.

I shook my head. "That's not how it is anymore. I'm full-in and I'm gonna be full-in until the end."

And didn't *that* turn out to be right? If I'd known how right, maybe I would've let her walk on out that door. But I didn't, and she didn't.

Instead, my client, Miss Gray or Miss Night or whatever I was supposed to call her, looked at me a moment. Then she took a step away from the door and stared out the window, into the night. "So," she said, not smiling. "What do we do next?"

"First, you sit back down and let me talk. Fair?"

She nodded. "Fair," she said, and glided back into the room, but didn't resume her place on the outer office sofa.

"It seems to me we gotta find out just exactly what you're in. I've gotten a glimpse, but only enough to make me ask a lot of questions. I can't get in there on my own, not with Menace's goons everywhere and that she-devil Damia Nyx prowling around." I took a breath before I continued; I knew neither of us would like what I had to say next. "*You*, on the other hand, can come and go from that world as you please."

She laughed again, still bitter and hurt, but with the faintest hint of warmth now. "How?"

I slipped an arm around her waist, tugged her close, then reached into her jacket pocket. I'd felt the small hard shape when I slipped my arm around her. I pulled the thing out and opened my hand to reveal the black ring with the fluid red band around it and the half-hidden barb, the twin of the one that'd drawn wet red lines all along my gut and shoulder and wrist.

"I think this is the key," I told her. Then I glanced up and got a good look at her face.

Her skin had gone as white and hard and brittle as chalk, her lips thin, drawn back into something like a snarl or a grimace. Her eyes burned with—what? Loathing, I thought. Or fear.

"Put it away," she whispered.

I dropped the ring back into the pocket I'd pulled it out of.

"I'm sorry," she said, sidling away from me. "I ... don't want to look at that thing."

"So you know what it is."

"No, and I don't want to. It's something awful. That's what I know."

"Then I'll get rid of it," I said, reaching again, "maybe that—"

"No!" she snapped, clutching the ring through a handful of her jacket, holding it to her heart like a precious keepsake. "I can't. I should—I want to, oh God. But I *can't*."

"I figured. I don't know how, but I figured." I took a breath, and the stormy tension in the air dissipated a bit. "So okay, we'll just have to figure out how to use it to get what we want."

"It's too dangerous."

I thought of the sting of my wounds. "I know it. Still ..."

"This is crazy."

"Probably."

She shook her head, managed something resembling a smile —but it was a broken thing, more pain than relief. All the same, it was the most life I'd seen in her yet, the brightest glimmer of hope. I wanted to leap to it—yeah, just like a moth to a flame.

Miss Night stared out the office window, out across the jagged skyline of the city where the dawn had begun to touch the clouds, turning them from the black of sackcloth to the gray of ashes. Not much warmth or light to be found out there, either, but I suppose it was better than nothing.

"I'm tired," she said softly. "So tired."

"Yeah," I said, and put an arm around her again. "Let's get out of here."

TWENTY-TWO

MEAT WAGON

I know what you're thinking but no, we didn't go back to my drab place, not that morning, and for the record, I spent the next few hours in my creaky Murphy bed alone.

This time it was the phone that shouted me up out of sleep.

It took me a minute to stagger over to it, a moment longer to decide if I was actually going to pick it up. I figured since I'd already dragged myself over there I might as well answer the damn thing, if only to make it shut up.

"Yeah?"

"You *are* there." The voice paused, and I could just about see Cass biting her lower lip the way she did when she was worried or scolding. "You okay, Frank?"

"Sure."

"We were supposta open the office five minutes ago. I was gettin' worried. Not that we had any business or anything, but still … It ain't like you, being late."

The genuine concern in her voice made me want to apologize, but then I got angry that she'd made me feel guilty and the response came out terse. "I had a long night," I said, rubbing red exhaustion from my eyes. For the first time in a while my scars hardly itched or ached at all, maybe because I was numb with fatigue.

"Yeah?"

"Yeah." Cass obviously wanted more, and probably she was entitled to it, but I let it go at that.

"You close the Night case, Frank?"

"Just about."

"She was here last night, huh?"

"How'd you know?"

"I just ... I walked in and I got one of my feelings. So you told her everything?"

"Everything I could."

"Good. Now you can stick that stupid case in the filing cabinet and get on with other business, taking pictures of cheating husbands and that sort of thing. Payin' the bills. And I'll tell you, Frank, I'm mighty glad. I don't like what this case was doing to you."

"Well, I'm not through with it yet," I told her, and I didn't much care for the way it sounded, like I was apologizing. Only I guess that was pretty much what I was doing. "Got just a little more work to do and it's gonna bust wide open."

"What else *is* there?" Cass said, voice sharp even over the fuzzy connection. "You found out who she is, that's what she was payin' you for, right? So it's over and done with."

"It's more complicated than that."

She sighed, loudly. "Frank, listen, will ya? Please? All this ... it was bad from the start, but it's gonna get worse if you don't get out right away. It's gonna get real ugly."

"One of your feelings?"

"Yeah. A strong one. Real strong."

"You know I don't believe in fortune tellers, Cass. No crystal balls or old ladies with pretty decks of cards—or secretaries with 'feelings.'"

"I'm tellin' ya, Frank. I'm scared. I feel sick, I'm so scared."

"Maybe you should take some time off then," I suggested.

"That isn't gonna help. *You* oughtta take some time off."

"Yeah," I went on like she hadn't interrupted. "I think that's an idea. Why don't you give yourself a week off? Take your mother down the shore, maybe."

I didn't say how much better I'd feel to put some distance between Cass and Mr. Menace's goons. No need to upset her more than I'd already done.

"That's not a good idea, Frank," Cass insisted. "You can't run the place without me."

"For a week I can. Anyway you said yourself business is slow these days. After this whole Evelyn Night affair is wrapped up we can get back to the everyday stuff."

"I don't need a week off," Cass said. "I just want things to get back to normal."

"I'll see you in a week, Cass."

"No, Frank, let's talk about this. Honestly—I have an awful bad feeling about what'll happen if you don't drop this case. I walked in the office this morning and you weren't here and I could tell she'd been here, and it just hit me, so hard I had to sit down, and I thought—"

"See you in a week, Cass," I said again, and set the phone back in its cradle. Then, on second thought, I picked it up again and dropped it on the table, off the hook, in case Cass tried to call back, which she was pretty much certain to do. Then I wandered back to my Murphy bed and flopped in, ravenous for a bit more sleep. The meager sunlight coming in the window above the sink was giving me a headache, and I needed some rest before I put my plan for the evening into action.

I climbed out of the cab in front of the Chandler Hotel around dusk, my head still a bit woolly with sleep, or the lack of it. Inside, my pal Geiger greeted me with a smile that twitched nervously. I didn't think much of it—the fella always looked like a plump mouse in a room full of hungry cats.

"She still here?" I asked.

"As far as I know," he said, hands clutching at one another.

"There a car parked here for me?"

"In the back alley, as you instructed. And, um, about *that* ..." His voice fell to a whisper. "I have reason to believe the gentleman who dropped it off for you was not, uh, shall we say, the 'rightful owner.'"

"You don't say."

The man wasn't exactly street-smart, but even he knew hot property when he saw it. Still, if I was going to make my plan work smoothly, I was going to need reliable wheels. That meant no cabs. So I'd called in another outstanding debt and had an old friend procure some transportation for me. I didn't care to know where he'd come up with it; as far as I was concerned I was just borrowing it.

"You have the keys for me?"

My pal slipped a set of keys out from under the counter and pushed them across the imitation marble to me with his hand cupped over them, like he was trying to be sly about it.

"I'll be pleased when you take it off the hotel's property. Having that particular vehicle here is bound to make our guests ... uneasy ..."

"It'll be gone before you know it."

He nodded.

"Better give me Miss Gray's room key, too. Or the pass key, if she's still got the one for the room."

I'd figured it was safest to keep her there under the alias I'd picked—no need to advertise her real name around, even this far from the west side.

The manager gave me a look as if to say this was just about the last rule he'd break for me, but handed me the pass key anyway. I gave him a nod and headed off upstairs.

I knocked on her door, loud, and waited.

Nothing.

I pounded now, not much giving a damn if the folks in the other rooms objected to the noise. No answer, but I decided I'd given her fair warning and jabbed the key in the lock and opened the door.

I had just registered the fact that the room was empty when a hard hand clamped down on my shoulder from behind me.

I whirled around. The bellboy with the epaulettes on his shoulders was mighty lucky I didn't deck him, luckier I didn't go for my piece. A fella just doesn't get away with sneaking up on a man who's about had his face sliced off.

"Hey, Mister, that lady you're lookin' for, I just saw her outside, leavin'."

"Which way?" I said, already starting toward the stairs.

"Headin' west," the kid said. "I swear I didn't see her go out —I was right on the door, I don't know how she got past me, but I wanted to let you know right away."

All this as we scrambled down the stairs and across the lobby. The kid obviously hoped he'd get a tip out of all this but I was too busy fishing for the car key somewhere in my pocket. I left the kid at the door and hurried around to the alley, hoping I hadn't missed my chance. I hadn't figured on her going quite so early—and how the hell had she gotten out without passing the manager, or me?

I almost stopped short when I saw the boosted car poking its nose out of the alley, but I didn't have time even to snort at the transportation my old buddy had come up with for me. Long and low and black, curtained windows in back. At least I could see why the manager had figured the car was stolen, and why he'd been so nervous about having it parked behind his hotel. Hearses tend to have that effect on people, I've noticed.

I climbed in and started it up without bothering to see if the back was occupied. At this point just about anything seemed possible.

The meat wagon moved surprisingly well as I swung it out into the westbound traffic, searching the crowd ambling along the sidewalks for Evelyn. Too many people getting off work, the twilight street a crazy ant-colony of secretaries and men in pinstripe suits, mingling uneasily with the bread-line crowd. My only hope was to point the hearse due west, on the bet I already knew where my client was headed. But the whole escapade was for nothing if I guessed wrong.

I slipped along at the speed of traffic, getting just ahead of the shoe leather crowd, scanning—and caught a glimpse of a well-dressed woman disappearing into the back of a possibly-familiar black car. I couldn't be sure the woman was Evelyn, couldn't be sure the car was the one driven by the gaunt chauffer, Ferryman, but I trusted my gut, and followed.

It was no fun task, trying to play inconspicuous in a hearse, but if the driver of the black car knew I was there he didn't show it. He made a few twists and turns through side streets but I guessed it was the usual game, the same precautions he always took. I kept my distance and a couple of times I lost him and caught him again a block later. Then he took a corner and I took it a block behind him, and the car was gone. Just plain gone, like it hadn't been there at all. I put on the gas and roared up to the next intersection, staring down every street, but the black car might've evaporated like fog for all I could see of it.

I took another gamble and steered the most direct route I knew to the West River Narrows Bridge. There were a couple other ways to that side of the river, sure, but I had to take the chance that they'd go the old familiar route.

Crossing the long gray hump of the bridge, I couldn't quite chase Cass's words out of my mind. Something about putting that sluggish black river between me and the halfway decent part of town felt like I'd just done what she said—like I'd gone that last step too far. Then the dark buildings of the west side were in front of me and it was too late to go back. If I could only find out where Evelyn Night vanished to every evening, if I could only untangle that much more of this sordid riddle, I could pull her out of it, give her back the life that was supposed to go with that name I'd found. I wasn't sure what it would mean for me—for *us*, if there was any us—but that didn't matter. And that was about the surest sign Cass had gotten it at least partly right: I had stopped looking out for myself and my business and was in this entirely for a woman I hardly knew. I wasn't myself, not one bit. But that felt okay. Maybe that other fella, the one Cass still expected to see at the office every morning, hadn't known quite as much as he'd thought. Maybe sometimes a man needed to take better care of someone else than he did of himself.

Or maybe I was kidding myself that I didn't expect to get anything out of saving Evelyn from whatever lurked here, on the wrong side of things. Maybe part of me was even keen to catch her at the kind of games Damia Nyx and I had played together. Sure—and not much question *which* part of me ...

I swung the meat wagon onto the narrow road that fronted the river and killed the lights. Unless they were looking for me as they came over the bridge, they'd never spot me in the shadows of the towering, soot-colored abutments. I kept the engine running and waited, hoping like a gambler tossing in his last chip that I'd guessed right. I had a feeling that if I'd gotten it wrong, I'd lose Evelyn for good.

I nearly held my breath, and it wasn't all because of the stink coming off the West River.

It seemed like I sat there a long time, but I couldn't read my watch in the dark to know for sure. Three cars passed, only one of them headed west, and none I recognized. I was about ready to give up, but then what? Go putter around the office? Head home and try again tomorrow night? I still had my doubts whether or not there'd even be a tomorrow night as far as Evelyn Night was concerned.

The Falcon came out of nowhere, shoving its way through a

grimy fog that'd risen on the river and now shrouded the bridge. It rolled past without slowing down and I had to jam the hearse into gear and slam the gas to get after it again. I left the lights off, hoping I could see my quarry in the gloomy streets without being spotted. Night had settled in and half the street lights around here stood as dead as trees after a forest fire, so for once I had the darkness on my side—at least for now.

I had quite the romp, trying to hang back a discreet distance and not lose the black Dashiell Falcon as it weaved in and out of the winding streets, up alleys and down back roads, deeper and deeper into the crumbling district of the Tartarus Syndicate's empire. I followed as much by luck and instinct as anything, but somehow I kept the other car's taillights in my windshield. I'd half guessed we'd end up at the club again, or maybe outside that weird stairway to Hell where Damia Nyx had tried to have my blood for a dinner cocktail. But when the other car crawled to a stop it was in no place I recognized, just more abandoned buildings and graffiti-scrawled warehouse walls. I watched the tall pale chauffeur unfold himself from the front seat and open the rear door, watched my client step out, offering her left hand for his assistance. Then the two of them vanished down an alley so narrow I hadn't even seen it. Either that, or they'd walked right through a brick wall together. From where I sat I could only guess, but at this point even black magic didn't seem all that unlikely.

I waited a minute or so then pulled up to the curb across from the Falcon and climbed out, leaving the door unlocked. I hoped my borrowed hayburner would still be where I left it when I got back. Not too many street toughs would go after a hearse, but in this neighborhood you could never be sure—and anyway, the thing had already been stolen once. Even so, I intended to be able to get out of here quick if it came down to that.

I put a hand on my piece, just to reassure myself that it was there, tucked away in an inner pocket since I'd left my holster in

Damia Nyx's den. For a minute, then, I hesitated. No one in my line of work is all that eager to step into the dark of a totally unknown situation, and even less when the one thing you *do* know is that the dark has teeth and claws. But, foolish as it was, I'd come this far and I'd be damned before I turned back. Maybe I'd fallen in love, or maybe it was something lower than that. Or maybe I was just stubborn. Whatever the case, I was determined to get Evelyn out of that world, no matter what it cost me. I thought about drawing the .38, but decided that would be a bit too conspicuous, even here.

Pulling my hat down over my brow, I crossed the street, headed toward the spot where the Falcon's passengers had disappeared.

TWENTY-THREE

DOWN

The alley I'd suspected but not seen was hardly more than a dark line between two empty buildings, one place that looked like a Laundromat, its windows soaped over, the other maybe a grocer's, years ago. Neither looked like it'd seen occupants in ten years or more, but things had a way of falling apart pretty quick in this corner of town and maybe it'd only been that many months.

I stepped into the alley and started along it, studying the shadows in front of me, the vacant windows on the floors over my head, my elbows just about brushing both walls as I walked. If someone decided to ambush me here I was pretty well cooked —no cover, no place to run except in a long, straight line. Made me appreciate that old chestnut about shooting fish in a barrel in ways I never had before. I pulled my piece and held it down at my side, somewhat hidden in the folds of my coat, but ready if I needed it. I really hoped I wouldn't need it. I didn't care to think too much about the last time I'd fired it. It bugged me to shoot a girl, even one who wanted to rip my throat out.

Up ahead, the alley dead-ended in a wall as straight and skinny as a chimney, and for a second I wondered where the hell Ferryman and Miss Night could've gone. Then I spotted the subtle outline of a door set in the wall to the right, painted black so it looked like nothing but another shadow until you got up close.

A red circle about as big around as a dinner plate had been painted on the black, right at eye level.

I slipped up beside the door and held my breath a minute, listening for movement, voices, whatever.

Nothing.

I gave the door a push. It didn't move. I looked for a handle and didn't find one. Didn't find a keyhole either, for that matter. I tipped the muzzle of my gun up and gave the door three quick raps, the way I'd seen Damia Nyx do on that other door.

Again, nothing.

Hell with it, I thought, and threw my shoulder into the door. The tiny alley didn't give me much room for a strong start but I didn't really need it. The door was thin and the wood was old and the frame splintered on my second hit, dumping me into a deeper darkness than what I'd had to put up with in the alley.

I swept my gun across the blackness, but no one was there to greet me, at least, no one I could see. Still, I didn't relax my trigger finger just yet.

I felt my way down a corridor roughly as wide as the alley I'd just put behind me, the fingers of my non-weapon hand wandering over a rough terrain of rotten plaster and naked lathing. The place smelled of neglect and decay, and again that something else I couldn't quite put a name to. Best I could tell, I was alone there.

Once or twice as I walked I thought I felt rats scurry over my shoes, but I managed to suppress the urge to take a few pot shots at them. Every fifteen feet or so I stopped and listened, making sure I didn't have any other company. At some point the passage bent at a right angle, then again, and then descended a short staircase, and another, and a third. I had no idea now where the hell I was in relation to the buildings on either side of the alley, or my morbid getaway car. I didn't much like the feeling of being lost, but I was getting mighty used to it. And anyway, as long as I hadn't missed any doors or branches, I was still on the track of Evelyn Night and the chauffer.

The next time I paused, I could hear noises up ahead somewhere. I inched forward until I could make out voices, and music. Familiar music. Even now it made my skin crawl. A bit of wayward light spilled in a few feet further along and I crept toward it. Another sharp bend led me into a hallway full of cigarette smoke and dim reddish light and that god-awful music, some kind of jazz written with snake venom and played by madmen on diseased instruments. I tightened my fingers on the Harpe's grip and stepped out into the half-lit room, knowing where I was even before I looked around.

Club Erebus.

It didn't make any damn sense—we'd parked at least a half-dozen blocks from this dive, and I would've bet a month's rent I hadn't been walking that long, even with all the twisting and turning. So how the hell had I ended up there? But there was no mistaking the place—the dark patrons, the smell, that damned music. It was either Club Erebus or its evil twin.

I surveyed the room carefully, trying to get my bearings. No sign of Evelyn, no sign of the chauffer or Mister Dapper and the harem. No sign of the thug doorman, either—Jimmy Porter, my client had told me during her brief lucidity, better known to his friends as the Doberman. Just the usual milling lowlifes and cocktail girls. I seemed to recall that the last time I'd visited this place, I'd found Radamanthus and his girls at a table not far from that poisonous jazz combo, so, despite the way that music drove nails into my brain, I stashed the .38 away and walked toward it, hoping I could remain somewhat anonymous in the smoke and shadows. I wasn't ready to deal with the Doberman, not yet, and for that matter didn't know how I'd handle Radamanthus or Ferryman if I stumbled over them.

One thing at a time.

I couldn't say why, but that infernal music got under my skin worse this time. The off-color moans of the sax, the sickly pulse-throb of the bass, the insipid broken-glass plinking of the piano ... it slithered over me the way a python slithers over its prey, slowly squeezing the breath out of me. I watched the faces of the patrons floating like party balloons over their tables, all hollow smiles and bright empty eyes, and wanted to shout curses at them—how could they put up with that grinding-gears clatter? I bit my lower lip and walked on, forcing myself to ignore the music—and the itch waking up around my left eye. All at once the damn thing was worse than ever. I tried to sell myself on the idea it was because of the smoke and the cheap perfume and stale-booze stink in the air, but knew better.

Seemed like I wandered for hours in that place, a rat lost in some scientific-sadist's maze, one room leading to another, then another, and all the time that rotten excuse for music ebbed closer but not close enough. I managed to duck two waitresses in fishnet stockings and no one else in the joint seemed interested in me at all. Next thing I knew I stood looking over the bar at old cue-ball, the tight-lipped hoochmaster I'd gotten nothing but careless glances from last time. I kept my hat low over my eyes and my back to the fella in case he hadn't warmed to me any since our first meeting. At the same time, I wondered how the hell I'd ended up at the damn bar—I would've bet dollars to doughnuts I'd been headed away from this room. I scratched at that clawing itch and stared around, discrete as possible. Four different doors out of here and my sense of direction was shot. How was a man supposed to think straight, anyway, with the smoke in his eyes and that music in his head? I picked a door at random and wandered through.

Somewhere not far off I caught a sound, a tattered shred of laughter, familiar but not familiar, a sound about as cheerful as nails down a blackboard. I seized on it and headed where it came from, trying to puzzle out how I could know it so well without knowing it at all.

Then it struck me I'd never heard her laugh before. That was the thing. And even though I knew her voice, I felt sure all the way down to my shoes that the woman I knew as Evelyn Night could never make a sound quite like that one.

I poked my head around the next corner and spotted an empty room. But the sound came again and I chased it, around another bend, down a narrow hallway with art deco sconces that cast no light and carpet the color of freshly spilled blood. The hall ended in a beaded curtain, faux-rubies the shape of teardrops. I slipped up, quiet as a fog, and peered through the swinging gaps between the strings.

Radamanthus sat in the middle, same as last time, probably the same as always. On either side, the girls fawned and flapped their painted eyelashes and cooed like doves. And there, right next to him, sat my client, giving him her long pale throat to nibble on. He indulged himself between swallows of wine. The pug-nosed .38 in my pocket whispered to me, but I fought off the urge to pop the fella between the eyes, not for the way he was looking at Evelyn but for the way he *wasn't* looking at her, even when he had his thin lips all over her skin. I didn't want to think about what he was doing with the hand that didn't have a wine glass in it, the one I couldn't see beneath the table, but the blond on his right had her eyes closed and her head thrown back, so I could imagine.

Everything inside me went cold.

The blond with the bedroom eyes. I knew her, would probably see her in nightmares for the rest of my life. The gashes she'd left in my skin still itched.

I admit I was never the best shot on the firing range, and a short-barreled gun like my .38 is worth nothing for accuracy past ten paces or so, at least not in my hands, but I'd taken two shots at that girl. Two at close range. I was sure I'd plugged her with both of them—I'd seen them catch her in that sexy shoulder of hers, and that shapely thigh. Even if I hadn't opened any major arteries and she hadn't bled out down there in the dark, she should have been out of commission for a good long time, not out and boozing it up with her pals. But there she sat, a trembling smile pasted on her delicate lips, her slender body swaying like seaweed in a tide. The table and her stylish jacket hid any hints of her injuries.

My head swam. Had I hit her at all? I'd been drunk, sure, and who knows what else had been swimming in the whisky, floating in the strange-smelling smoke? Had I hallucinated the whole damn thing? The gashes on my wrists insisted I hadn't, to say nothing of the love nip on my neck and the slashes on my stomach and shoulder. And I'd checked the gun in Doc's car as we jostled our way to my office, to make sure I'd gotten it right. Two chambers empty.

So that much had been real, too.

All the same, there she sat, smiling and fawning, having a fine old time.

My stomach lurched like I might bring up lunch. I gave a moment's serious thought to finding that band and kicking some teeth out just to shut them up, or to maybe clawing my left eye out to stop that itch. Suddenly those two ideas seemed about as rational as anything I was dealing with in the world.

Familiar eyes flickered my way. I slipped back into the hall out of sight, hoping against hope the girl next to Damia Nyx hadn't actually seen me.

I don't know how long I stood there, slouched against the wall just inside that bead curtain, trying to pull my head together. It seemed like an hour or more but for all I know it was only a few minutes. Finally I sucked up some little bit of courage and spied through the dangling ruby teardrops again.

The room was empty.

I didn't take time to wonder how they'd slipped out without my hearing a sound, but stepped right in and had a good look around. Theirs was the only booth in the alcove; on the other three walls hung musty-smelling red velvet curtains. The door was behind the one opposite the booth. The red circle on it looked a lot like it had been scrawled there with something other than paint.

I reached for the knob.

Someone big came out of nowhere and grabbed my shoulder. He spun me around and I found myself face-to-face with Jimmy the Doberman. Looking at that mug of his, I could appreciate his nickname more than I cared to.

"Where you think you're goin', pal?"

That voice, thick as a slab of lard. Last time I'd heard it, the big Bruno had been standing over me in the dark of my office. I could hardly imagine he wouldn't recognize his own handy work stamped all over my face, but on the other hand he didn't come across as all that bright. I gave some thought to the piece in my coat, and whether or not I could pull it and fire before this lug clobbered me. I hoped I wouldn't find out.

"Isn't this the john?" I slurred my words some so maybe he'd get the impression I'd been tying it on for a while.

"I think I better show you the street, pal."

He started to lead me away; the hand on my shoulder pinched like a vice.

"Now it doesn't have to be like this between us," I said as he took me into the next room, back toward the bar. "How's about I buy you a drink?"

"Zip it, Mac, and I won't snap you in half before I toss you out."

I caught a break just then, managed to grab the elbow of one of those half-dressed cocktail girls. "Bourbon for me and a scotch for my friend here—Hume and Culloden, if you got it." I gave the big man a nod. "Best brown plaid you ever swallowed, trust me."

The goon faltered. The bargirl raised an eyebrow at him. He slung me into a chair and crouched on the one opposite me. "Make it a double," he told the girl.

She nodded and slinked off into the cigarette haze.

"I don't usually drink with the customers, 'specially when I'm about to evict 'em," the Doberman explained, none of the hardness leaving his granite voice. "But I s'pose I can make an exception one time."

I nodded, touched the brim of my hat at him. Seemed Evelyn had gotten this much right, the fella was a sucker for Hume and Culloden. Pricey stuff, but if it'd grease my way through that secret door I'd buy a round for the house.

"Don't I know you from somewhere, pal?"

The Doberman was squinting at me and twitching his big nose. I drew away some, despite myself, thinking of my .38 again. Was this goon actually sniffing at me, trying to get my scent? A fella could take his nickname too far, I thought. But then, the deeper I got into this twisted game, the less all the strangeness surprised me.

"Could be," I said, clinging to the dwindling hope that he was the kind of fella who forgot a face as soon as he'd finished pounding on it. "I been in here once or twice."

"Uh-huh." He smirked, cocked his head at me. I think it was on his mind to say more but just then the girl came and put our drinks in front of us and took a wad of cash off me.

"Here's gas in your tank," I said, raising my glass before the goon could put another two thoughts together.

"Whatever you say," he agreed, not bothering to lift his glass to mine. We drank. He put it away fast, exactly like I'd counted on. I tried to think about getting to Evelyn on the other side of that door, and not about how this lug was gulping down what little money I'd wrung out of this case so far. Time was when the money would've concerned me a lot more than the woman beyond that door—more than any woman, for that matter.

I watched him settle his seventh glass on the table, moving with the great and painstaking care only drunks have, and knew I was getting close. The Doberman was a big fella but that was a lot of booze for anyone's blood and he was sinking pretty quick. I ordered another round for him, nursing my third bourbon. I could've taken a good deal more but I was determined to keep some kind of edge on the man.

"Ah, hell," the Doberman said, plucking his fresh glass off the barmaid's cork-lined tray and swallowing half at a go, "I remember now where I metcha before. You're that dumb sap I put the lights out on in that office across town. Sure. That, uh, private dick." He downed the rest of his scotch. "Prob'ly you shouldn't oughtta be here."

"How about I buy you another one of those?" I asked, thinking how much I wanted to put a slug in the fella's midsection ... or maybe just a shade lower. It would've been quite a kick, putting some hot lead into the goon who'd made such a mess of my face. But I figured gunfire would be a bit too conspicuous even in this place.

The Doberman shrugged his meaty shoulders. "Sure," he muttered.

The ninth Hume and Culloden put him under the table, lights out—a gentler method than he'd used on me, but ultimately as effective, and pretty sure to leave him regretting whatever he could remember of our little tête-á-tête whenever he came to. I dropped a couple bills on the table to cover the tip and slipped away back down that hallway, around into the private room behind the bead curtain. I tugged the red drapes aside and tried the door. Locked, as I figured. Time now to find out if my little hunch would work as well as the other trick Evelyn Night had taught me, plying Jimmy the Doberman with H and C.

I slipped the red-black ring I'd clipped from Damia Nyx around my third finger and grabbed the knob again. I couldn't feel what slot the ring's thorn slipped into, but it had to be something like that because the lock tripped and the door yawned open.

I didn't especially care for the odor drifting up out of that dark passage, but I went inside anyway.

TWENTY-FOUR
CARNAL

The stairs were steep as some Tibetan peak, and with the red curtain back in place and the door shut behind me all I could do was feel my way down with my hand and my heels, keeping my piece out ahead of me, tilted at what I guessed was the angle of the staircase. I tried to breathe soft so I could hear any noises coming at me, but all I heard was the rusty-nail whine of boards under my feet. My free hand traced the rough brick wall at my side. The air stood stock-still and stank of mold and decay and growing things—and again I caught that whiff of something black and familiar under the rest. I reviewed my life up to this point to see if I could find another moment when I'd been so totally in the dark, in every possible sense of that phrase. Nothing came to mind. I tried to forget the unbreakable gloom and focus on what my fingers, feet, nose and ears were telling me about this passageway. Not much, was the answer. I thought about the lighter in my coat pocket but, even in the silence I didn't especially want to light myself up like a beacon.

I guessed at how many strata of the city I might be passing through—down past the tangle of power lines and the phone lines and all that electrical spaghetti the Consolidated Westing-house boys were always tearing out of the streets, past the steam pipes and the gas lines. Down past the subway lines, too, I figured. Down to the level of the sewers, the wet rotten breeding grounds of rats and roaches and who-knew-what else.

Things like Mr. Menace?

Had I really bought all that wild nonsense Hally Thersis and Evelyn Night or whoever she wanted to be had told me about the Tartarus Syndicate and the Big Boss? Aides Clymenus, aka Mr. Menace. Not just a gangster, not just an ice-hearted man with all the brutal power bad money can buy, but a genuine monster, a beast who could end a man's life with a few words? A thing that could kill people without killing them? All of that was the waking nightmare chatter of a straight-jacket candidate.

And here in this grave-smelling pitch black, I found myself believing every syllable of it.

There was Damia Nyx, after all. Damia Nyx who should've been stretched out on a slab with her hands over her fine chest and two powder-burned holes in her. Damia Nyx who I'd seen half an hour ago drinking wine and rolling her eyes in the queer bliss of Mr. Dapper's company.

As a precaution, I added a little pressure to the .38's trigger. Not that my longtime pal had done me much good so far … But that was something else I didn't care to think too much about.

Some other smell joined that cellar damp now, something like the miasma of smoke in the club, but stale, dead. It made my head bob and sink like a buoy in rough seas.

The stairs ended abruptly and there was water pooled under my feet on what felt and sounded like a cobblestone floor. I paused, listened: a slow, steady dripping somewhere ahead, and that was all. I might've been in my own tomb for the all the icy silence around me.

Yet another thing not to think too much about.

I decided to risk a look with the lighter, so I fished it out of my pocket and gave it a flick.

The flame cast a second's worth of yellow light, turning

everything around me the color of old newsprint, and then my fingers went numb and the lighter clacked to the floor at my feet. I should have cut and run then, gotten the hell out, but for a minute I stood frozen there, turned into a statue by what I'd seen in that eye blink when I'd chased the shadows back. There's no rational way a man could've seen as much as I did in that flashbulb instant, but nothing about the world I'd entered was in any way rational and the picture lingered complete and vivid in my brain like an afterimage singed into my eyes by lightning.

Bodies, the pale yellowish-white color of spoiled milk, twisting and writhing all around me like worms in a bucket. Couplings of men and women, groups of three, clusters of four, their flesh entangled, their wasted bodies bent and crouched and merged in ways that made my stomach roll over. I saw a shape dangling from chains, saw three other figures gathered about it, moving their teeth. I could still feel the ragged wall at my left but it seemed like they were all around me, flailing and flexing— and all in total silence, as if I'd wandered into the silent movie of some madman's nightmare fantasy. Even in that instant, I recognized faces in the throng—Radamanthus, and Damia Nyx—and I finally understood that odor, the one I'd caught beneath the cellar smell and the smoke.

Sooner or later, most of us learn the peculiar perfume of carnality.

Somewhere in that awful jumble of writhing bodies was the woman I'd called Miss Gray and Miss Night. I'd spotted her pretty face pressed close to some anonymous flesh, but in the wink of my lighter I hadn't seen so much as a twinkle of doubt or grief in her bottomless black eyes. Only a kind of naked hunger that outstripped the nudity of her body by a mile.

Then the darkness slammed down on me like a lid and I couldn't see, hear, feel anything. I couldn't trust the crazy picture in my head. In the dark I felt—hell, I *knew*—I was completely alone. The silence practically insisted, and while that odor of sweat and flesh hung on, it suddenly smelled old, the kind of stink that clings to a worn-out mattress.

I stood there breathing deep, squinting at the black, sweeping my gun back and forth, waiting for even a hint of motion, ready to squeeze off as many rounds as I could before they took me down. I thought I might close my eyes when I did, to keep from seeing anything the muzzle flash might show.

Nothing.

No movement, no mutters or moans of the sick revelers, only that steady *plink ... plink ... plink* of water, someplace else.

I knew they'd seen me, their red rats' gazes had leapt all over me in the instant the lighter's flame had lit the place up, but the rush I'd expected didn't come. I backed up the hallway, going how I'd come, or hoping I was—the wall still dragged along under the fingers of my left hand but I didn't much trust even brick walls down here. My gun flicked back and forth in front of me like the tail on an angry cat. I couldn't move too fast for fear I'd tangle my feet up in each other and go down in a heap. Probably lose my gun if that happened, and I'd almost surely lose any last tiny shred of my sense of direction.

An arm, soft and cool as a fall breeze, slipped around my waist, from behind. An invisible hand traced its way up my chest and stroked my chin. I couldn't see it but I knew it was hers—Damia Nyx's. My knees threatened to buckle under me. I poked the darkness ahead of me with the gun, impotent to protect myself.

"Leaving so soon, Frankie?" Her voice was right in my ear, her mouth must've been close enough to nibble my earlobe, but all I could feel was that wandering hand. It felt like some kind of vile reptile but I didn't want it to stop. "Someone here would be terribly disappointed if she didn't get to play with you before you flew the coop on us, Mister Detective. Wouldn't you, sweetheart?"

"I'd never forgive myself," another voice answered. I knew it even though it didn't sound anything like the voice of the woman I was falling in love with.

The voice I'd just heard sounded as impervious to love as a lump of frozen rock. I've never much believed in a soul, but I was sure I hadn't heard one in those words.

I pulled the trigger, pulled it, pulled it again. Fire blazed, stark and white, blinding after the blackness. The thunder of the first shot echoed on and on in my skull, hammering away anything else. I pulled the trigger until the hammer slammed down on empty chambers. I pulled the trigger until some unseen fingers wormed around my hand and worked the gun out of my grip, easy as that.

I fought to blot out any thoughts of what all those hands were doing on my body, those lips. I struggled not to imagine Mr. Menace in his chamber somewhere not far from here, smiling blackly at what he and his puppets had waiting for me. I did all I could not to feel their devilish ministrations. And I tried not to like it. Whatever else anyone thinks about me, I want that much known: I tried not to like it.

The last of my gunshot deafness faded away—I could hear that endless dripping again. The denizens of these tunnels swarmed me like ants, and still they didn't make a sound. Not one damn sound.

Despite the total darkness, I closed my eyes.

I may've made a few noises of my own, there in the black.

TWENTY-FIVE

RED

I woke up like I was clawing my way out of my own grave. The sunlight falling across my face came through a shroud of fog, but even so it stung my eyes like sweat. The room looked familiar enough—my digs, plain as a brown paper bag. My unopened mail scattered across the table in the kitchen corner, my coat dangling like an executed man from the wooden hat rack by the door, with my fedora for his head. Same water-stained plaster ceiling I'd stared up at on a thousand nights, same window with its view of the building's brick airshaft. The bed was mine, too, sheets tangled, the one pillow bunched off to the side. And I wasn't the only one in that bed, now I had a look. Despite myself, I jerked away from the woman asleep beside me like she might be rabid.

Like she might bite, you could even say.

Squinting against the morning light, I slipped out of the creaking Murphy bed and backed away from the woman. She didn't so much as stir. I didn't think about the fact I was naked, didn't ponder just then what'd happened to the clothes I'd had on beneath that coat and hat. I had more pressing concerns.

I stumbled my way into my tiny bathroom, feeling somehow

more at home among all the broken tiles and mildew. I left the door open so I could keep a watch on my guest out of the corner of my eye. The bottom of the scuffed bathtub had a bit of water in it. Well, at least we'd cleaned up after … whatever.

I leaned over the yellowed sink and took a good long look at myself.

What a mess.

Scars, the old one around the left eye and a bunch of new ones around the nose, straggling across my right cheek. They ran down to lips that were still puffy-tender from their meeting with a fast-moving fist in the recent past. I saw a few newer additions around the throat, on the chest, the wrist, still just red-black scabs. That poor sap staring out of the glass at me was a sorry heap of bricks in need of a wrecking ball.

I sat down on the narrow lip of the claw-footed tub and wondered who that fella was and how he'd come to be such a walking disaster.

Memories drifted around my mind like old snapshots dropped in a pond. I saw a door with a frosted glass window, saw a woman I knew, but didn't know. A red light pulsed on and off in my skull. I saw a girl slender as a new-born foal smiling sweet depravity at me. Darkness, and muzzle-flashes. A random procession of faces marched by and I put names to them without knowing exactly how I conjured it all up—Hally Thersis, Myles Ferryman, Jimmy the Doberman, Radamanthus. Somewhere in the gloom between the ruddy pulses, another face hovered, just out of sight, a face I *needed* to see to snap everything else back into place. A face that sank fear straight to the deepest places in me. My thoughts groped at it, then shrank back in terror, lunged and retreated again. I couldn't. I couldn't drag that image out of the shadows even to shake some sense into everything else. But I could put a name to it, oh yeah. It was Clymenus, better known as Mr. Menace, the man with a hundred eyes and a thousand ears.

I stood up and shook my head at that poor beaten-up bastard in the mirror. I could remember so many random names, why couldn't I think of his? I ran two fingers down the side of my face, watched the sap in the mirror stroke the ugly half-moon curve of that old scar over his eye.

Frank. That was the dumb palooka's name. Frank Orpheus. Licensed Private Detective. Office at the Cain Building, in midtown. Suite number 513.

The rest of it came fluttering back then, too, as that whirlpool in my brainpan died down and the photos settled where I could see them. Not quite all, but enough.

Almost enough.

I looked again at the long slender shape in my narrow bed, saw in the corner of my eye the fella in the mirror frowning at her. Just how had we ended up here, like this? How had I gotten so tangled up in this craziness? How had I so completely lost my grip on all the most basic rules of my profession, starting with the one about not letting your feelings get in the way of business? I poked around for traces of last night, but something had blown a big ragged hole in the middle of my recollections. I remembered tossing back high-quality hooch with the goon who'd done his best to make my face look like something Picasso might've painted, and I vaguely remembered the big dumb thug sliding down in his chair and flopping to the floor on his knees like he was shooting dice or maybe praying. But between that moment and the sunlight stinging me awake, someone had torn out all the pages.

I ran some water, scrubbed my face with my bare hands, raked my fingers through my hair, and walked back out into my living room-kitchen-bedroom. Slowly, I sat down on the bed and gave the soft figure there a nudge. When that didn't get any response, I gave her another, and another, then a push, finally a shove. That did it. She rolled over and opened her eyes, blinked, shut them again, then opened them much more slowly. Her brow furrowed, then she looked me up and down and her eyes widened. It hadn't even occurred to me to get dressed, but since she was every bit as naked under those sheets as I was on top of them, it didn't seem worth making a fuss over now. I saw her hand wander up and down the contours of her shape, assessing her state of undress. She sighed. It was a very small, somehow unsettling sound.

"Morning," I said.

She stared at me.

"Frank?"

"Yeah, and you're Evelyn. Evelyn Night."

"Of course." She said it like the name was just another fact, like the price of lima beans in Peru, neither here nor there as far as she was concerned.

"You remember ... anything?"

She went blank, might've been no more than a department store mannequin for all the life in her eyes. Then that plastic look crumbled, and she shook her head like she was answering no to a question, but not the one I'd just asked.

"Frank ... oh, Frank ... You were there, weren't you?"

"Was I?"

She scrambled up into a sitting position, forgetting any modesty she might have left and kicking the sheets away, pulling her knees up to her chest and touching my shoulder with one soft cool hand.

"I ... I can't see everything, but ... some of it ... I can remember some of it because you were there. I don't know why that is, but it's true. I can remember some of it because you were with me. I ... we ..."

She broke off, closing her eyes and turning her face away from me. I slipped closer to her and curled an arm around her long, tapering back, ran my fingers through that forge-fire hair of hers.

"What?" I said.

"You were ... you were supposed to be ..."

"What?"

"… my first."

"First what?" I asked, but I knew, and understood she didn't mean it the way girls usually do when they gab with their gal pals about their firsts. "You mean I was supposed to finish up like Guilio, or Hally Thersis?"

I felt the far-off stir of memories, of carved thorns and polished nails, and teeth.

"It was what they wanted … Mister Radamanthus … and …"

She couldn't bring herself to say that other name, and she didn't need to. I knew it well enough and I didn't much feel like hearing it just then. But what she'd said made it a bit clearer why Jimmy the Doberman hadn't killed me that night in my office. I'd thought they meant to scare me off, but maybe this Mr. Menace had me figured better than I'd realized. Maybe they knew exactly how to keep me on the hook, to make sure I'd stick to the case no matter what. Getting rid of some troublesome photos was just the gravy.

"Yeah, okay," I said, pulling her tight to me, enjoying the sensation of her soft warmth alongside me more than I had any right to. "Maybe that was how things were set up, but somehow it didn't end that way. I've still got a pulse and from what I can tell, so do you."

"I guess we should count our blessings."

Her voice sounded more damned than blessed, but I nodded.

"Yeah, and we should do something else, too. We should figure out a way to end all of this, for both of us. We should figure out how we can wake up from this nightmare, once and for all."

"We can't. *I* can't."

"Like hell."

"How?"

She slumped against me, breathing very deep and slow.

"I'm not sure yet, because I'm only just figuring out what we're dealing with. But I think I'm starting to see all the stuff I couldn't at first, all the stuff that made your case such a puzzler. When it was just a case."

She looked at me, but the surprise in her eyes faded almost instantly. She knew that she was a lot more to me now than a name and case number at the top of a file. More than a one-night stand, too.

"He's some kind of ... monster, isn't he?" I continued, each word as heavy as if it were cast in lead. "The man running the show. Mister Menace." I saw her flinch at the name. "And I think he can take your life away in pieces and only give you back the ones he wants you to have. That was okay for your friend Miss Nyx, because she wanted to be what he wanted to turn her into. So she gave in to him and when he'd torn out anything decent and innocent in her, she still had her name and everything else that made her look like good ol' Damia Nyx, uptown society girl.

"But you ... Maybe you wandered in on your own, even asked to be let into the party. Only then you realized you didn't want what Radamanthus and his boss were selling, and you didn't go in smiling like little Miss Nyx did. And when they tried to take all the good out of you, you held onto it. You hid it somewhere, and after you got away from them, it came back to you, but full of holes. You were a person again, unlike the rest of that strange flock, but you'd lost your history, your home, your family—even your name. But you knew enough to go looking for it. So you came to me."

I wasn't sure where the thoughts all came from; I had a feeling they were percolating up from whatever part of my mind remembered all the details about last night, the stuff the rest of my brain had wiped clean. All I knew for sure was that as I said all these crazy things, they made perfect sense to me. It was the raving of a madman, and I knew beyond any doubt it was true.

Evelyn just slouched there against me, cool and light as a feather pillow.

"I can feel him," she said, her voice so quiet it might have come from across the sea. "I can feel him pulling on my soul, trying to … to tear the rest of it out of me. I … Frank, I can't keep hold of it much longer. Pretty soon … he'll win. And I'll be just like Damia."

"No. We won't let it get that far. We'll stop it first."

She held me in her haunted gaze a moment, then sank back onto the bed, not even troubling to cover up those splendid, naked curves of hers.

"I need to sleep."

I shook my head, despite the damn near overwhelming desire I had to settle there beside her. "We need to think. Sleep can wait."

"I'm so tired, Frank. Let's just sleep a while."

With every word she spoke, I found it harder to keep my eyes open, and my whole body felt like a sack someone had filled with wet concrete. The thought of sliding back under the sheets with her and letting the thick gray fatigue in my skull have me sounded like the closest a guy like me might get to heaven. But I shook it off, got up to put on some strong coffee.

"We can't waste time," I said, rattling pans, filling my tall black coffee pot with water and lighting the stove to start it boiling, making noise to keep us both alert. "Gotta think, if we're gonna walk away from this."

"I can't Frank, it's too late for me." I heard her words slur toward a doze. "You can … you should … Let me go, Frank. Walk away and let me go."

I ignored the pot and dropped back onto the bed, swept her up in my arms.

"Enough of that talk. We get out of this together, or not at all."

"Don't say that."

"I said it. It's how things are now, like it or not."

"I don't like it," she murmured. Her eyelids kept fluttering shut then bursting open, then fluttering shut all over again. "I let you go last night. I don't remember much of what happened, but I remember that. He couldn't make me kill you. Please ... I saved your life, don't throw it away for me."

"I said, we'll both walk away from this."

She sighed, leaning against me, heavy with exhaustion now. "How?" she muttered.

"We have to face him," I said, slumped against her as she slouched against me. "Face him and ... finish him. Cut off the head of the Tartarus Syndicate, however we can."

"No," Evelyn whispered, and I heard an edge of near-terror in her voice I'd never heard before. "No ..."

I pried an eye open, hardly aware I'd let them close, and looked down at her, asleep in my arms. So beautiful.

From somewhere a thousand miles away came the rich fragrance of coffee brewing. I figured I'd better go take it off the stove in a minute.

Shifting to get up, I rolled over beside beautiful Evelyn and didn't quite make it off the bed.

The air stank of burnt metal and incinerated coffee.

I opened one eye.

Twilight. Damn.

And ... something else.

The bed beside me was empty.

I sat up and stared around my crackerbox apartment. I was alone.

Only I wasn't. I felt her there, somehow, as if I could tell just by the feel of the scorched air that she was still in the place.

Then I saw her, standing at the window, dressed and tidied, staring out at the gathering night. How I'd missed her the first time I couldn't guess; it was like I'd looked right through her. Like she'd been made of glass.

"Hey," I said, getting up now, switching off the burner under the boiled-dry coffee pot. "Hey."

She didn't turn. I stepped up next to her, studied her phantom reflection in the window. I hated that look in her eyes —it was the same one I'd seen before, at the hotel, in the office. The look of someone desperate to be someplace else. The look of a hop head half out of her skull for a fix.

I put an arm around her neck, tried to draw her to me but she wouldn't budge. She just stood there, watching dusk deepen to night behind the jagged concrete and steel skyline of the city.

"I ... need to go ..."

"Not yet."

"Yes. Before something else happens to you."

"Crazy talk. I'm fine." I tried to ignore the itch around my eye and the aches in my face so that I could maybe believe it. "You're staying here with me until we can figure out our next step."

"No. I ... I can't stop myself ... I hear his voice in my head, right now. I hear him whispering for me to ... to give up, stop pretending ... stop pretending I don't belong to him. And I can't ... I can't keep saying no.

"And if ... *when* I finally give in ... Frank, he wants me to kill for him. He wants me to kill *you*."

"You had the chance. You didn't do it."

"But ... I had to fight so hard ... I can't fight it for another night. I need to leave here, now, before I break down. I should never have come to you at all."

"Listen, if you go out into that city, what do you think will happen? Maybe you won't kill me, but it'll be someone else, some poor sap who'll fall hard for those red lips of yours, and then *two* people will die. That poor sucker, and you. The part of you that monster on the West Side couldn't get to. Radamanthus's boss is trying to take everything from you, everything that matters. I'm not about to let him get away with it now."

Now at last she turned to face me, her eyes full of darkness. She shook her head, slowly. "It's too late."

"No."

I wrapped her up tight in my arms and kissed her, kissed her deep and for a long, long time.

I guess it was that kiss that finished me, completely and for good—and Evelyn Night, and other, innocent people. That kiss that never seemed to end, that spiraled on and on into the black. We toppled into bed and my hands were all over, frantic to uncover her skin again. We rolled and thrashed and moaned in a kind of insane chorus that made me think distantly of that endless music in Club Erebus. And then I got to thinking that we were at Erebus, our naked bodies tangled together in a booth while the music thumped and groaned, and maybe we kept the beat to it or it kept the beat to us; the rhythm was the same in any case. Cocktail waitresses and cigarette girls drifted past, giving us politely uninterested gazes, pink ribbon smiles, as if our contortions were nothing all that interesting. Customers in pressed suits and fancy dresses gawked at our performance, grinning, appraising us like showdogs, but we kept pushing and relaxing, flailing and flexing. Polite applause broke out and I wanted to snarl at all those freakshow escapees to get their filthy eyes off us, what the hell were they doing in my place anyway? Only then we weren't in my place, or at the club either. We were back in that sweat-stinking tunnel, twisting on the floor while other couples or trios or groups did the same and more, and I couldn't hear either of us anymore, but I could still feel her, and all those eyes on us, and that brutal hunger twisting in my gut. Even this bestial abuse of our flesh couldn't soothe that hunger, and I thought I felt teeth tearing flesh and couldn't tell whose teeth or whose flesh and didn't give a damn anymore. Someone else had joined the fun now, a blonde girl, writhing and squirming with us like an angry white snake. It wasn't enough. I wanted the taste of blood, of stolen vitality, and I knew it clung to my skin, maybe my own maybe not.

But suddenly in the depths of all that, I couldn't. Something deep in the pit of me forced me back, screamed sanity at me. My bones hummed with pent-up, ravening hunger, but I held it off. Still not sure where I was, only half sure *who* I was, I pushed myself away and into a darkness that obliterated everything for a long time.

TWENTY-SIX
CASS

Somehow, it was dawn again. Or was it the same dawn? Was that twilight only a dream, and everything that happened after it?

Just what the hell *had* happened after it?

I sat up in bed, slowly, my eyeballs throbbing in my skull the way they used to after a night of bourbon, back before I'd learned to hold my booze. I rubbed at my face, trying to get the aches out of it and massage some clarity into my brain. I groped for some recollection of what had happened, or what had seemed to have happened, but kept coming up empty, with nothing but crumbs of memory and sensation. I didn't care too much for the flavor of those crumbs, I can tell you—not at all. They left a thick, ugly taste in my mouth.

The bed beside me was unoccupied again. And this time, I knew I really was alone. My place had that cool, echoey quality of emptiness to it, like a spent shell casing.

Evelyn was gone.

I climbed to my feet and staggered to the sink, ran some water and rinsed my mouth, trying to chase away that god-awful taste. It went, mostly. I saw water in the tub again. It looked a bit pink, even in the yellow light.

I turned my back to the bathroom and looked around the rest of the place, all four-hundred square feet of it. Everything was the same as always, every inch of wall space taken up with shelves and cupboards to keep my meager belongings, kitchen stuff and a few books, the couple of framed pictures I'd held onto from my legitimate policework days. The unmade Murphy bed took up most of the floor space and my desk, an organized mess like always, claimed much of what was left. But even so, something had changed, something too big for me to see right away. Something huge and vital. I studied my familiar digs and searched for it and didn't find it.

But I did find something else.

It was folded neatly in two and tucked under the lamp on what had been her side of the bed, and I knew even before I picked it up pretty much what it would say. At least, I thought I knew ...

On the outside was written, *Frank* in neat, efficiently elegant script.

What it said inside set my heart pounding extra hard.

Dear Frank—

I'm sorry I left you as I did, alone in the night. But it has all gone too far—for me, perhaps for both of us. I tried, Frank. I tried to warn you that I could not refuse Him any longer. His voice was too much inside my head and I had to answer. I thought to do it without destroying you, but I fear I have done just that. I am surely lost now, as He always wanted me to be. Lost in the dark. I suppose that last glimmer of humanity still in me, the tiny light by which I write this to you, will soon flicker out forever. It will be better that way.

Forgive me, Frank. Forgive us both.

E ~

The name trailed away as if she'd forgotten it even as she wrote it.

I stared at the letter, read it again. It didn't make any sense, and it made perfect sense. Some part of me understood every word, but the alert portion of my brain couldn't unlock what the rest had already figured out. Didn't want to, most likely. I stood there, planted beside the bed, rooted in place with that letter in my hand, the words circling around and around in my brain. I needed to react, to do *something*, but I had no idea what. Hunt down Evelyn Night? Where? Search a thousand alleys and strange doorways and dark passages on the west side? Roust all my informants, bribe or bully them into coughing up information none of them could possibly have? I picked up my .38 but it only made me feel that much more powerless—what the hell could a gun do for me now?

All at once I remembered darkness, and too much silence, and pale white shapes glimpsed in the flicker of a lighter's flame, soft voices and cold fingers. And I remembered emptying my gun into the black.

I remembered trying to blast Evelyn Night into oblivion.

When had that been? Last night? Two nights ago? The memories all seemed woven together into one senseless tapestry of visions. Whenever it was, I knew all my bullets had been wasted, and I was glad. The fact that I hadn't shot Evelyn down in a panic was about the only comforting thought I could find just then.

At last I folded the note and put it down on top of my gun, then I got dressed and slipped the gun in my belt. If I stood around in my place even five minutes longer I would lose whatever I had left of my marbles, so I figured I'd do the only thing I could think of, the same thing I did most every morning. I'd go to the office. Maybe there, in the mundane sanity Cass so expertly maintained, there where I did my best thinking, the world would start to make some sense again.

I got to Suite 513 of the Cain Building well after the usual time we opened, but there was only gloom behind the frosted glass door with my name on it. For a moment I wondered what was going on, and I felt my muscles tense for some new brawl. Then I remembered that I'd given Cass the week off. Just as well. I could've used some extra work, but right then I didn't feel much like taking on any new cases. Probably a little spouse-chasing or insurance fraud would do me good, but I couldn't bring myself to care. All I wanted was that sensible, familiar space where I was Frank Orpheus, PI, not the lonely fella who occupied a dingy place in a cheap building wedged in among much nicer ones. Frank Orpheus, PI, could handle things that other fella never could.

I opened the door and stepped inside and all that sanity shattered into a thousand jagged, cutting pieces.

Cass was there, after all.

Most of her.

Her body lay sprawled across her desk, her arms flung to her sides like a portrait of the crucifixion. Her legs spread much too far apart. Her shirt and camisole had been torn wide open and her small white breasts lay flat against her ribs like lumps of unbaked dough. Her skirt was hiked up around her waist and all she wore under it was a girdle of thick red blood. Jagged gashes X-ed across both wrists, and more blood pooled in her palms and dripped through her fingers to the floor. Her head flopped to the side, her eyes wide, like she was looking right at me. Wide and glassy and dead.

Beneath the line of her pretty jaw, her throat was gone.

With all that crimson, it took me a minute to spot the single bullet hole in her chest. It didn't seem to fit with everything else that had been done to her—too neat, too quick—but all I could really think about right then was how much of it Cass had been alive for. Enough to keep her blood flowing for a good long time.

I'm not sure how long I stood there, staring at her and feeling nothing. I kept waiting for something to come over me —horror, grief, shock, anger—but nothing did. Cassandra

O'Clare—who'd been typing my reports and answering my phone and keeping my sorry excuse for a life in order since she was barely more than a kid—was dead, and that was all there was to it.

I turned around and closed the door and locked it behind me and walked back to the elevator and got on and rode it to the Cain Building's lobby. Then I walked out onto the street, and never went back in again.

TWENTY-SEVEN

OILED

I sat alone in some anonymous midtown blind pig and ordered a double bourbon, neat, and told the barkeep I didn't want to see the bottom of my glass anytime soon. The only other people in the joint looked like full-timers, fellas who managed to keep themselves embalmed around the clock. I wondered what their stories were—not that I had any interest in asking. Still, I bummed a cigarette off one of them and popped it in my mouth. I hardly ever smoked anymore, but right now seemed a good time to drive another nail into my coffin. It took me a minute of patting down my pockets before I remembered I'd lost my lighter ... somewhere. I had a vague recollection of dropping it in the dark, and the sound of dripping water. I begged a book of matches off the bartender when he brought my drink, lit the smoke and took a long, deep drag. The smoke burned like brimstone in my lungs. I dropped the matches in my coat pocket where the lighter used to be.

The first glass went down dangerously smooth, and I started to think, as much as I could. The picture of Cass O'Clare sprawled over her desk was as bright and stark in my brain as something painted by Hieronymus Bosch. I tried to study it objectively, to read the clues in it, but all I could see were her eyes, aimed right at me but not seeing me or anything else, not then and not ever again.

Anyway, I didn't need to find a scrap of evidence in that scene to figure out who murdered my secretary.

It looked pretty clear right then what "forgive me" meant.

I tried to figure how Evelyn might've gone about luring Cass to the office, how she could've known Cass's home phone number. No doubt Radamanthus or someone else in the Red Circle of the Tartarus Syndicate knew how to get any kind of information they wanted. Mr. Menace had a thousand ears, after all, and eyes that saw into the darkest places. A phone number was nothing for a monster like that.

Or maybe it'd just been bad luck. Maybe Evelyn had gone to my office for some other reason and Cass just happened to be there, picking up something she'd forgotten …

Did it really matter? Was Cass any less dead, one way or the other?

I swallowed the second glass and wondered if Maurice Guilio and Hally Thersis had looked about the way Cass had when they'd been found. I wondered if they'd been posed the way she had, their limbs arranged like a department store dummy's, to show off all the brutality that'd been done to them. That made me reach for another glass.

Somewhere between the fifth and the sixth, the callous, brutal reality of what had happened started to penetrate my dazed numbness. I suppose that was why I'd decided to hit the bottle so hard—not to forget what I'd seen, but to shake myself loose enough to feel … something. Anything.

I tried to picture her face—not slack with death like I'd last seen it, but attentive and vibrant, those hazel eyes bright with intelligence. I tried to grasp the idea that I would never hear her voice again, never be on the receiving end of her gentle chiding again. I'd hardly bothered to wonder about her life beyond my office walls, and now the question no longer mattered. I'd had something great in her, and not just as a secretary—and I'd taken

it for granted. Taken *her* for granted. I could never undo that
now, could never make myself worthy of the trust she'd put in
me, of her kindness. The poor kid had loved me in some innocent way. Now that, and all the other stuff I'd never tried to find
out about, was over.

She'd tried to warn me. She'd tried so damn hard to warn
me. And I'd been deaf as a stone and half as smart.

I swallowed more hooch and tried to grasp the ideas of *never*
and *forever*, but they stretched away out of my reach and I came
up empty, over and over. Empty.

My glass was empty, too. I tapped it loudly on the bar. The
barkeep frowned.

"Don'tcha think ya had enough there, Mac?"

"I'll say when I had enough, *Mac*," I answered. "You pour,
and lemme worry about when's enough."

I dropped some greenbacks on the bar to make my point
for me.

He shrugged and swept the cash into the till.

"It's your funeral," he said, tipping another three fingers of
lovely amber liquid into my glass.

I thought about telling him it wasn't *my* funeral, but
managed to hold my booze-lubricated tongue.

Sometime during that bourbon-hazed morning I made an
anonymous call to the cops and reported a murder at the Cain
Building, suite 513. I knew they'd want to talk to me sooner
than soon—my secretary dead, my office the crime scene—and
they'd no doubt get mighty suspicious if they couldn't find me.
But I had no intention of being found. Not yet.

Right now, I was going to play the hunter, and let someone
else be the prey for a change. Whatever happened next didn't
matter one damn bit. I would finish this even if it killed me.

And just how do you plan to do that?

The voice in my head sounded too much like Cass, prag-
matic and direct, but kind. Always kind.

What do you plan to do, Frank? Kill Evelyn? Persuade your cop pal to send the vice squad after the Red Circle crew? Saunter into the Tartarus neighborhood and kill Clymenus, the invisible puppet master? What?

I didn't know and didn't much care. I had to find her, that was all. I had to find her and tie up all these loose ends before they strangled me.

My glance swam down to the ashtray at my elbow and I saw it was heaped with twisted butts, like a pile of dead maggots. I could only remember smoking one, but I knew these were all mine.

If I didn't find Evelyn Night damn quick, I'd go finally, totally over the edge.

So I told myself, anyway, not quite getting it then. Not quite realizing that the edge was already behind me.

TWENTY-EIGHT

CROSSING

I found the borrowed meat wagon parked in that same alley behind the Chandler, found the keys still in my pocket. I couldn't remember how it had gotten back here and I really didn't care. I climbed in behind the wheel, slammed the door and locked myself in. I was too drunk to drive and too tired and didn't have any clue where I was going, but none of that mattered, either. I felt like a shark, like I had to keep moving or drown in everything that'd happened the last few hours. I closed my eyes a minute and rested my head against the hearse's over-sized steering wheel.

A heavy tapping on the window beside me brought my eyes snapping open again. I took an instant's sideways glance before I turned my head. A beat cop stood staring in at me, his arm cocked so he could lean on the top of the door frame. His knuckles still rested against the glass.

Everything in me went cold. How long had I been out? I gathered from the angle of the shadows it was late afternoon already. So it'd been a few hours at least. All that time, sitting here waiting for the law to find me. I wondered what their line was right now—*we just want you to come in, answer a few questions for us* ... Or were we already at the cuffs and mugshots stage? All I knew was any time I spent sitting in a box or a cage while the cops beat their gums at me was time I wasn't out on the streets, time I wasn't moving. I thought for a second of cranking the engine and putting the pedal to the floor, but the keys were still in my hand and just how far was I likely to get in a hearse, anyway? I'd be the funniest thing the radio dispatchers had heard in ages.

So I cranked my window down, slowly.

"Hey, buddy, ya can't park this thing here. Gotta keep the alley clear."

I figured it was best not to open my mouth, not to let the fella smell the booze on my breath or catch me in some clumsy lie, so I just nodded and started up the car. The cop nodded too, and walked away and didn't look at me again. I saw him turn right out of the alley. I pulled out and headed left.

Later on when that poor cop realized he'd let a murder suspect drive off, he'd have a hell of a story. I'd be the best damn fish tale of his career—the big one that got away. In a hearse.

I wasn't sure how long I'd been out, but sleep had sobered me up almost too much. The ice in my veins had begun to thaw and if it got too thin I'd have to stare down what I'd let happen to Cass, and face the idea that the woman I'd slept with—the one whose case I'd insisted on sticking with after all the times Cass begged me to back off—was a brutal killer, a creature every bit as nasty and bloodthirsty as that maneater Damia Nyx. I didn't much like dwelling on either of those things, so I focused on driving. Driving west, of course.

A steady, tired gray rain was falling, but it couldn't blot out the stink of the river. The odor of sewer-sludge and dead fish was stronger than usual today. I smelled it from two blocks away and it churned my guts like a warning. The scar over my left eye itched constantly now, maddeningly, but I gripped the wheel tight and drove on. The slender gray towers of the West River Narrows Bridge poked up in front of me, their crowns lost in the low, roiling clouds. I urged the old car onward, ignoring the coughing coming from under the hood, not thinking about much of anything but getting to the other side, building up all the power the rumbling hearse could manage—then slammed on the breaks and shuddered to a stop. There was a car parked in the shadow of the bridge abutment, next to a payphone.

I knew that car, and the lanky man behind the wheel.

He must have been waiting on orders from one of the bosses, Radamanthus or some other player in the Red Circle gang—or hell, maybe from the big man himself, if the big man could be bothered to make his own phone calls.

I swung the hearse around, bouncing the passenger side wheels up over the sidewalk and coming down hard, the hearse's shocks protesting, and in a second I was parked beside that familiar car and jumping out of the hearse, the Harpe .38's muzzle surprisingly steady on the shadow behind the windshield.

The driver's window was open and I shoved the gun in, up against that bony skull.

"You're gonna take me to Evelyn Night," I told the chauffer.

He said nothing, but, moving slowly, stuck out one hand, palm up. He twitched two long knotty fingers in a "let's have it" gesture.

I thought the fella must be a nutcase—was he asking me to put a bullet in his brain? One tremor of my trigger finger and that bald head would have a .38 caliber hole in it. Then I realized what that finger-wave meant. It didn't make the man seem any less crazy to me, but it meant there was a chance he'd take me where I wanted to go—something he couldn't exactly do with his brains blown out. So I dug into my pocket and pulled out two bits and dropped it in that outstretched hand. The tarantula-leg fingers wrapped the coins up and vanished into the car. Then the back door swung open like maybe he'd pulled some hidden lever inside the driver's compartment, and I climbed in.

The seat still smelled a bit like Damia Nyx, but I tried not to notice.

The driver started the car and pulled onto the bridge. I kept the gun where he could see it in his rearview mirror, so he'd know its deadly stare was still trained on his chalky dome. Funny thing was, I couldn't see his eyes in the mirror, just shadow under the shiny black bill of his driving cap. For all I could tell, he didn't have any eyes.

"We're gonna play this straight," I said, squinting at that blank face. "You take me where I wanna go and I don't turn your brains into oatmeal."

Myles Ferryman drove on in silence, without any hint of reaction to my threat. I slumped back in the seat, keeping the gun raised as we drifted off the bridge and started wending our way through the meandering streets of the west side, the Tartarus neighborhood. Menace's domain. He was there, some-where, hiding away in some basement or back room, pulling all the strings, hearing anything anyone said, seeing anything anyone did. I could feel him, just like Evelyn had said. I could feel him like a chill in the air, a slime on my skin. I wanted to spit the taste out and take a good long shower. But I wasn't about to turn around.

I watched faceless buildings roll past, and faceless people, whores and dope pushers and wasted hopheads and petty crooks who had no idea how small they were. We passed Club Erebus and turned down a narrow street, and after that I lost all track of where he took me. And it struck me that maybe he hadn't been waiting for orders from Mr. Dapper or the Big Man or anyone else.

Maybe he'd been waiting for me.

Maybe it was some staggeringly simple trap and I'd jumped right in with both feet. And I was fine by me.

After what seemed like hours of aimless twisting and wind-ing, crossing and re-crossing our path, we rolled up outside a crumbling building with a Gothic façade that might've been impressive in its day. The arcing letters painted in the front window against badly faded red velvet curtains said Hotel Avernus.

I got out and marched into the dingy, cigarette-smelling lobby, the humid air unmoved by the limping ceiling fan. The scrawny man behind the cracked yellow Formica desk was all wrinkles and wide black eyes and looked about two hundred years old.

I grabbed the cheap tie around his neck and dragged him about halfway across that counter to me, his flailing hand landing on the brass service bell, making it ring with absurd cheerfulness.

"Evelyn Night, good lookin' redhead. Where is she? Which room?"

The fella looked as if he was considering saying he didn't know, so I made the knot a little tighter.

"Two-B," he coughed, waving one hand at the narrow staircase just off the lobby. I dropped him back onto his feet and left him smoothing out his shirt, his face all twisted up with shock and bewilderment.

"Thanks, pops," I said, already on my way out of that sad stub of a lobby.

The whole place smelled of mildew, the wallpaper yawned with yellow water stains, and the carpet felt cheesy-soft under my feet. I found 2-B right around the corner from the second-floor landing and pounded hard, then again. I waited half a second for an answer then stepped back and gave the lock a good hard kick with the bottom of my black loafer. The bolt was cheap and the frame was cheaper, and I had all the extra strength of pure fury burning in me. Wood splintered and the door slammed inward, recoiled, jittered on its hinges. I shoved past it and walked inside with my piece out in front of me, hammer cocked.

Evelyn Night lay peaceful as a corpse in repose on a filthy bed, stretched out on her back, arms at her sides. Her smart linen suit was immaculate. Her face was virgin white, her lips the color of blood. She didn't even twitch as I thundered into the room and put the .38's muzzle against the pure skin of her forehead.

"Wake up," I told her. "Wake. Up."

Her eyelids trembled like she was dreaming, then fluttered open. I caught a glimmer of terror in those dark eyes, but somehow I didn't think it was because of the lethal hardware aimed at her brainpan.

"Are you going to kill me, Frank?" she whispered.

"I ought to."

"I'm already dead."

"I can make sure of it."

"I wish you could. I wish a bullet were all it would take to get me out of this."

"You killed Cass. Murdered her, in cold blood."

She said nothing.

"Why? Dammit, why her? She wasn't anything to you."

"Not to *me*, no."

The words twisted my gut into a tight knot.

"You're saying you murdered Cass because of me?"

"He wanted me to." She didn't say the name, of course. She didn't need to.

I came close, then. I came within a hair of pulling the trigger and splashing her brain all over that stained bed. I wonder if it would've made any difference.

Instead, I eased off, dropped the gun to my side.

"Why not do it?" Evelyn asked, not moving except to turn her head just enough to look at me. "Why not try? It's what I want. It's the *only thing* I want now."

"I've seen too much death for one day," I said. "Anyway, killing you won't do Cass any good. Or me either, for that matter."

I stared out the dingy window, at the brick airshaft. I saw rats squirming through the garbage at the bottom.

"I must be crazy," I said, with my back to that beautiful murderess, "'cause, see, I still want to get you out of this. And I still think I can."

"It's impossible. It was impossible the minute I gave the first little part of myself to Him. I was damned then, that very second. Maybe, if you leave here now, you can still escape. But not me. I'm in Hell where I belong. And I'll never leave."

"He made you kill Cass," I said. Something about the statement tasted wrong, somehow, but I kept going. "He's been behind all of this. This Mister—" But I couldn't bring myself to say the name any more than Evelyn could. Somehow it felt almost poisonous forming on my tongue, and I spat it out unsaid. "Him. Radamanthus's boss. Whatever power he has over you and all those other dumb saps and thugs, he can't use it if he's dead."

"You can't kill a thing like Him," Evelyn said, voice stretched tight as violin strings.

"Unless he's the Devil himself, I can."

"What if He *is* the Devil himself?"

I didn't answer.

Evelyn sighed.

"He'll kill you, if you ever get close to Him. But you'll never even get close to Him. His ... people ... won't let you."

"Maybe not ... But they would let *you* get close to him. You've been there before."

"I don't remember."

"You could get us in. You're one of his favorites, his ... chosen. You could walk right in and take me with you."

"I don't know where He is," Evelyn Night said, shaking her head. "I can't remember. And I don't matter that much, not enough to get close to Him unless He wants me to. Not enough to get *you* close to Him."

"You can do it. You can find him, you can get to him. I know it."

"I ..."

"It's the only way to set things right. Even if he kills us both, it's the only way."

She sighed.

"When?" she murmured.

"Right now."

"You're crazy."

"This whole thing is crazy."

She sighed, stared up at the ceiling like she could find some sanity there. I wasn't sure if I wanted to comfort her or kill her. Maybe both.

"Let's go," I said, and took her hand and pulled her to her feet. She looked at me then, looked into me in a way she'd never done before, and for a moment I forgot what she'd done to Cass, and all I saw was that lost soul who'd wandered into my office about a thousand years ago. Despite everything, I took her into my arms again and held her, tight, and kissed her on those firm red lips, long and deep. It felt like goodbye.

Then the kiss ended and we broke apart and walked out of that room together in silence.

TWENTY-NINE
SUBTERRANEAN

Ferryman was still waiting in the long black Falcon as we walked out, his hands on the wheel, his face dead ahead under the shadow of his chauffer's cap. The back door swung open and I ushered Evelyn in, then got in beside her.

"Take us to Him," Evelyn whispered.

The lanky chauffer nodded and the car rolled away from the curb. Just like that, no questions, no backward glance. Like he'd expected nothing else.

For a while we wandered the streets again, lost tourists on a day trip through of hell. Maybe they were the same streets as before, maybe they were different, they all looked the same and I didn't bother paying attention. It was late afternoon, but the low black ceiling of smoke and fog made it look like night had come early and planned to stay. The dirty clouds spat a feeble rain, just enough to give everything a slimy sheen. I couldn't shake the feeling we were going down, twisting around into some low point in the city where the streets ran below the West River's water line. The buildings all looked shut up and forgotten, two- and three-story brick jobs, their windows blindfolded with plywood, unhealthy yellow weeds poking out of their cracked foundations. I saw fat black smokestacks from some abandoned factory pointing like accusing fingers at the grimy sky. I kept thinking someone was watching, kept thinking I saw eyes staring down at us from the gaps in the planked-over windows, the shadows in the doors. But when I turned to get a good look all I saw was dark.

The car stopped at a corner and the back door swung open, although I don't remember anyone actually touching the handle. I climbed out of the car with my gun in one hand, Evelyn's fingers clasped in the other. She stepped out holding my hand like I was taking her to a show at the Century City Music Hall. Even here, even now, she couldn't help being that kind of lady.

The Falcon's door slammed shut behind us and the big car drifted away, silent as a boat on still water. A minute later the veils of tired drizzle swallowed it until even its staring red tail-lights were just a memory. I had a feeling deep in my gut that I'd never see that car or the man behind the wheel again. Somehow, I wasn't relieved.

"Which way?" I asked.

But it was obvious, even as Evelyn pointed and said, "There."

The sign carved into the concrete lintel over the gaping black maw at the bottom of the steps said Tartarus Station. The words were hard to read because someone had painted the word CLOSED across the sign in straggling black letters. I could smell a cold damp stink coming up from that place, something a hundred times as rotten as what I'd smelled in the other pits I'd visited in this wretched neighborhood. Even that underneath-odor of sweat and carnality smelled thick, putrid, like everything including lust itself had died and turned to carrion somewhere down there.

My snub-nosed .38 suddenly looked tiny in my hand, like a kid's cap gun, and I felt almost stupid holding it, but it was all I had. I thought for a minute how stupid I was, going in there with nothing more than that one little peashooter and no plan at all. But something in my gut knew damn well that all the planning in the world wouldn't add up to chipped beef on toast, that

I could've been walking down those steps with a couple of Tommy guns in my hands and it wouldn't make one bit of difference.

"You've gotten me far enough," I told Evelyn, as I took a long look down the wide stairs. "I'll take it from here."

She shook her head. It was a small gesture, but unarguable.

"You're only here because of me. Because I dragged you into my nightmare. I never meant to—Frank, you have to understand that. I never meant to get you caught up in any of this. You were my last hope ... so I thought, anyway. I didn't know when I first walked into your office that I had no hope left—that it was already too late. I'd hoped you could bring me back into the light. But instead, I dragged you into the dark."

I said nothing. Waited.

"That's not all," Evelyn said, her voice flat now. Not even hurt, just ... dead. "Somewhere down there is where ... is where He murdered me. I asked you to find me, and you did. As much as you could. I think whatever I'm missing is down there. So I'm going with you. I really don't want to. But I have to."

Maybe I should've tried to talk her out of it. Maybe I should've put her lights out for her and left her slumped in a neglected doorframe like some well-dressed stew-bum, if she wouldn't listen to me saying no. Maybe I should've trusted Cass's warnings in the first place and let all this play out without me. Maybe a lot of things.

But what I did was nod at her and start down the steps.

I saw a rusting metal fence just inside the mouth of the old station, but off to one side the bars had been bent enough for even someone my size to slip through into the dark. I poked the gun in first then followed it through. Evelyn came after me, quiet as a breeze. I tried not to gag on the stale air sighing out of the derelict dark. Again I found myself wishing I'd gotten in the habit of carrying a flashlight with me. I patted my pockets and felt a square lump—the matchbook I'd grabbed from that nameless bar. I guess some part of my mind had known well enough

I'd end up in the dark again. In the pale light at the edge of the subway gloom, I counted the white match-heads. Thirteen. Enough to get us inside, maybe, but not enough to get us out again. And I had a feeling I'd better save a few, in case of … Well, I wasn't sure what. But it seemed like a good idea.

Feeling Evelyn close at my back, I took a few careful paces down the curving tunnel. Something under my foot squished loudly, but I ignored it. Another sound came from nearby, a slow thick sound, almost like a dog panting. It was so soft I could almost believe I was only hearing some weak breath of wind blowing through the station. I wanted to strike a match but I'd need two hands and wasn't all that much in the mood to put my gun away then. I reached back to Evelyn, planted the matchbook in her hand.

"Only light one at a time, and only when I say."

In the gloom, I could just see her silhouette nod.

I listened a minute. I couldn't hear that breath sound anymore. That worried me.

"*Now,*" I whispered.

I heard her scratch the matchhead on the matchbook's cover, then yellow light flared into the passage, shockingly bright in the black ink of the tunnel.

I got one good look at Jimmy the Doberman's eyes, blazing with fury, and then the big goon was on me, like he'd been in my office that night.

This time, though, I saw him coming.

I pulled the trigger once before we hit the ground, and then one more time while I was still sure I wouldn't miss the thug and hit Evelyn. Then we were rolling and flopping across the floor, and he was slamming me hard against the cement, making all sorts of crazy lights flash and fade in my skull. And the whole time he was snarling like a rabid animal—like a dog that needed to be put down. I knew if that knife came out again I couldn't stop him from slashing my throat, doing what pretty little Damia Nyx had only tried.

The Doberman tossed me to one side and I caught a glimpse of Evelyn, somewhere a few feet away, standing stock-still with the dwindling match over her head, as if she'd turned into some kind of statue. Then I was on my back again and in the last flicker of the flame I saw the fatal glint of metal and knew the Doberman was about to finish what he'd started with my face.

I jammed the gun up under his armpit and pulled the trigger and pulled it again and pulled it again, hoping my bullets would make more of an impression on him than they had on the bloodthirsty blonde.

The thug twisted off of me and went down, then lay there on the ground, flopping like a tuna in a fisherman's net and cursing me and God and anyone who might be listening. Then he started to gurgle and spit and I knew he was finished, even if it might take a while. I thought about putting one more bullet—my last bullet—in him, to get it over with, but maybe it felt too cold-blooded. Or maybe not cold-blooded enough. Maybe part of me took some satisfaction in listening to him die, nice and slow, feeling every ragged inch of his descent into eternity. Either way, I didn't finish him. I should have, but I didn't.

Instead, I started on down the passage again, prodding my way through the dark with the Harpe's blunt nose. One more shot, if I needed it. I hadn't even bothered to grab the thug's knife, but I really didn't think it would help. Whatever waited up ahead—or down below—wasn't going to care about bullets or knives.

A hand closed over my arm but I knew that touch too well to flinch away from it.

"Are you hurt?" Evelyn asked, close to my ear.

"Not as bad as the other fella," I said. "Light another match, will ya?"

She struck another one and in the brief sodium-yellow glow that followed I could see that the tunnel curved again right in front of us, and started down another flight of stairs. Somewhere behind us, the Doberman's flailing grew quieter, but not yet silent.

"Stay close," I said, and in the dark Evelyn and I started ahead again. I trailed my free hand along the wet, broken tile wall and groped my way forward, through dark too solid for my eyes to adjust to. I felt Evelyn at my back, heard her shoes on the concrete. I wished I could catch just a whiff of her perfume but the rank stench of corruption blotted all other scents out of the stagnant air.

A minute later we emerged together into a space full of hard echoes that made it sound large and open. Evelyn lit another match and I saw we were at the old train platform, the turnstiles and token booths still in place, the city's forgotten outposts. I thought I heard rats and maybe other things scuttling away from the light. In that heartbeat's instant before the flame faded out, I noticed there was nothing else down here, only the platform and the tunnel where the trains used to prowl.

"Must be down the tracks," I said.

"That way," Evelyn said, and waved the guttering match at the tunnel that forked off to the left.

She lit another match and together we crept to the edge of the platform. For a minute I hung up there, looking up and down the tracks. I couldn't quite chase away the thought that maybe these tracks weren't disused, that as soon as we jumped down into that cement alley a light would blaze out of the shadows and hundreds of tons of metal would thunder down on top of us and spare us the trouble of ever facing the demon called Mr. Menace.

Probably we would've been lucky if it had.

I held my breath a second. Silence, except for the skittering of roaches and rats, and that familiar plink of water dripping. Even the Doberman's agonies didn't carry all the way down here —or maybe he'd finally given up the ghost. Either way I was glad not to have to listen to him.

Steeling myself against I didn't know what, I sat down on the edge of the platform and jumped onto the tracks. The trough was deeper than I'd guessed and I hit hard, lost my footing, and fell across the rails, all three of them. I had a split-second's anticipation of being fried like a strip of bacon. But this station and this train line were long dead and the third rail was just cold metal now. I picked myself up, wiping oily slime off my hands and coat, then helped Evelyn into the pit with me. Then we started walking again.

I can't say how long we walked. Down there in the dark, in the long straight spaces between matches, time stretched out like saltwater taffy, lost all meaning. It seemed like an age, but it may've been five minutes. Either way, it ended when we came to another wide space, a place with its own sepia light. I looked around for the source but couldn't find it.

There was another platform here, but nothing else to suggest this was another abandoned station. Instead, heavy crimson draperies dangled, moth-eaten and black with mildew, from the vaulted tile ceiling. Looking at the place, I couldn't figure it for the hideout of a mob boss, a man with money who'd want folks to see that as far as he was concerned, crime *did* pay. All the same, I knew He was there, behind those moldering curtains. The man with a thousand eyes, the man with ears in every dive and back-alley in the city. The one who liked to make his enemies bleed.

Mr. Menace.

I grabbed the edge of the platform and started to haul myself out.

Evelyn's hand snagged my shoulder and tugged me back down, back to her.

"Frank—don't. This ... we should get out of here. You should. You don't ... you don't want to know what's behind that. Oh God, you don't want to see. I know ... I know things you don't. Please, get out of here while you still can."

And I knew she was right. Some black instinct in my gut

knew for an absolute certainty that I didn't want to find out what was on the other side of that curtain.

Whatever waited back there would destroy me. Probably both of us.

But I had to go. I was in too deep, that was all. I was in too deep to turn away. If I didn't end this now it would never end.

I wanted to kiss Evelyn for a final bit of reassurance, but instead I turned away and climbed up onto that platform. When I turned to help Evelyn, she followed. Her face had an expression I'd never seen before. That horror, that loss was still written in her dark eyes, but all the sadness and misery had gone. She'd surpassed all that, and now the only thing left in her was fatality.

I turned away from her, and pushed through the red curtains.

THIRTY
MENACE

Somewhere between rotting shrouds the color of old blood, I hesitated. My shoes were filled with lead, my legs turned to cement posts. A secret waited for me back there, a nightmare, something worse than I'd ever imagined, far worse than all the cheating husbands and small-time thugs and insurance fraud cons I'd ever dealt with. I didn't dare look it in the face. And I couldn't go back. I thought of the one bullet in the .38's cylinder. That was one way out, but it felt like a path straight to hell. Then again, so did what waited before me—and what was behind me was nothing at all. Void, oblivion. I was damned. Damned if I did, damned if I didn't, just like the saying goes.

So I shoved aside the last layer of red velvet and stepped into Mr. Menace's lair.

I wasn't too surprised to see Evelyn Night standing inside, waiting, as if she hadn't been somewhere behind me only a minute ago. It was impossible, but it also felt inevitable. Nightmare logic was the only sort of logic that applied here.

The room was low and deep, full of shadows that hung as heavy as Marley's chains. Candles burned here and there, in recessed sconces on the walls, on wrought-iron candelabras. Somewhere in the gloom at the back of the place, stone steps led to a darkened dais. The details swarmed my senses, and all at once it struck me what this place was.

It was a church. A temple consecrated to the city's crown prince of darkness.

"This is it," Evelyn whispered, staring around her, those luscious eyes wide, black. "This is where He murdered me."

"So where is He, huh?" I heard the capital letter in my own voice now, and hated it, but couldn't stop myself. "Why doesn't He show Himself?" It hadn't exactly escaped my attention that the Big Man had apparently only posted a single guard in his den. Whatever the hell He was, He wasn't some run-of-the-mill crime boss.

I started into the shadows on the dais. Evelyn grabbed my arm—with her right hand, I noticed.

"Frank … This is Hell, isn't it? We're in Hell."

She was nodding at a series of long, dark arches along one wall, rough wet stone. The kind of thing you find in a very old catacomb, not some abandoned subway stop.

I wandered nearer, not wanting to see, and still unable to keep myself away.

Under the arches, someone had haphazardly arranged a dozen or so beds—old things with carved feet and fancy head-boards. They looked absurd here, and perfectly at home.

And … there were shapes on the beds. Corpses. Not especially fresh ones, mostly. They looked like they'd been badly mummified, shrunken brown limbs and collapsed faces and stringy gray hair falling from stretched-tight scalps. I saw one in the tatters of what could've been an expensive suit, and another with the dangling remains of tight bleached curls in a style that looked years out of date. I knew I couldn't be looking at Mister Dapper, at Damia Nyx and the other girls, but that's who they were. The whole harem, laid to rest long before I'd ever encountered them at Club Erebus.

All the ones I never saw in daylight.

The thought swam drunkenly around my brain, and I felt

the last of my grip on reality lurch away. I was a man overboard in a merciless sea, drowning, nothing left to cling to, nothing solid to keep me from sinking into the abyss. But also, strangely, completely free.

Other revelations came rushing to me then—that Radamanthus had been the shadow I'd seen over the Doberman's shoulder that night in my office, that somehow his ... condition ... had made it possible for him to get past the locked doors, to let his goon inside to do the physical labor ... Somehow, the ones on those beds only had real power here in the Tartarus district, on this side of the river. That was why Damia Nyx had needed to lure me over before she worked her seduction-and-destruction number on me. Only poor old Jimmy had been flesh and blood —and muscle, his most valuable asset. His bad luck to be the one member of the Red Circle vulnerable to hot lead.

That part of me that still thought of himself as a detective congratulated himself on putting the last few pieces of the puzzle together. But the satisfaction drained away in an instant when I got a decent look at the last bed in the row.

It was vacant. But by the look of it, I guessed someone *had* used it, and not too long ago. Even in the feeble light of that ghastly place, I could make out a couple of strands of hair on the pillow. Hair the color of bedded embers.

"Frank ...?" Evelyn asked, from a few paces away. She had her eyes closed, her head turned slightly away from me, like she was expecting a slap in the face.

"It's nothing. Empty."

She nodded as if she knew precisely what that meant, then turned away from me. Hiding something. Hiding what she knew.

But it didn't work, because even in that glimpse, I read it.

Evelyn's bed lay empty because she wasn't like those others. She'd caught herself halfway between life and death—had clung to me to hold her suspended there, dangling over her own grave, keeping her alive, or half-alive. She hadn't become another of

Menace's marionettes like Nyx or Radamanthus because she still hadn't made her first kill for him.

Because *I* had killed Cass, not Evelyn.

That single tidy bullet hole in her chest amid all the carnage made perfect sense now. Somewhere in the middle of Evelyn's murderous frenzy, I'd had just enough wits to end Cass's agony —and save Evelyn from Damia Nyx's fate.

"God," I moaned, and sounded pitiful even to myself. "Oh my God."

Evelyn just stood there, still as a marble angel on top of a forgotten crypt.

I could only think of one thing to do for her, for either of us.

"Clymenus!" I shouted. "Where are you? Where are you, you damn disgusting freak? Show your face!"

The stone walls threw my voice back at me in cackling echoes, mocking my outrage. I snatched one of the candelabras and waved it at the gloom, not caring as some of the candles fell and others winked out. I spun in a drunken lurch and spotted the dais again, something atop it shrouded in gloom under a cascade of gaudy crimson draperies. The throne room of a king desperate to impress his subjects with his dark power. And at the top, the man himself, the faceless tyrant, the spider at the center of the web. A shadow among shadows, watching us in silence. Watching the futile thrashings of a couple of bugs he'd ensnared, confident he could finish them off whenever it suited him. Savoring our helplessness.

I cocked the Harpe's hammer and strode toward the motionless shape.

"I have something for you," I said, my voice an almost comical growl—a kid playing at being tough.

"Frank—" Evelyn said, but the plea had no strength left in it.

I marched up the stone steps onto that unholy altar, thrusting the struggling flames ahead of me with one hand, pointing the .38's snub nose at the ridiculous throne with the other. The few remaining candles pushed back the shadows at the deepest part of the dais, sending them fleeing like greasy black rats.

And then I saw Him. Mr. Menace. The black heart pulsing all this darkness to life. Grinning at me.

Aides Clymenus sat in a high-backed red satin chair, driftwood fingers steepled under his bony chin, a death rictus stretched across his leathery face. His clothes were an elegant confusion of eras, all long past.

"Don't look at him!" Evelyn screamed. "Don't look at his eyes!"

But I had, I did, and I went on, staring.

His eyes were gone. Just two gory pits that hadn't seen anything in a very long time.

His eyes ... they were black, like empty wells, Evelyn had told me. *As if there was nothing human behind them ...*

She'd spoken more honestly than she realized.

The thing in the ersatz throne was dead. I wasn't all that sure it had ever been alive, not in anything like its current form. It looked like someone had stuffed a bunch of old bones into a nonsensical costume and propped them up there like some spook-house gag. One good hit would turn the shape in the rags to a pile of dust and skeleton-shards.

I turned back toward Evelyn, very slowly, like I was moving through tar.

"He's dead."

"I know."

There was no more confusion in her voice, no more fear or pain. Her words were as lifeless and cold as the bag of bone in front of me.

"He was a myth, wasn't he?" I asked. "He was a myth all along."

"Yes."

And there it was—the end of the big lie. There was no Mr. Menace. There never had been. The paper-dry mummy in the old clothes was nothing but an ugly joke, a fairytale boogeyman in effigy. The corpse of a man who'd never actually lived. There'd never been any dark kingpin running things in Tartarus, never any demonic puppet master pulling everyone's strings. Only a story these bored dilettantes told themselves because of who—because of *what*—it allowed them to be. A falsehood so dark and powerful it had taken on a life larger than all of them—larger than life itself. A falsehood that created a kind of hedonistic gravity they hadn't even been able to escape by dying.

No one had dragged Evelyn Night into the dark, or Radamanthus or Damia Nyx or any of the others. No doubt they'd believed in their underworld god when they first heard his name—believed because they'd wanted to, believed because being his toys cut them free from all taboos, shattered every barrier to unfettered debauchery, gratification with no thought to the cost. Every one of them had bowed before this debased idol willingly, eager to give themselves up to all the evil that lurked in their own hearts. The evil that lurks in everyone's heart.

And doing it, they had evoked something darker than Mr. Menace could ever have been if he'd actually existed. Something that kept their shadow-selves around even when their flesh had gone cold, their hearts still and silent.

I stared at Evelyn, the woman I'd fallen for. The woman I'd more than half believed I was falling in love with. And I saw a smile on those red cupid-bow lips, a smile that had nothing to do with happiness and certainly nothing to do with love. It was the smile of someone truly and inescapably hellbound. And in that terrible expression I could read every word of my own obituary: how eagerly I'd plunged into this twisted world, the nonchalant way I'd handed myself to Damia Nyx, the school-kid giddiness with which I'd followed Evelyn into the labyrinth, pretending I could save her. The way I'd let her and the others play their games with my flesh and whatever I might have of a soul, here in the never-ending night of this infernal urban underworld.

Something else came to me then, a memory sharp as a knife wound.

"You made *me* call her, didn't you?"

Evelyn's face was porcelain, hard and cold and completely without feeling. "It had to be you."

I could almost see myself dialing Cass's number, telling her I needed her to meet me at the office right away, not tomorrow morning but now, *right now*. Luring that innocent kid into Evelyn Night's snare so she and I could share her, could really dig into the thrill of the slaughter. I gave Evelyn that so I could have her. I'd done it then banished it from my mind, locked it away in the place where nightmares go to fester until they rot your sanity.

But here, in the emptiness at the heart of everything, I couldn't hide from it, couldn't escape from the sheer bewilderment on Cass's face as Evelyn had wrapped a hand around her throat and torn it open with the nasty little barb on her cruel little ring. Even knowing my bullet was the one that had ultimately cut Cass's life short didn't gut me the way that new memory did, not by half.

I thought about those dead things between the arches, coffin stuffers that looked too much like the figures who peopled Evelyn Night's shadow-life. Just how long had I been wandering in and out of the abyss myself? Just how long had I been mingling with phantoms? Ever since I'd first followed her across the West River Narrows Bridge, maybe.

But even knowing that wasn't the worst of it.

All this time … All this time, we'd pretended it was this Mr. Menace we were fighting, Lord of the Underworld, don of dons, thief of souls. But that had been pure fiction. Clymenus was a false Satan. We'd been fighting ourselves.

And we had lost.

I stared at Evelyn and saw that smile stretching a bit. She

knew. Probably she'd known before I did. There was no mistaking that look. It was a confession. The helpless smile of someone with no way out. Shattered. Fatal. Damned.

It was an invitation, too.

I raised the Harpe, leveled its blunt muzzle at her head. Evelyn watched me do it and never flinched.

The bullet I'd been saving made a wet red hole where her left eye belonged. She took a single stumbling step toward me and her smile broke into a grin and her grin wept blood. Then she crumbled to the wet stone floor and lay very still.

EPILOGUE

There's not much more to say.

After I killed Evelyn Night, I stood there alone in the dark—I don't know how long. If I'd had another round in the chamber, I might have put it to good use.

But, no. That would be the easy way out. The cheater's way. Whatever I'd earned in this pitiful game, it wasn't a quick escape.

So finally I tucked my gun away and made my way out of that cathedral of depravity, back through the labyrinth below the city. Probably I was walking in total darkness; I don't remember taking any light with me but I can't say; the whole journey is nothing but a black void in my memory. I vaguely recall finding myself outside in the rain, in a bad part of town I didn't recognize.

I wandered around until I found my way across the bridge, back to where there used to be a trace of sanity in the world. I felt like I'd walked a thousand miles, but when I saw a cab parked by a curb, the driver obviously waiting for a fare, I went on by.

A few minutes later—or maybe they were hours—I found what I'd been looking for.

I strolled up to the black-and-white and rapped my knuckles

on the driver's window. The cop inside rolled it down and looked up at me like he didn't know me from Adam, and didn't want to.

"Yeah? What can I do for you, Mack?"

He had no idea how much luck had just come his way. He was about to close a couple of big cases, with no more work than he'd put into sipping his morning joe.

Assuming he believed even a single word of the crazy yarn I was about to spin for him.

"I want to confess to murder," I said. Then I handed him my gun and told him everything he needed to know.

AUTHOR'S NOTE

This book started as a screenplay, evolved into an experiment in narrative voice, and finally became what you have here—a sort of a love letter to the genre of film noir and the hardboiled crime novels of days gone by. I hope you have even half as much fun reading it as I had writing it. Writing a novel is often a hard slog; this one rarely was.

As is always the case, there are people who deserve a lot of credit for numerous things that made the book possible, from giving me feedback to just keeping me going as a writer, and as a human being.

Many thanks to the members of the Gainesville Fiction Writers group who offered some excellent critiques that really improved the book—Lina Langley, Matthew Schramm, Heysel Marte, and Elsa Peterson. Thanks also to the excellent crime writer and all-around good guy, Bret R. Wright, for his expert opinion. A million thanks to Marie Whittaker (who you may know as Amity Green) for finding this book a home, and to everyone at WordFire Press. Thanks for years of support and friendship to Christy Shorey and Morgen Leigh, two unreasonably talented writers who have given me so many invaluable insights into any manner of subjects. Thanks also to the many awesome members of Fiction Foundry and the Colorado Springs Fiction Writers Group, as well as to the members of the BHS Speech and Debate team for making me care so much about my day job.

Finally, of course, thanks to my wonderful parents, in particular my mother for raising me as a fan of the great old movies that inspired this book.

ABOUT THE AUTHOR

R. Michael Burns is an October child and Colorado native with a background in theater, creative writing, philosophy, and other dark arts. He has published short stories in the horror, science fiction, fantasy, and mystery genres, as well as the horror novel *Windwalkers*. After earning degrees  in English and Philosophy, he taught for the better part of five years in Japan, both in public schools and in a private English conversation school. During that time, he traveled extensively around southeast Asia. Three of his Japan-based fantasy tales have appeared in *Heroic Fantasy Quarterly's Best Of* anthologies, and his articles on the craft of fiction have been recognized by Predators and Editors and are taught in several college creative writing courses. He currently resides in Florida where he teaches English and coaches his school's speech and debate team.

IF YOU LIKED ...

If you liked *Mr. Menace,* you might also enjoy:

Zomnibus
by Kevin J Anderson

Lady Sherlock
by Brooks Arthur Wachtel

She Murdered Me with Science
by David Boop

OTHER WORDFIRE PRESS TITLES

City of the Saints
by D. J. Butler

Selected Stories: Horror and Dark Fantasy
by Kevin J. Anderson

Rescue From Planet Pleasure
by Mike Baron

Our list of other WordFire Press authors and titles is always growing. To find out more and to see our selection of titles, visit us at:
wordfirepress.com

CPSIA information can be obtained
at www.ICGtesting.com
Printed in the USA
LVHW110101201020
669244LV00024B/808/J